D0966646

The Tower Struck by Lightning

    The image shows a tower half destroyed by a lightning bolt that strikes the top section (the head). This tower is the column of power. The bricks are flesh-colored to denote that the structure is a living construction, the image of a human being. The playing card demonstrates the danger involved in any excess of self-assurance, and of the consequence: pride. Megalomania, the pursuit of chimaeras, and narrow dogmatism establish the context of the symbol.

—A Tarot card

Fernando Arrabal

The Tower Struck
by Lightning

Translated by Anthony Kerrigan

VIKING

VIKING
Published by the Penguin Group
Viking Penguin Inc., 40 West 23rd Street,
New York, New York 10010, U.S.A.
Penguin Books Ltd, 27 Wrights Lane,
London W8 5TZ, England
Penguin Books Australia Ltd, Ringwood,
Victoria, Australia
Penguin Books Canada Ltd, 2801 John Street,
Markham, Ontario, Canada L3R 1B4
Penguin Books (N.Z.) Ltd, 182-190 Wairau Road,
Auckland 10, New Zealand

Penguin Books Ltd, Registered Offices:
Harmondsworth, Middlesex, England

First published in 1988 by Viking Penguin Inc.
Published simultaneously in Canada

Translation copyright © Anthony Kerrigan and
Fernando Arrabal, 1988
Foreword copyright © Anthony Kerrigan, 1988
All rights reserved

Originally published in Spanish as *La torre herida por
el rayo* by Ediciones Destino, S.A. © Fernando Arrabal, 1983

LIBRARY OF CONGRESS CATALOGING IN PUBLICATION DATA
Arrabal, Fernando.
The tower struck by lightning.
Translation of: La torre herida por el rayo.
I. Title.
PQ6601.R58T613   1988   843'.914   87-40467
ISBN 0-670-81346-X

Printed in the United States of America by Arcata Graphics
Fairfield, Pennsylvania
Set in Garamond
Designed by Julie Quan

TRANSLATOR'S FOREWORD

by Anthony Kerrigan

I first *saw* Arrabal (I haven't seen him since), naked, on a poster which he, or his underground friends (or enemies, police provocateurs?), caused to be plastered up on the walls of an old section of Madrid, where *el pueblo* mingles with the *aristos* (nobles with titles and no funds) in the last years of the Franco regime. If it was not over-life size, his phallus (undoubtedly his own: no signs of any photomontage) was. He himself was in France and was not allowed over the border by the Customs Service. This *cartel*, this *affiche* was apparently his most artistic, his most bohemian, reply in the circum-stances. He could thereby cry *Presente!*, in the Hispanic ritual of both Left and Right. And: "The Style is the Man"; and style may be physiological.

When I went to seek him out in New York in 1987, at a "collective" opening in a Greene Street art gallery with the guerrilla-sounding title of M-13, where I had been assured by a New York agent that he would appear, my destined

(Yiddish *Bascherte*) companion and I searched among a faithful, and faintly (only faintly) compulsive-chic conglomerate, attempting to espy his quite definable physiognomy, but found not a single striking example of an anarcho-contra, or even of a true (non-New York-uniformed-*narodniki*) bohemian. (The paintings didn't merit a searching look or any espying: most were the latest nothings, already dated, "collectively unified" by a jejune phallic-worship which made the phalloi [*sic*] look unlovely menaces. And some "ridiculous pudenda": shades of Dahlberg's *The Sorrows of Priapus*!: "cloacal nihilism." *Kitsch*—in all its variant definitions—was everywhere. Arrabal, in his persona as painter—and priapist—did well to stay away.)

We then made a tour of "in" eateries, following the path of some Spanish painters who knew him by sight, and wound up in a "thirties" pub back on the same Greene Street, where we regarded much sheer anachronism (and my companion tried on a beaded hat from the "flapper" décor). We felt we had at least found something he might have mined: anachronism itself. (Moreover, not to find whomever one is looking for is a constant in the Theatre of the Absurd, of which Arrabal—his very surname means "outskirts"—was a dramatic practitioner.)

As for the city in which we sought him: after some months of life in New York in the early seventies, Arrabal wrote a poem in which he sees himself "back again in post-Civil-War-Madrid, in 1940, amid the ruins." And he adduces gangs (The Young Lords), "anti-Yankee" Puerto Ricans, "rats, cockroaches—and infinite nostalgia!" (*Le New York d'Arrabal*, Paris, 1973).

In a piece written from New York and published in Madrid in 1986, "*Manhattan español*," Arrabal speculates on what would have happened if "the Jewish genius from Genoa,"

Columbus, had followed his originally intended route and discovered *Manhatta*. "The first wave of Jewish emigration would have been made up of *conversos* from Spain, of knights-errant, of avid readers of books of chivalry": those Don Quixote read. New York would now be speaking good Spanish, officially. That's one view: only proper for the founder of *théâtre panique!* Moreover, there might be more hierarchic good manners, and less scrum and scrimmage. Everyone would be, with formality, late. And one of the two sexes might not be wearing pants, *contra-natura*, even indoors. New York (*Nuevo Madrigal de las Altas Torres?*) would not be the "Wonder Bread capital of the world." But then, doubtless there would be no Faustian "work ethic" or Puritan skyscrapers.

And in this book with a title from the tarot deck we find much of the same anachronicity, but with ancient themes brought up to date. East vs. West. But what an East ("eastern" ideologies infiltrated into French Academe, as well as the dogma of a Stalino-iconic Russia, all of it lodged in Paris, mainly), and what a West (the detritus of Christendom, the debris of Christianity in France and Spain)! The West also includes a neo-Mormon (South of France Spanish bohemian) *ménage-à-trois,* and the East (or is it only part of today's West?) a Left-of-Mao Parisian splinter group of terrorists, many of them dressed like Chinese *narodniki.*

And the chess game is politically as well as criminally cosmic. Is it even a grand-master game? Or an idiosyncratic construct? Arrabal himself is a championship chessplayer, sometimes taking on multitudes, as on the day in 1987 when he contended with as many as forty schoolchildren champions in a single afternoon in a Spanish city.

Chess games have been played before to settle cosmic disputes. Borges adduces two from universal legend (in his *Extraordinary Tales*, New York, 1971: my translation):

I

When the French laid siege to the capital of Madagascar in 1893, the priests of the native religion participated in the defense by playing *fanarona,* a local variant chess, and the queen and people followed the moves of the game—ritually played to assure victory—with greater concern than they did the efforts of the troops.

II

In one of the tales which make up the series of the *Mabinogion,* two enemy kings play chess while in a nearby valley their respective armies battle and destroy each other. . . . Gradually it becomes apparent that the vicissitudes of the battle follow the vicissitudes of the game. Toward dusk, one of the kings overturns the board because he has been checkmated, and presently a blood-spattered horseman comes to tell him: "Your army is in flight. You have lost the kingdom."

A paradigm of these rites is adumbrated in the present book.

As regards his view of the world, Arrabal is singularly marked by an absence of "conspicuous compassion" (which replaces the old "conspicuous consumption," according to Allan Bloom in *The Closing of the American Mind*). Arrabal limits himself to a kind of oneiric blessing for all bedeviled men and women. He reflects their nightmares (especially in his well-known plays), which cannot count on dogma.

While the motley "committed" battalions invade the pages of literature with their predictable (how utterly predictable!) polemics, he could and can take potshots as a free *franc-tireur,* an irregular, a true guerrilla without a compromised, contaminated, *engagé,* cause.

If Arrabal is not an anarcho-counter-revolutionary, an anarchist *contra* (meaning someone against both sides, on principle: an antinomian), he is practically an heir (at least in the attitude of "A plague o' both your houses!") in the line of the most individualistic Hispanic liberalism. This attitude is most notably, and nobly, represented, in peninsular Spain, by the humanist Ortega y Gasset, who was under a cloud in Franco Spain as an anti-"Traditionalist" Man-of-the-Left, and is now denigrated as an "elitist" ("elitism—what a dreary superstition," says the novel's narrator in Saul Bellow's *More Die of Heartbreak,* who goes on to laud "the exception," the exceptional people). Ortega is now denounced by the *"Progres"* (the "Progressives" of Academe) and their students-in-the-streets. And the same highly individual stance as Ortega's was also that of Unamuno, who was ousted as Rector of the University of Salamanca, first by the Red "Popular Front" government in Madrid, and then, a couple of months later, was ousted by the other side, in an edict signed by Franco at the behest of the University's Council of Professors: the "with-it" thirties professors in the Movement (*el Movimiento*), à la mode "national" socialists, drummed him out. So that he became an outcast banished by both camps in the Civil War.

The title of an Arrabal film (written and directed by him), *Viva la Muerte! (Long Live Death!:* the mystico-religious-warrior cry of the Spanish Foreign Legion and as much Spanish-Moorish as Christian), is more than an echo of the cry launched against Unamuno at his last public appearance by the head of the Spanish Foreign Legion: it was *La Legión's* battle cry. General Millán Astray, their commanding officer, added a variant anathema against Unamuno, the famous *Muera La Inteligencia!,* ("Death to the Intelligentsia!": *sic*).

Unamuno was a classic (nineteenth-century) Liberal (not

one of the dogmatic late twentieth-century sort) who lived and wrote at a time when Spain boasted that apparent paradox (looked at from the 1980s), a political party liberally called *Partido Liberal-Conservador:* the Liberal Conservative Party. Where are culturally conservative liberals available today, for instance?

For his part, Arrabal takes an exceptional stance: he takes exception to almost everything. In his work as a whole he is as far outside the "mainstream" as it is possible to be.

Late in 1987 (in a theatrical piece written on the Yale campus), Arrabal prefigures ultimately developed egalitarianism at "Yale in 1999," where, once "elites" are in mass disgrace, doctorates in the Yale School of the Drama are awarded to . . . horses (after centuries of human "oppression" and reactionary privilege), to honor "their sense of rhythm, their rolling gate, their 'occupancy of space,' their neighing. . . ." In " '*La cucaracha*' at Yale," he postulates that USA cockroaches (already possessing a mouth and two eyes, just like anybody else) surely possess, looked at rightly (from the left), rights, too. Cockroaches of the world united with all the oppressed deserve degrees from the Department Without Rime or Reason, as well as in philosophy (the Department of Disequalization), along with those from the School of Drama.

As regards his plays (which I first saw, in French, off the lumpen-pimp Place Pigalle quarter in Paris), he is certainly an original. And if one "places" him by calling him a paraphrase of the spirit of Beckett, or of Ionesco, say, it could only be because they are all of them originals.

They may be compared only in the sense that none of them has any truck with any permanent organization or government or bureaucracies of any kind. They are *sui generis* when it comes to classification, no matter how Ph.D. theses may link them.

When Arrabal's *Le cimitière des voitures* (*The Automobile Graveyard*) was staged at the University of Texas, the authorities—administration and campus security—held up production, ruling that a *functioning* automobile (actually it was a hulk) could not appear on stage for fear of fire, or some other unspecifiable catastrophe! The incident could have been written into the play, as a Prologue, say, in the Elizabethan way. A stage policeman could have been introduced into the script, and appeared on stage at the outset to announce that the car was a threat to public safety, to security, and that the audience, if it had any sense, should disperse and go home.

Of late, Arrabal, the once proto-Leftist, has taken on the government of Cuba, as any libertarian or ex-young-communist would most naturally do, in the case of Armando Valladares, whom he housed upon Valladares' arrival in France, fresh from twenty years in political prison in Cuba and from an official greeting staged by the Socialist President of France. Arrabal offered the lodging and space the Cuban *zek* required to set down and also record the poems he had been unable to write out but had perforce only memorized in the Cuban Gulag.

As to the translation into English: in a finely calligraphed private letter from Rue Jouffroy in Paris to the present translator, the author says he is glad merely to arrive in a "sedan chair" before the public, though, once Englished, he might "seat his behind on a throne . . . for Parnassus has already yielded such outrageous surprises." He is free of any responsibility for a single syllable of the English in this version.

Special thanks are due the sensual novelist William O'Rourke, future memorialist of Dahlberg, and to Professor Angel Delgado, man of the world and *gran maestro*. To the playwright John Barnes, filmmaker and connoisseur of Casanova, and of Dahlberg. And to Judge Jerome Frese, who played *the game* with Mohamed. And to the telluric Lisa Kaufman, editor.

Anthony Kerrigan
Senior Guest Scholar
Kellogg Institute
University of Notre Dame
(Siberia, USA)

The Tower Struck by Lightning

ELIAS TARSIS DOES NOT RAISE HIS EYES, AND therefore they do not meet those of the implacable robot in front of him. If he did look up he would not be able to suppress the impulse to throw the chessboard and its pieces in his opponent's mottled face.

He reeks of assassination, Tarsis thinks to himself. *For two months I've been living with his assassin's scent. He's a criminal . . . and I could prove it.*

He could prove it, but who would listen? Who would be interested in verifying the indisputable (to him) proofs accumulated in the course of a year? The real truth was that he was more interested in wreaking vengeance on Marc Amary than in seeing him brought to trial. This inexorable machine, this vile automaton has caused him the blackest suffering. Whenever he thinks of him he can feel a bubble of incandescent mercury traveling from his heart to his brain and back again. He realizes that he must calm down if he is to win the chess duel begun two months ago. He must use his active intelligence to guide him through the vicissitudes of the action without letting his thirst for vengeance lead him astray.

To the others—the judges, the spectators, and the members of the chess federation—Marc Amary is not the "bloody robot" imagined by Tarsis but the very image of self-possession. And of Science with a capital *S*. He could probably demonstrate, like Leonardo da Vinci, that a bird is an instrument which functions according to mathematical laws.

After the strange and sensational kidnapping of the Soviet Minister for Foreign Affairs, Igor Isvoschikov, in the course of his stay in Paris, the press's interest in the World Chess Championship has diminished. Nevertheless, the curiosity of chess players everywhere has reached its apogee now that the denouement is in sight. The Beaubourg Center theater, scene of the action, continues to be filled to capacity at each session, but now the spectators are made up of the most ardent enthusiasts, those for whom the usual five hours (so brief!) of normal play are compounded of instants in which they discern new marvels, in which radiance falls upon them like manna in the desert. The spectators who had invaded the hall during the first days most certainly now preferred to follow the astonishing adventures which the abductors of the Soviet dignitary continued to conceive and distill with expert economy. The terrorists took pride in an epistolary genius and a fine dramatic talent. The abduction by a so-called Comité Communiste International of a Kremlin bigwig constituted a premier performance which could not fail to fascinate in the larger theater of the world.

In the course of the twenty-three games Tarsis has played against Amary in this championship duel, he has been contemplating with great irritation the obsessive cycle of maniacal ceremonies performed by his adversary; the rites of a castrated eunuch, as he calls them. Now, after two months of contention, thirteen games declared nullified, and five victories apiece, the next victory (the sixth and last) will decide the title of world champion. And Tarsis is afraid that his fury will affect his mind and cause him to lose his head or, what is worse, his concentration.

Marc Amary seems to remember the minutes and the seconds as they pass, so that he neither needs nor uses a timepiece. On Tuesdays, Thursdays, and Saturdays—days with scheduled games—he presents himself *systematically* exactly at fifty-five seconds to four. The computer governing his blood and his subconscious functions automatically, tick-tock, tick-tock. Or almost so. And the unvarying process begins: he allows ten seconds to move from the door leading to the scene of play to his chair; twenty seconds for noting down the date, his name and that of Tarsis; ten seconds for checking whether the two official clocks have been wound to the limit; the remaining fifteen seconds are given over to arranging the figures and pawns (already perfectly placed on the board in compliance with the rules of chess) according to his own magical measure or, as Tarsis would say, according to his "assassin's whims." Each one of the sixteen pieces must occupy the exact center, to the millimeter, of its square: the knights' heads lined up toward him (in adoration?), the bishops' grooves precisely in front of his eyes, and the arms of the small cross crowning his king parallel to the invisible line traced by his two elbows on the table. "Load, aim, fire!" At exactly four o'clock, at the moment the judge starts White's clock, thus marking the official commencement of play, Amary becomes motionless and considers the board and its pieces with such intensity that one would think that he was seeing them for the first time. He is simply discovering them. Whenever he is playing White he begins, exactly at four, with exactly two minutes of reflection . . . pointless as far as the onlookers are concerned inasmuch as these lucubrations inevitably end with a meticulous and discreet move which the world of chess already knows by heart: the king's pawn advances two squares, 1. e2-e4. He takes hold of the pawn—as he does all the pieces in the course of the game—with the tips of his bloodless fingers, between the index finger and the thumb. He carries out each and every one of his moves, whatever the prevailing tension, with a deliberate coldness which might strike one as indifference and which has the added value of infuriating Tarsis: *He is a crafty sadist. He conducts himself with such composure merely to exasperate me. He tries to show that he need not lose his sangfroid in order to finish me off. That's the way he sets all his traps. And I'm the only one who knows the depths of his malice!*

Marc Amary is a Swiss investigator for the CNRS (the National Center for Scientific Investigation), resident in Paris. His colleagues would not be surprised if the Stockholm academics were to give him the Nobel Prize for Physics as a reward for his discoveries relating to the *soliton* or the *Great Unification,* but they certainly *were* disconcerted by his sudden dedication to chess. And not because they disdained the game. Probably not one of them would have suspected that their brilliant and prudent colleague (who had nevertheless been a militant member of the outlandish Dimitrov Faction for several weeks) cared less, at this point, infinitely less, about chess, physics, the Nobel Prize, the World Championship than he did about what he called the creation of the "New Man." On only one occasion, eight years before, in the presence of third parties, during a symposium on elemental particles, did he make a declaration which could have betrayed him. It did not betray him only because the savants around him might as well have lived on the moon. In fact, they were at the University of Heidelberg, and when a Danish researcher asked him to sign a petition in defense of Professor Yefim Faibisovich, imprisoned in a Soviet labor camp, Amary declared: "If I were directing one of those 'centers,' I'd order a new punishment. I'd give the prisoners pencils and enough paper to last them as long as their prison sentences. I'd ask them to carry out the factorial of 9,999—without a calculating machine."

What an amusing thought! Something a pharaoh might have dreamed up, a matter of multiplying 9,999 by 9,998, the result by 9,997, the new result by 9,996 . . . and so on, until the unit was reached. It was a joke, his colleagues thought, which might be interpreted as a subtle criticism of labor camps . . . No one imagined that such interminable torture could be his solution for eliminating the enemies of his cause, who were already numbered in the billions.

Elias Tarsis, the son of Spanish parents, was born in Andorra la Vella . . . "by chance," he always specified, as if one did not inevitably come into the world by chance, whatever the city of one's birth. In his case, "chance" went all the way and his mother ceased to exist the moment he was born. His father burned on for another nine years; upon his death, Elias was taken in by his Aunt Paloma in Madrid. In those years of triumphant nationalism devoid of complications, yearly competitions were held to select "super-endowed" youths. They were held in the same naïve spirit that caused Spain to "Christianize" cognac by christening it with a name from the national baptismal font. (The French paid this no notice. Whenever they encountered a super-endowed Spaniard, like Picasso, they asserted he was French.) Tarsis obtained one of the ten scholarships for the super-endowed, enabling him to pursue his secondary and university studies under the best conditions: in short, free Catholic school, free books, and free room and board. Tarsis's aunt, so as not to overdo it, was happy to accept half of the last allowance, and Elias became her boarder, with bed, breakfast, and supper. But to Paloma's consternation (she had meanwhile been designated his official guardian), the boy neglected his studies and dedicated himself to reading comic books. "Comic books are my meat," he said.

And they served him splendidly. He stayed locked up in his room for more than a year, beneath the only picture of his father left to him: a photograph of his progenitor as political refugee, courtesy of the French. When he finally abandoned his room, the floor lay deep in dirty clothes, garbage, empty food tins, worn comic books, and some filth which his aunt never mentioned because she was a modern woman who understood how things should be. At fourteen, Tarsis ran away to Barcelona, where he began his life as a proletarian, an apprentice in a jeweler's workshop, before being promoted to machine operator.

For no particular reason, on the eve of the World Championship matches, Tarsis was able to meet with three judges, and he blurted out the following warning: "Marc Amary is an assassin! En garde! No one is to be allowed into my resting room. That's all I have to say."

In truth, he was at a loss for any more words. As far as the judges were concerned, he had already said too much.

Prey to rage, Elias Tarsis puts his head between his fists and sinks into an abyss of analysis over the first move.

"I should have foreseen it! He could not continue with the Spanish opening, which has gotten nowhere against my Berlin defense. He's such a coward! His only tactic is a stab in the back. What a filthy move! Fit for a slug. No momentum. Typical of him. But he could be preparing a trap. Let him try."

The International Chess Federation was unable to get the

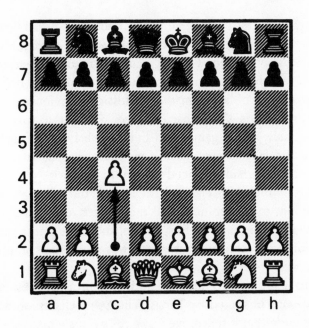

I. C2-C4

two contenders together before the match. To represent him at the preparatory conclave, Amary sent his colleague Jacques Delpy, a fellow researcher in physics; Tarsis simply sent the president of the federation of Andorra. It was clear that they would appear in the field only on the day of battle in the trenches of the chessboard, and that they refused absolutely to waste any of their energies in the guerrilla war of communiqués, in bureaucratic skirmishes, or in committee-room salvos.

This standoff brought into the open the clear hatred existing between the two rivals. It came as a surprise, given the total lack of knowledge, even in the world of chess, about the lives of the two men. A sensationalist English weekly had insinuated, two months before the tournament, that Elias Tarsis had been a procurer in Barcelona and that Amary had murdered his mother, headlining a two-page spread devoted to the tournament with the daring title "Are a Procurer and a Parricide Vying for Chess Champion of the World?" But in fact, all that was known of them for sure was their *Elo coefficients* as published in the professional reviews, and the dates and results of their participation in various tournaments. Occasionally, their games had been published and analyzed in the specialized press. Their victories in national and regional contests had advanced them both, following the aircraft accident which had claimed the life of the reigning world champion, to the point where their status as finalists in the candidates' tournament had now become a contest for the supreme title. Two years before, they had been completely unknown.

Amary probably did not open this round with 1. e2-e4 for the reasons imagined by Tarsis. The Swiss champion was of the opinion that if this move was not obviously malign, it was profoundly combative.

To those who did not understand his "cult of truth," Amary might appear arrogant. A fortnight after beginning his studies for a master's degree in physics at the University of Geneva, he arrived at the conclusion that none of his teachers could teach him anything and that it would be a waste of time to attend their classes, whereupon he definitively took leave of them. In a parallel move he registered in the Department of Mathematics—and repeated the process. All of which did not stand in the way of his gaining both degrees with top grades. He spent part of these years, years in which he stylishly made short shrift of his university studies, in reading through the work of the various Nobel laureates in physics and mathematics. The English chess master D. P. Hawksworth published an interview, in the English journal *Chess,* with Raoul Santini, a colleague of Amary's in Geneva, which includes the following dialogue:

RAOUL SANTINI: Marc Amary has said that, just as he suspected, the Nobel laureates in physics and mathematics are simply beasts of burden.

D. P. HAWKSWORTH: Did he really use that phrase?

R.S.: It was so long ago! Certainly he must have used one of his typical hatchet phrases, without much emotion, no hatred, icy. He must have stated what he said as a fact, some kind of proof or evidence, and I have only recalled the gist of it. If I'm not mistaken, he said that most of the Nobel laureates contribute nothing of a decisive nature to the development of either science or humanity.

D.P.H.: Did you agree with him?

R.S.: None of us who were students then would have dared to vent any such criticism seriously, unless it was meant as a joke or a bit of bluster.

D.P.H.: What was he interested in doing at that time?

R.S.: I wasn't a friend of his. Nobody was. He led a solitary life and only rarely spoke to any of us. There were rumors about his mother, who was said to have died insane at that time. To tell the truth, most of us thought that he must be like her, a bit mad.

D.P.H.: Why did he go to Paris?

R.S.: Probably he went there to get his DEA [Diploma of Intensive Studies], a necessary passbook to enter the CNRS, which was at that time the glorious goal of every European researcher.

Amary, then, along with one hundred and twenty physicists from France and other countries (doubtless the best European physicists of their generation), all of them bent on scholarships, enrolled in the Faculty of Sciences at Paris. On the first day of the academic calender they were welcomed by Pro-

9

fessor Lajos Lukacs, an old and original researcher who was in the habit of interrupting his lectures to heat up some coffee in a small pot over a spirit lamp which he carried in his ample briefcase. He regaled them with the harangue for newcomers which he used each year with few variations. (He belonged to the old school. His colleagues considered him a gross vulgarian.) He spoke as follows:

There are one hundred and twenty of you. Most of you will get your DEA. Now, this diploma is no more than a piece of paper . . . not much different than a piece of toilet paper in a public lavatory on the outskirts of town. So what kind of dream are you pursuing? Do you mean to break into the Paradise of the Elect, a CNRS laboratory, the ideal connection for every canny student who is already arranging for his retirement? What kind of fate is in store for you during the coming year? Do you expect to suckle the milk of science rather than that of your girlfriends? What's it all for? To reach the land of El Dorado, I suppose, the goal of all bums and vagrants, and, of course, the title of state functionary, for a lifetime, with social security, transportation bonuses, an assured retirement, all kinds of promotions, all kinds of extra pay, academic honors, free summer camps for the kiddies, a guaranteed insurance policy for permanent erections . . . and infinite boredom until you die, doddering worse than poor Oppenheimer at Princeton. Some flaming youth! And is this, then, the ideal of the young who were once hailed by our noisiest poets in the exalted time when verse was possible and people knew how to dance the tango? I will be honest and tell you that in the best of cases perhaps five of you will land a job as researchers for the CNRS. But what's the point of being a researcher if you don't publish? A zero, a naught to the left! And one becomes a robber who steals from the state the loose change needed to make the neutron bomb and honorary sashes for deputies, one becomes a mugger who robs the taxpayer of the savings he needs to buy lottery tickets and pornographic magazines. Who among the five heroic and glorious researchers—a new Homer will sing their virtues—will go so far as to publish? If we have recourse to the statistics based on the curriculum vitae of your predecessors—and this is a secret more tightly guarded than the plans of NASA and which I reveal to you most confidentially—two of every five will make it, that is, publish, and that's out of the entire one hundred and twenty of you! And yet, where have these two statistically lucky people, privileged by fate and favoritism, published, up to now? In French or Italian journals. And that's so much pipi and caca, sheer excrement! These journals are about as prestigious as Swedish ones on *tauromaquia,* on the bullfight. One can call oneself a serious scientific scholar and accept one's pay without shame when one publishes in the *Physical Review* or in *Physical Review Letters* or, being generous, in that English journal for snobs *Nature,* that is, assuming one is able to write, in this case, briefly and for public consumption. But see here! Who among you is about to make himself at home in the House of Science? Apart from your humble servant, one man in every ten generations achieves it in this region of barbarians and illiterates. I'll give you some friendly advice: don't waste your time—a whole year can be endless. Join some laboratory in Basle and masturbate rats, or make your way to Johannesburg to help build missiles for the defense of the white race. You can earn money that way and win honors. On the other hand, you may choose to dazzle some rich, rotund, romantic Norwegian woman to whom you may want to explain the theory of relativity by telling her of the train which climbs . . . and climbs . . .

Amary listened to the discourse without blinking. At the end he took out his notebook and wrote down *Physical Review,* nothing more. He then took refuge in the Science Faculty Library and began to go over, on his own, the problem of dual amplitudes which the Theoretical Physics Laboratory of the CNRS was attempting to resolve; he put the DEA completely out of his mind. Five months later, when his colleagues and teachers had assumed that he had renounced any further work for the coveted diploma, the CNRS was astounded to learn than an unknown researcher, who had nevertheless sent his signed article from Paris, had just been published in the *Physical Review.* Even more astounding, the article was an answer to the very problem then being investigated by one of the most prestigious laboratories of the center. The title of the work read: "Dual Amplitudes with Coupling of the Omega for Six Pions and Gyrating Bosons," and its author was Marc Amary.

Amary added a handwritten note to the copy of the magazine forwarded to him from the United States:

Too much importance is attached to it: a generalizing work. Banal problems. Mere calculation. Not difficult. Tempting: a mathematical formula on strong interacting properties. Supertechnique: dazzling. Stupid problem: I thought about it for a fortnight. Within a year everyone will understand it. Physics will evolve: just like athletic records.

He signed the note: "The Master." [The "Kid" would not have been able to help him write it, nor "Teresa," nor "Mickey":

they were frivolous beings who thought only of making jokes or of laughing at him all night long, so that he couldn't sleep.]

At the end of three minutes into the first move by Amary, Tarsis is still sunk in his analysis. A spectator in row 17 has unfolded his copy of *France-Soir* and is contemplating the front-page photograph of Igor Isvoschikov, a member of the Politburo and Minister of Foreign Affairs of the U.S.S.R., under a flag with a five-pointed star, and a banner which reads: COMITÉ COMMUNISTE INTERNATIONAL. According to the paper, the photograph (like all those sent punctually every Wednesday by the abductors) was taken with a Polaroid camera in order to establish the date of its development; moreover, the Soviet leader is holding a copy of the day's paper under his chin. The prisoner sports an ecchymosis around his left eye, which demonstrates, according to the journalists, that the interrogations are not nonviolent. Since the accompanying communiqué from the Comité does not speak of a "confession," the police have deduced that the Russian Minister is not cooperating with his abductors. Along with the photograph, the terrorists have sent a document of great length in the name of their organization; its title is "Theoretical, Political, and Strategic Solutions." The newspaper has printed a summary of the piece.

At three minutes and twenty-six seconds on the clock, Elias Tarsis brusquely moves his king's pawn just one square forward (1. e7-e6). The contrast between the vehemence of his gesture and Amary's permanent calm is startling. Following his move, he gazes at the wall boards with a sardonic smile. If he were not fearful of the effect of any untoward incident, he would have turned on Amary and given him a look that said: *So you thought you'd surprise me? Suck it! You weren't*

13

expecting that! He leans back as if to get a better, more triumphant perspective of his move.

Amary had opened with a certain flexibility and Tarsis, counter to all expectation, had replied along the same lines. Nevertheless, with such apparently mild moves, the latent virulence of the opening has reached psychologically wilder heights than if they had followed the lines laid down by what is considered more forceful play: Spanish or Sicilian openings.

Tarsis is thinking: *Amary is an intellectual, pure and simple, a homicidal machine. As a chess player he belongs in a café. He doesn't know the essence of the game. He merely applies the schema he's learned, all of which he recalls thanks to a prodigious memory. This equipment is useful in preparing an* attentat, *but not in front of a chessboard. He has won five games through sheer bore-*

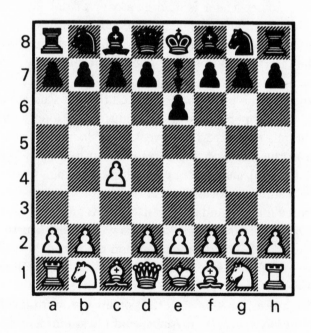

2. . . . . e7-e6

dom . . . This robot never tires, and he is able to take me by surprise, me or anyone who is dealing with the secret of chess.

The duel between Amary and Tarsis was as good as a lesson in philosophy. Chess consists of an unvarying infrastructure (its laws, scheme, norm) and a variant structure resulting from the combinations on the board. Tarsis, like Fischer, Steinitz, or Morphy, understood the law and knew that perfection is achieved through serenity amid disorder. Amary, like Karpov, Euwe, or Petrossian, was a master of variants, of mutations, and therefore he avoided all signs of chaos.

While Tarsis makes his way to the rest area he tells himself: *Amary has the instincts of a shark. He kills with stealth. He's done it before and he'll do it again.*

Isvoschikov, though seventy-two years old, was the youngest member of the Politburo, the supreme Soviet institution, where men like Peche pound ahead with great audacity, albeit with some ills, toward a nonagenarian age of revolutionary activity. His abductors were fully aware that among the Soviet leadership he was the most likely to succeed the present Secretary-General of the Party, the number-one man in the Soviet Union. (Actually, the Politburo contained two members younger than he was: Aliev, who was only sixty-nine, and Solomenstsev, who had just become a septuagenarian. But their ethnic origins—the former from Azerbaijan, the latter from Kazakhstan—precluded access to the highest reaches of power in the Russian state.) The Soviet constitution has not made any legal provision for the Dauphin: there is no Prince of Wales. The prevailing system of succession creates the most varied personality conflicts and often degenerates into a free-for-all, with the most deleterious effects on the working masses.

One Communist country had resolved the problem: North Korea. There, the Party's Secretary-General, Comrade Kim Il Sung (who vied with his Albanian counterpart for the record in length of permanence in supreme command), had been named, by acclamation, "President-for-Life" of his country, thanks to a sensational referendum in which he achieved the enviable figure of 100 percent of the votes in his favor. It was insuperable. Ever attentive to the well-being of his people and in order to save them from confusion the day of his death, he appointed his own son to be his successor. His infallible knowledge of historical dialectic envisaged thus the creation of an original and renewing figure, that of a Communist monarch linking the past with a most radiant future.

Certain Kremlinologists speculated on the possibility that the kidnappers were not attempting to obtain compromising state secrets from the two-month interrogation to which Isvoschikov was submitted, but that they were simply trying to convert the most likely candidate for top power in the U.S.S.R. to their own revolutionary cause by means of brainwashing techniques. A devious double benefit would accrue when Isvoschikov, duly indoctrinated and subsequently freed, and then miraculously basking in the false prestige attendant on his "heroic" resistance to his kidnappers, achieved added renown to help him to power in the democratic, popular, proletarian state.

The confidential report which the cleaning service of the Beaubourg Center produced at the request of the International Chess Federation noted that while Amary always left his room and adjoining private bath in a perfect state of cleanliness and order, Tarsis on the other hand had transformed his quarters into a lions' den or, more precisely, his two rooms into lions' cages: the bathroom stools would be found upside down in the tub, the bidet suspiciously stained, the bed looking as if it had endured an assault by a dozen cats, the easy chairs overturned, the napkins bloodstained as well as wet, always strewn about the floor, mixed up with trampled underwear and, on one occasion, a ripped-up brassiere. The Chess Federation was fearful of any clandestine visit, and the rest areas for each player were set up for the express purpose of providing some respite for one player while his opponent was busy analyzing the board. But there was always the possibility that Tarsis, despite the numerous precautions, might entertain a woman in his quarters, a woman who might provide him with some outside help, destroy the champion's isolation, or upset the balance of resources between the players. The report also pointed out that Tarsis had blocked the closed-circuit television screen with a metallic Christ figure nailed to a spectacular construction of black wood on a black pedestal, an obstruction placed so as to blot out the filmed image of his opponent.

Elias Tarsis was meant to be called Komsomol Tarsis, following the will of his father, who dreamed of internationalist fêtes and proletarian Elysian fields. Nationalist Spain (*Una, Grande, y Libre*), where he found shelter when he was nine, did not countenance such red dreams, and his Aunt Paloma was merciless in assigning the younger Tarsis a God-given baptismal name. In those years, Madrid was more than ever itself and less than ever like the Andorra where he had been born or the South of France, where he had lived until the death of his father. All the more to its honor, as Unamuno would say.

A contest for exceptional children brought the country's outstanding boys of ten, eleven, and twelve years of age to Madrid to compete for the ten available team openings. During a fortnight of examinations, young Tarsis, who was having great difficulty in adapting to his Aunt Paloma's tiny flat and to Madrid as a whole, felt a resurgence of life. Closeted in the classrooms where the written examinations were held, totally absorbed in solving labyrinthine intricacies, he seemed to glide between consolation and hope and thereby was almost able to keep at bay the horrid crow of anguish. He felt . . . as if he were still in Céret, on the French border with Spain, with his father, who, in his unforgettable accent, patiently provided some pointers in geometry, or taught him the names of the Visigothic kings of Spain, or explained how a grain of wheat became the bread he ate.

Step by step Tarsis worked his way through the selection tests: he was able to find the correspondences between heteroclites, he reproduced a geometric figure with the help of some cubes, he calculated the direction of movement provoked by various interacting levers, he evaluated systems propounded to him, he translated incomprehensible phrases thanks to an impromptu code, and he deciphered hieroglyphics as only an exceptionally endowed person might do. At the conclusion of these feats, the twenty remaining youths had to endure the final test, the unique oral trial.

When Tarsis entered the hall where the examination was held, he found himself alone, facing five professors. The man in the center of the tribunal, who seemed to be presiding, said to him, with a certain air of solemnity: "This final examination is a test of creativity. Listen to me carefully: NAME ALL THE WORDS YOU CAN IMAGINE. I repeat: NAME ALL THE WORDS YOU CAN IMAGINE."

As he scrutinized the objects in front of him, Tarsis quickly named them: table chair notebook glass bottle water pencil tie shirt jacket button . . . His litany was so fast and furious that he was quickly confronted with the notion that he would soon stumble, stutter, and come to a halt . . . when suddenly the list of the Visigoth Kings of Spain which his father had taught him flashed before his eyes and he rattled them off, as if he were singing them out happily at his father's side in the village of Céret, among the snails and the cigalas: Ataulfo, Sigerico, Walia, Teodoredo, Turismundo, Teodorico, Eurico, Alarico, Gesaleico, Amalrico, Teudis, Teudiselo, Agila, Atanagildo . . .

When the jury stopped him in the middle of the roll call, Tarsis could guess at the outcome. The tribunal was apparently pleased with such games.

Thanks to the Exceptional Student Scholarship granted him, he was able to enroll for half board in the college of the Piarist Fathers of San Antón, doubtless influenced in this choice by his Aunt Paloma, who was overawed by the fact that among its alumni was a Nobel laureate in literature, a dramatist who was all the rage at the moment, and that among its "house painters," literally, was the great Goya, Francisco de Goya y Lucientes himself. Among the numberless students in this school in the middle of Madrid, Tarsis got lost. He vegetated on the fringes, like a wild animal wandering in the jungle, all hope of finding its comrades gone forever.

Two weeks after beginning his second year at the Colegio de San Antón, Tarsis managed to transform one of his fellow students into a "slave." The student was an extraordinarily obese boy who was spending a year in the capital of Spain. Since his family was apparently French, he was known as El Francés. Tarsis would punish his slave by locking him in the most remote toilet, in a dark and abandoned cellar beside the third patio, and making him stay there all through recreation periods. It was a toilet in the Turkish fashion, with a single hole in the floor, filthy and vile.

It was impossible to understand how Tarsis had come to form such a relationship. Along with the other boys in his class, he would play Basque pelota against the wall under the arcades or soccer in the central patio, but every quarter of an hour he would run off to make sure that his prisoner had not moved from his dungeon. It was a useless precaution, for his slave could easily have escaped had he the will to do so. During each of his visits Tarsis found some reason for anger, and this served to increase his fury: sometimes, because El Francés had not stayed exactly in the corner he had assigned him, smack against the back wall; other times because the prisoner appeared to look at him too dully or, on the contrary, with too much daring. Whenever he imagined that his prey was at the point of complaining to the priests, Tarsis cuffed him mercilessly or whipped him with his belt.

Tarsis hypothecated confusedly—and therefore absurdly— that El Francés was to blame for the death of Tarsis's father. He seethed with a barbarous hatred which took the place of mourning. In the end, he was convinced that, given the circumstances and his victim's guilt, he, Tarsis, showed more patience than Job. He chose to issue orders by means of the most abrupt signs, never deigning to speak, and finally he forbade his slave to raise his eyes and look at him. When the filthy toilet wasn't filthy enough, when its odor wasn't evil enough for his taste, he was frustrated, and he himself wallowed in the world's injustice. In class he spent his time thinking up new plans for mortifying his victim as he deserved, that is, more and more: by the use of nettles, nails, his knife, or tying him up so he couldn't move, or half gagging him with a scarf so that he could scarcely breathe. Sometimes Tarsis was overcome with an infinite desire to cry, in the knowledge that he was alone and abandoned.

This relationship with El Francés lasted two school terms, and would have gone on, if Tarsis had not attempted a fatal move. At the beginning of the third term, El Francés's younger brother appeared at the school. Tarsis, by way of making his point more forcefully, decided to make this boy his second slave. But the younger boy balked. Tarsis was forced to employ all his guile to get him into the latrine next to his brother, and as soon as his back was turned, the boy escaped. Tarsis tried to argue him into it, to overcome him with presumed reasons, and then, when he ended by using force, the boy defended himself tooth and nail. The ensuing struggle grew so furious that a watchful priest was drawn into the affair.

A ball of yarn is already unwound when one loose end becomes unraveled, and the relationship which Tarsis had established with El Francés came undone. Expulsion from the school was rumored, to which Tarsis was indifferent. His aunt was of another mind. Goodbye, Goya, Nobel laureate, and the Feast of San Antón! The Father Superior, after receiving the two protagonists in his quarters, astounded everyone by his decision to expel the two brothers while merely denying Tarsis the afternoon collation for a week. Tarsis thought this a model of justice. The Father Superior's singular reasoning, which led to this bizarre disparity of punishment, was never made clear; neither was it ever learned why the name and surname of the slave (Belgian, Swiss, French?) were expunged from all school documents.

Father Gregorio was the man chosen to show the strayed sheep where the right path lay. When Tarsis was ushered into the priest's office, he felt like a trapped cat and was ready to scratch. But the priest, who had a reputation for severity (it was well known that he had been in attendance when firing squads operated at the Colegio de San Antón in the years just after the Spanish Civil War, for the college was used as a prison), immediately evidenced a certain complicity with the boy.

"You won in the competition among exceptional students, and I'd guess that you would be very good at chess. Do you know the rules?"

"No."

"Would you like me to teach them to you?"

"I won't tell you anything more about the matter of El Francés."

In that epoch of Faith-Hope-and-Charity and of apostolic Roman Catholicism, such a provocative answer might have cost any student of the school quite dearly. But this particular turbulent lad had somehow fallen into the good graces of Father Gregorio, who displayed a paternal compassion toward the boy from the start, not only bearing his insolence but teaching him how to play chess into the bargain.

Only a short distance from the catacombs on Noviciado Street, where the Protestants awaited without cover the hunt for heretics so fashionable at the time and so devoutly practiced, Tarsis and Father Gregorio carried out uncommon conversations, considering the time, and doubly uncommon in that the boy sometimes made his point with great heat—and sometimes even with some logic.

"You know, Tarsis, you're my devil's advocate."

"Tell me, Father, why is it that of the four Evangelists, only one of them mentions the Good Thief? It seems to me that none of it is true."

"Why do you tempt me?"

"Another thing I don't understand is that if the Son has a human side, a human as well as a divine nature, as they tell us in the class on Apologetics, how is it that the Holy Spirit, who is the love between the Father and the Son, possesses only a divine nature?"

"Tarsis, what you must do is pray, go to Mass, receive Communion . . ."

"And avoid thinking . . . like the devout ladies who service the Church. You just want me to be as smug as most Catholics."

"Stop it. Don't talk nonsense. You're only a child."

"Well, I'm not a baby and I'm not an idiot, and I can't be taught the way the missionaries do it, with a saint's picture and tin foil."

"Don't you believe in God?"

And the boy, though a mere lad, fully calculating all the risks attendant on his reply, and as if he were happily committing suicide, imitated his father's accent and way of talking and very slowly fired a broadside: "Everything that stinks, everything that's sick, everything sordid, everything abject, can be summed up in one word . . . God!" And he ended by belching.

Father Gregorio seemed more sadly bewildered than horrified. After a long pause he honestly confessed: "You surprise me . . . I'm astounded that at your age you can use the word 'abject' so correctly."

At the end of two minutes and five seconds of study and analysis, Amary accepts Tarsis's challenge and plays 2. d2-d4,

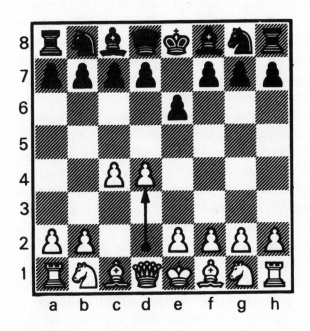

2. d2-d4

thus occupying the center, controlling e5 and c5, and demonstrating that he is venturing on the Queen's Gambit, an opening which does not suit him in principle.

Immediately afterward he stops his clock and thereby automatically sets Tarsis's clock in motion; he scrupulously marks down his move and fixes his gaze between his adversary's eyebrows—a ritual with him.

Tarsis begins his reflections under the heavy weight of his rival's unbearable stare. But if he should look up, he will only provoke an incident that would disconcert him, as Amary hopes will happen. Nevertheless, it may be that Amary is contemplating him with real curiosity, even with a certain admiration, as he would a wild horse, or a jailer.

On his worksheet, Tarsis grudgingly notes Amary's move. Two types of writing appear on this sheet: the first, detailing his own moves, is not only legible but even polished; the other, an account of the moves made by the "assassin," is a series of scrawls or furious strokes. For Tarsis, to call Amary an "assassin" or a "robot" is to assimilate him, to appropriate him; and to write out his name with any care would be as repugnant as to caress him.

The most well-established taboo in chess is the one forbidding touching. "A piece touched is a piece played," according to the rules. Thus we see the irrevocable nature of the act of touching. If a player's fingers graze a piece, he is obliged to declare *"J'adoube,"* a French term originating in the Middle Ages used in solemnly dressing a knight in his armor, and which today may signify "Pardon!" or, more precisely, "I am arranging," or "I am disposing." For some psychologists, among them the American ex-champion Fine, this taboo against touching masks the two threats menacing every champion: masturbation (according to these experts, the figure being touched is a penis, which is why, after touching it, the player excuses himself) and the homosexuality "latent in chess players." Tarsis finds these theories as absurd as they are outrageous. Most chess players are of the same opinion. [During the Montreal tourney a Canadian woman poet asked Portisch his opinion of Fine's thesis; in reply the Hungarian champion turned his back and went off in a huff; he did not strike her, because she was a woman.]

As things went, the first public "hand to hand" encounter between our two rivals could not have been more exemplary. The occasion was the draw to determine which player would use white in the first game. For reasons that might be considered either mythical or magical, Tarsis wanted to win: he thought that it would demonstrate that he had Luck (or Nature? or Fortune? or God?) on his side. With equal zeal, Amary wished to win the first skirmish for quite reasonable motives: to be able to count on the small advantage given by possession of whites would provide the initial benefit, which he would know how to exploit to deliver a telling blow. After the official speeches and the patriotic hymns, the two players faced each other: Amary was ashen, while Tarsis's face was inflamed. Amary accepted the pawn offered him by the president of the federation, whipped it behind his back, and then extended two closed hands in front of his rival: one fist held the fateful pawn. Tarsis was about to tap one of the hands, but suddenly held back, raised his index finger, and made a pass at the other's left fist, which was precisely where the white pawn lay hidden. This gesture—a symbolic victory for Tarsis—would have been enough to justify the theoreticians who see in chess a playing out of narcissistic conflicts, but it went unnoticed. Perhaps Fine might have maintained that Tarsis had brandished the phallus of triumph during the above ceremony in mock-sodomy of his competitor, but that at the last moment, in fear of being masturbated by Amary, he managed to wave his finger so close to his enemy's hand that everyone thought he had touched it when in reality he had not even grazed it.

Family conflicts, especially the antagonism between fathers and sons, are projected onto the chessboard and its figures. In Amary's case, his childhood might well yield every kind of interpretation.

When Amary was twelve, his mother entered a private clinic on the outskirts of Nyon (some fifteen miles from Geneva, Switzerland). In other epochs such residential clinics were simply called madhouses. Inasmuch as their father had abandoned the family hearth two months before his wife's hospitalization, Marc and his ten-year-old brother, Gabriel, found themselves abandoned in a spacious apartment in the center of Geneva. To say that they were "abandoned" is an overstatement: Gabriel occupied the ground floor and Marc lived alone on the floor above (alone . . . but secretly with the Kid, Mickey, "El Loco," and the "Others"). The demands of office on Marc's father in the course of his diplomatic career caused them to move frequently, from city to city, changing climates and schools along with the years. Finally the boy had the opportunity to stay put he had longed for, along with the Others. He had been born in this city but had resided here only during his father's brief vacations.

Marc took charge of their economy: their father sent them a monthly remittance, which allowed them to live modestly, not to say narrowly. He divided their income in six portions in six different envelopes marked: "Food," "Gas, electricity, and telephone," "Books," "Cécile's clinic" (their mother was called only by her Christian name), "Transportation," and "Miscellaneous." Their father continued paying the rent on their apartment from his own account, but he was so careless and distracted that there were months when Marc made his little brother call Father on the telephone to remind him of his forgotten obligation. Minute calculation made clear that the Transportation fund would be better spent on buying two bicycles on time payment to visit their mother in Nyon instead of taking the train there. The saving involved, given the scarcity of means, was not only an economic gain but meant more than thirty miles a week of biking excursion in the countryside.

The fact that neither his father nor the neighbors, not to mention the authorities, paid any attention to (or did not care to notice) the state of abandon in which the boys were left following their mother's confinement was an unmixed blessing for Marc. Thus abandoned, he lived free and independent, in a state which years later he would call one of "self-management," or "autogestation."

This condition of total autonomy did not prevent him from continuing his studies. Even though he was in a position to commit all the mischief possible for one of his age, he limited himself to forging the signature of his progenitors on the official documents that came his way or in his class grade book, and he received an excellent, though without fanfare or eulogies. He did not enforce or even recommend any particular type of conduct for his younger brother; the only restriction was a prohibition against entering his bedroom (in deference to Mickey, Teresa, and the Others). The younger brother followed a course of action which had nothing to do with that of his elder; years later he would end up in the film industry as a sound engineer, after two unsuccessful attempts as a director of documentaries.

Before they acquired the two bicycles, Gabriel one day wheedled his brother: "All my friends go fishing in the lake. I made myself a rod, but I haven't got any fishhooks."

"We don't have money for toys. But here are the envelopes, and they're yours, too. Take a look . . ."

"The one for Food is good and fat."

27

"Well, we have to eat. And there are still thirty days until the next letter from your father." (Marc never said *our* father.)

"I'll go without supper . . . if you like."

The next day, the two brothers went to a store called Le Grand Passage in downtown Geneva. Marc had instructed his brother to make a scene. He was to let out a wail and call for his papa. "Papa, Papa . . . I've lost my papa." The clerks quickly surrounded the poor boy and there was a great stir. Marc took advantage of the confusion to appropriate a dozen fishhooks. His brother had no further demands. Besides, once the savings from the Transportation envelope were realized, there was money to cover his needs in comic books, trifles, and snacks.

Whenever he contributed papers for his courses at the institute, Marc Amary, perhaps by way of amusing himself in his solitude, would invent quotations, texts, authors, cities, rivers, or nonexistent theories. Or perhaps he engaged in these flings of imagination to demonstrate to Mickey or the Kid that he was above the matter in hand. It was true enough: he was beyond the limits of the studies offered him. In the course of a written test in a philosophy class given by a Marxist, Marc quoted passages from the correspondence between Marx's son-in-law, Paul Lafargue, and a transported British prisoner in Australia, whom he called Robert Ass. This bit of hocus-pocus was the only one nearly uncovered, when the professor, who decided to write up the matter for *Les Temps Modernes,* asked him for further references. But Amary's *sang-froid,* his cool, allowed him to get away with that hoax and a whole series of similar operations, which took him to the end of the school year, at which point he was saved by the bell.

He once used much the same tactic at a now-defunct chess club, The King's Knight. The in-house champion was displaying his talents before his admirers with a certain air of grandeur. After an hour of respectful silence, and addressing the cock of the walk with infinite modesty, the boy asked: "May I play with you?"

"How old are you?"

"I'm twelve."

"That's the best age to learn. All you have to know in chess is that books are useless. Practice makes perfect, it's the only way."

Marc began the play with a psychological trick: he moved two pawns forward simultaneously, as only the most ignorant neophyte, someone who knew nothing of the rules, might do.

"Double moves are forbidden since the time of Methuselah. Did your papa teach you so badly?"

The boy made an effort to blush. And soon he was playing as he knew he must, without a fault, and checkmated the champion in twenty-seven moves. He left the café-club precipitously, before anyone had time to congratulate him or ask him any questions: these unshared pleasures were like secret gardens where he cultivated all his joys. [He told El Loco everything, but furtively, so as not to be overheard by the Kid or the "Three Condors." They were simply cheeky, and spent their nights playing poker in the dormer window.]

Considering his extreme youth, Marc treated his mother with surprising condescension. The night his father disappeared, he saw her on her knees, praying "to God" to bring him back; but she didn't cry, not even when she asked Gabriel and him to kneel with her. While his begetter and his brother gave vent to sobs, Marc limited himself zealously to repeating the prayers his mother was mumbling; his sole meditation centered on the wonder of a person who had proclaimed herself an atheist resorting to prayer. It was something he was never to understand.

During the weeks that followed, while his mother sank

into hopeless madness, Marc Amary was in full control of himself, acting as if exotic events were only natural, even when his mother claimed that the neighbors were stealing her coffee spoons and that the tradesmen were poisoning the curds of her cottage cheese. But one afternoon he announced to his brother: "Grown-ups have no integrity, no dignity, no honor."

He was beginning to delve deeper. He observed that his mother fondled him as she never had before his father's disappearance. And he began to go out to watch the flight of gliders, one of the few spectacles that could draw him away from abstract scientific speculation. The day his mother was put away he jotted down these notes:

Up until now scientists have only described mysteries and enigmas. And not resolved them. Majority of men believe statement of problems is resolution. Industrial era over. Scientific era begins. Solutions at last. With no interpretive delusions.

He signed: "The Master." [Mickey and the Kid laughed maliciously on the bed.]

Isvoschikov's kidnappers allow the plot to thicken and the suspense to intensify: they have dispatched a communiqué to the Central Press Agency, "a text of 32 lines with 90 signs each, that is, the equivalent of two full newspaper pages." In it they affirm that the protagonist of the revolution is the metropolitan proletariat, "a class which has nothing to gain within our world of production." They conclude with a reference to the "collusion of the Soviet Union with terrorist groups who represent only armed neorevisionism." In spite of which, they again demand, as the price of setting Isvoschikov free, that the Soviet Union bomb the Saudi Arabian oil wells.

Tarsis, whose turn it is to play, remains in his rest quarters throughout the entire break, something he has never done before. When he emerges, his shirttail showing beneath his jacket, he strides decisively up to the board and, still standing, moves 2. . . . d7-d5; he then cuffs the clock. Amary watches in satisfaction: in his mind it marks his first victory, for not only has Tarsis taken six minutes to carry out his two initial moves (of the 150 minutes in which he must execute the first forty) but he has demonstrated that he was not prepared for this opening.

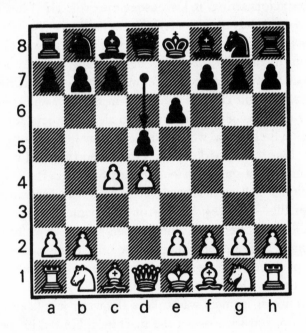

2. . . . d7-d5

The novelty of this championship match lies in the fact that in it two antagonistic world concepts confront each other. Tarsis is a player with the temperament of an artist who internalizes the structure of chess, as he would that of the world, but when he is faced with tactical problems, as at this moment, he reacts like a technician. Amary, on the other hand, is a man of science who analyzes in an objective fashion, placing his faith in statistics, but who in a crucial situation can only fall back on hypothesis, whereupon this logical fanatic is obliged to proceed in an irrational manner.

Irrational . . . that's what Tarsis's reasoning would seem to be—if anyone had known what he thought. For Tarsis is convinced that Amary is responsible for Isvoschikov's abduction. It is, he believes, the last of a long series of outrages. Behind the textual verbiage published in the newspapers by the abductors acting "in Defense of the Proletariat" he detects traces of his adversary's mentality.

As for the proletariat and their world, Tarsis was to know it from the ground up. When he was fourteen, he took the railroad from Madrid to Barcelona, almost comfortably, hidden in a freight car. Once arrived in the Catalan capital, he spent three rough nights trying to sleep in the station, the Estación de Francia, while during the day he lived out of the waste bins in the market area. On his fourth day of flight, he encountered a sign on Viejos Baños Street, in the center of the city, which read: APPRENTICE WANTED. He was found acceptable—on a test basis—for employment in a jeweler's workshop, located in a rented room on the third floor of a building. The oral agreement between himself and the boss (one of three craftsmen working in the shop) bore no similarity to a modern labor contract.

His first assignment was to keep the water jugs filled, sweep the shop, and wipe down the machines. He did his best. A week later he was assigned a mission requiring some trust.

He was given a leather pouch to hang around his neck, and was told to transport, to and from the shop, all the stones used in the trade—rubies, diamonds, agates, sapphires, etc. He took them to the artisans who worked for the shop: to the setters, who inserted the stones in the jewelry; the engravers, who designed the artistic prints; the polishers, who heightened the polish; the gem-cutters, who carved with precision; or to the bathhouses, where the gold or silver dipping was done. He also showed clients the models conceived as possible designs by his boss. Since even modest buyers had their own preferences and ideas regarding types of jewelry, each modification in design sent him off on a new trek.

In those days, the entire guild of jewelry workers lived in the center of Barcelona, mostly in slum quarters or in cheap rented rooms on such streets as Petritxol, Baños Viejos, or Boquería. The typical freelance artisan often lived in a tiny room in which a studio couch or divan filled the space left near a desk whose drawers held the tools of his trade—and like as not some lewd "French" photographs in lieu of a woman. The different trades were all plied by men, except for that of polisher, which was reserved for women, and these ladies inhabited the dreams of all romantic craftsmen, for they were young and single, lovely and perverse, with fairy hands which rubbed and rubbed, as they busied themselves stroking away like odalisques, on into eternity or delirium.

Step by step, slowly but steadily, the boss allowed Tarsis to try his hand at small jobs during these early apprentice days: he began by welding broken chains, then making simple repairs, and finally cutting brooches and rings. This last operation required a small saw, which broke easily and often. One day it broke in the boy's hands and the two ends were driven into his thumb and middle finger. Because it was a common accident, the shop was equipped with an acid bath, which served not only to wash away the black stains from soldering but also to stanch the blood in such wounds. Tarsis made an awful scene: his fellow workers thought that he must be having an attack. The figure of El Francés loomed in Tarsis's mind, and he howled: "I can't stand the pain!"

He boarded in a *pensión* established on one floor of a building by a widow who also worked elsewhere as a maid and who had a deaf-mute son a little older than Tarsis. The new apprentice did not find his work onerous, and he appreciated the confidence shown in him when he was entrusted so soon with the precious stones. In that epoch, apprentices were no longer formally taught their trade by foremen and fellow workers, something which suited Tarsis; there was a great difference between being taught and learning on one's own, and he learned through his gifts of observation. As soon as he began to carry out the simpler tasks on his own, working the silver (gold was too costly to entrust to a beginner), he quickly demonstrated his skill. Each step forward amounted to a conquest, and when he finally gained access to the gold stocks, he was unreservedly pleased: he even imagined that his father was watching him with satisfaction.

He soon acquired the habits of a craftsman in his trade: he would brush himself after work to recover the powder adhering to his smock, and he would wash his hands carefully so that the filter might strain out any particles encrusted in his fingernails. (These filters were then bought by the recuperators, who managed to separate the gold from the filth.) Though there was nothing majestic about the shop, Tarsis experienced an irrational exultation whenever he touched the gold. It might have been akin to what men felt centuries before when they worked at discovering the philosopher's stone.

He was interested in every detail of his job; he might have called it magical, if this word had been current with him. He was enchanted as he watched the gold being cast into the small clay cubes, fused under a small gas flame. The blowtorch caused an occasional accident among the apprentices in other workshops, and they sometimes wound up in the emergency wards of hospitals in a semiconscious state. Tarsis, however, never breathed in any of the poisonous effluvia, though he kept the rubber hose containing the gas in his mouth without letup; he managed to blow on it skillfully at all times and to keep the flame at exactly the proper height. At the end of his first year in the shop, he had some cards printed which contained a verse in the local Catalan language:

> *Moltes felicitats*
> *moltes prosperitats*
> *vos desitja*
> *l' aprenent*
> *que treballa*
> *molt diligent.*

> (Best wishes
> and prosperity
> are desired thee
> by the apprentice
> who does his work
> with diligence.)

He distributed the cards among clients and artisans, and since the message was a hit—especially because it was written in the Catalan language of Barcelona by a boy who was apparently from Madrid—he was the recipient of generous Christmas and New Year's gifts. As a result, he was able to buy the tools he needed. Apprentices and craftsmen had to acquire on their own account the necessary implements (saws, pliers, measuring instruments). They could not use those of their fellows, which were unsuited to their own personal requirements. Tarsis was soon granted permission to draw out the gold threads to make rings. With infinite precaution he would make the minute measurements, cut and form the threads, and round each one with a wooden mallet prior to sending it to the polisher for the final touches. He preferred working with gold alone to constructing brooches from a drawing. The foreman, a man scant of words, one day spoke a short phrase which filled Tarsis with more satisfaction than he had received from being named an exceptional student: "You are going to be an outstanding craftsman."

A year later, he was in charge of appraising gold, and of determining the carats of each piece. Although the technique was simple enough, the evaluation depended on instinct. The gold was rubbed against the black stone and a little acid was then dropped upon it. The number of carats was determined based on the relationship between the color which appeared and yellow. Tarsis's ability to grade the difference instinctively astonished his colleagues. But to him, his skill was no more noteworthy than the fact that he and his two fellow workers did not require the magnifying glass used by the foreman.

He never wrote to his Aunt Paloma, nor did he ever again read the cheap illustrated books of his youth. Every Sunday morning he played soccer with his landlady's son; they were both members of the Barcelona team for deaf-mutes. It was an outstanding team within the Honor Division of the Catalan Amateur Championship League. Tarsis played right forward, and was the only one on the team who could hear. The umpire in these matches did not use a whistle but instead a large white handkerchief. Just when a professional club showed signs of signing him up for its junior team, Tarsis quit soccer for good.

On his third move, Amary advanced the queen's knight 3. Ktb1-c3), maintaining the pressure against the center. He

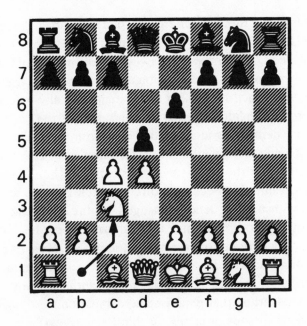

3. Ktb1-c3

placed the horse so that it faced him, as was his custom, so that it could look at him . . . so that it might worship him . . . or so that it might be able to kick his rival in the face. But by then Tarsis had absented himself, and was in his quarters, observing the play, perhaps from between the arms of his enormous Christ figure, watching Amary's maneuver on closed-circuit television.

The favorite topic of conversation in the jewelry work-shops and among all the workers in the trade was: women.

At the end of his first period of some three months in Barcelona, and along with one Antoni Puig, a shop technician, Tarsis went for the first time to a whorehouse, the Top Hat, not far from the site where in 1907 Picasso had met the models for his painting of the whores of Aviñon Street, an unfinished symphony which passed into the history of Cubism and the mannerism of affectation under the title *Les demoiselles d'Avignon.* Since he looked older than he really was, it did not prove difficult to get by the plug-ugly at the door, who was busy demanding identification cards from the really young, his job being to keep minors out. That first visit Tarsis savored thoroughly; at the same time, it also affected him like a first hit of cocaine. He began to stiffen and felt choked, weighed down with unease. And it changed his life. The place was, he thought, both glory and abyss, a place where he suffered pleasure, where he found joy amid darkness. Most of all, he had found a drug he soon could not do without: he was astonished that he had been able to live without it until then. He soon learned that paradise and damnation were made up of various seasons or states. Within a few weeks, along with his fellow traveler Puig, the exploratory expedition had become a daily pilgrimage, either prodigiously wondrous or awful. The nightly round would begin on the Street of Mud Walls, Calle de las Tapias, where the most salacious and amusing whores hung out, then proceeded along the highway to Sarria, where the more exquisite and costliest professionals carried out their office, and might end in the black lands, Tierra Negra, where, behind the Ciudadela Park, the virtuoso on duty, or rather the *virtuosa,* for less than a five-peseta piece, would void whoever might be her parishioner, while he, by way of exalting his transports, would encase his most dextrous hand in the she-samaritan's crotch, while with the other he would caress her nipples. Afterward the pilgrim might swab himself against the wall.

Each of the brothels boasted a large sitting room which opened out on a dramatic scene, a velvet cord separating the

38

audience from the artists. Some of the latter indulged in banter with a piquant bravura and brazenness, others simply but not innocently would move their limbs with a show of elegance, the better to display their charms. But the truly triumphant were the psychological geniuses who grossly and openly mocked the onlookers and voyeurs. Some were dressed as if for a stroll on the street, others covered their nudity with a towel or two, while the sauciest wore only panties and brassiere. It never occurred to any of them to be so indiscreet and senseless as to sit there naked. Payment was in advance and was made to a bawd who kept her back to the spectacle and spent the night reading the *Lives of the Saints*. The she-sacristans would give each client an open-sesame (in the form of a copper token more than half an inch in diameter) upon payment of the charitable contribution. To avoid controversy, the majority of these temples boasted posters, prominently displayed, upon which the basis of the contractual arrangements were clearly enunciated. Regular lay: X amount; French: so much. Each metal disk gave one the right to one servicing—which ended with the first flood tide. Sometimes the insatiable and needy consumer, after his first outburst, in a rapture of exacerbation would have to finish off the herculean task by himself in the toilet.

The experts, who were legion, would deliver large commentaries, without any show of jealousy, regarding the virtues of each executrix, and would compassionately advise the novices:

"The one in the transparent blouse does it like a house afire and she swallows the smoke."

"Watch out for the one with the flat nose, her teeth are deadly in maneuvers."

"That redhead does a customs search while she's playing your flute."

Every Wednesday at two in the morning, Tarsis and his friend Puig would attend the film showing at the Principal Palacio, a special session for the city's gamblers, their support system, and other authorized members of Barcelona's netherworld. (The showing was known by the name of *"Las Golfas,"* the "She-Bums.") The import of the film itself almost never surpassed the loud improvisations delivered with salty wit from the audience in that hall packed with bedmates and panderers.

On a parallel course to this nocturnal errancy steeped in fornication-without-a-human-face, Puig was spending some part of his days shadowing a neighborhood girl for whom he sighed but to whom he did not dare declare himself. One Sunday morning, following his soccer game with the deafmutes, Tarsis deliberately and ridiculously got him drunk on dry aniseed brandy in the hope that he would screw up his courage to ask for the hand of the girl on whom he had focused all his senses, or almost all.

For his part, after his discovery of the life of the night, its delights and its nightmares, Tarsis spent days retracing in his mind and savoring his excursions from house to house, where he spent most of his time as one of the voyeurs. He daydreamed at work, and his eroticism became a delirious obsession:

. . . on the stairs I fondle her behind and caress her pomegranate and push her on the floor and go in without taking off her underwear she kisses me and her tongue is thick and smells of jasmine my mouth fills with a torrent of saliva we get to the loft and she envelops my cock with her mouth her tongue she breathes me in her mouth like petals and puts her breasts in my mouth and I cover them with saliva and spume and caress her and tremble and fill her mouth with bubbles and swallow them slowly so as not to lose a drop while I nibble she kisses my backside and I boil as she puts her tongue into my behind I see stars and shiver and want

to bite her and rend her kiss her and console her trumpets resound as a fire rages and the flames reveal her and I'm sweating and mount her from behind and feel her legs fine and white alongside my testicles and am aroused all over again my blood flows with wasps in my veins I see her in the subway and lift her skirts and my cock goes all the way into her heart the people look at us as she lets herself go as if in a dream between waves in the roar of the tunnels the other women caress me and one after the other I enter them the train setting the tempo all of them licking me everything balls ass cock and rub themselves against my hands knuckles elbows knees I'm going to die my marrow is inflamed burning inside they lick my feet install me on a wheel so that one after another they can be entered my cock my head splits my belly is out of control it palpitates on its own they all kiss me one after another their lips wet in a frenzy hundreds of women thousands millions of women like archangels . . .

His delirium often ended with the image of God, while his constant erection caused him unstoppable pain.

Tarsis does not accede to the Queen's Gambit proposed by his rival and plays 3. . . . Bf8-e7 with apparent recklessness. Amary announces *"J'adoube"* to the referees in a firm voice, and immediately moves the bishop a fraction of an inch, for, in actual fact, Tarsis had not placed the piece in the proper center of its square. With his action, Amary believes that he is giving his opponent an irrefutable lesson.

The number of possible combinations by which to carry out the first ten moves in a game of chess attains the figure of 169,518,829,100,544,326,897,235,000,000. But frequently a champion player must analyze more than ten moves as he sits before the board. Time, therefore, is precious and concentration fundamental. Any distraction may lead to an irreparable catastrophe. Nevertheless, Tarsis and Amary, as if they were challenging each other to a Ping-Pong duel, au-

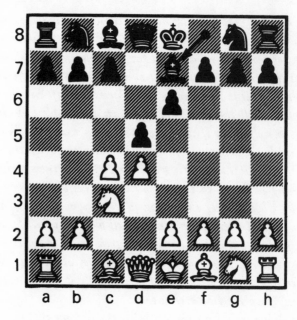

3. . . . Bf8-e7

tomatically carry out (apparently without any reflection whatsoever) five moves each.

(Marc Amary:
4. Ktg1-f3, 5. Bc1-g5, 6. e2-e3, 7. Bg5-h4, 8. c4xd5.
And Elias Tarsis:
4. . . . Ktg8-f6, 5. . . . 0-0, 6. . . . h7-h6, 7. . . . b7-b6,
8. . . . e6xd5.)

Or perhaps they move in this fashion so as to put a quick
end to their first, tacit, agreement, which they both endorsed
by adopting the line of the Tartakover Variant to Queen
Gambit Declined, the object of so much study on the occasion of the Karpov-Korchnoi encounter.

Tarsis has made his last move (8. . . . e6xd5) with such disdain that he flings his rival's pawn, which he has just taken (which

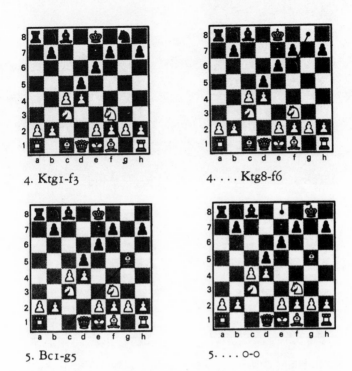

4. Ktg1-f3

4. ... Ktg8-f6

5. Bc1-g5

5. ... 0-0

he has "eaten," as the game's followers might say, using the suggestive cannibalistic term), down hard on the table. It lands off the board and falls prone. Amary notes the move parsimoniously and sets the pawn upright. With rising fury, Tarsis grabs the piece violently and hurls it into the seventh row of spectators.

The officials contemplate the incident with amazement, as livid as the Swiss champion himself, if that were possible. The rules did not foresee such a situation: pieces retired after being taken are outside play. At the very most, the judges may decide that an aggressor's gesture, because of its vehemence, might perturb his opponent's powers of reflection. But Tarsis might then argue that his rival, by righting the piece, disconcerted *him*. The officials hate these troublesome imbroglios.

6. e2-e3

6. . . . h7-h6

7. Bg5-h4

7. . . . b7-b6

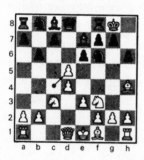

8. c4xd5

8. . . . e6xd5

44

For the first time since the beginning of the match, the two players observe each other fixedly, both of them immobile. Tarsis appears to be fretting, in a fury, while Amary maintains his familiar lack of expression. And the exchange of looks between them seems to continue without letup. Tarsis is repeating to himself something he has said since the beginning of the championship: "I didn't have to play him. I should have killed him when I got the letter from de Kerguelen. And if he provokes me, I'll do him in right here and now." The officials stand up ready to intervene, but look and remain hieratic, paralyzed by their sense of responsibility. The audience watches the interminable, muffled battle in total silence.

At the end of fifty-eight seconds, Amary lowers his head, beaten in the visual duel, and advances his queen without thinking of the consequences to b3 (9. Qb1-b3).

The amazement felt by the critics analyzing the game in the adjoining hall is only natural: Amary has committed a beginner's vagary. It might be said that, hypnotized by his adversary's play (. . . b7-b6), he attacks a black queen wing not yet defined, assuming that the bishop will occupy b7.

Amary goes to register his move on the board, when suddenly his hand stops: he examines the board and discovers his mistake . . . too late. The inner commotion to which a champion is prey following a false step like this one has been recounted by the Estonian player Keres in the following manner:

I always ask myself "How could I have played so badly?" The blood seems to drain out of me. There are players who seem on the contrary to marshal all their red blood cells on their forehead and cheeks. I try to keep calm and struggle to hide my dismay and my desire to give up.

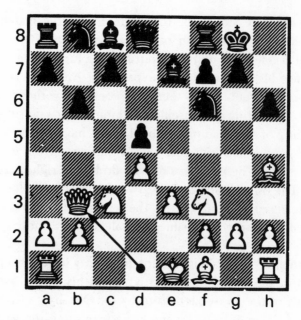

9. Qb1-b3

Amary makes his way very slowly to his quarters and locks himself in. He wants to think over his error in private.

R. M. Gudmundsson approaches Tarsis and tells him: "Maestro, it would be preferable if in the future you were to avoid throwing pawns into the audience. The next time, my colleagues and I will find ourselves obliged to reprimand you in an official manner."

Tarsis, who is humming to himself, condescendingly nods his head. He accepts the fact that the judge, in violation of the rules, addresses him during the period set aside for reflection.

The official breathes easy and Tarsis, grown smug and haughty, stands up; he is off to reflect as usual on his own moves in the small suite assigned to him for that purpose. The scene now offers an unexpected development: a chess match in which both players are absent.

Suddenly quite fatigued, Amary rests in an easy chair in his quarters. He has lost his impassivity because of an incident he would normally consider insignificant. The like has happened to him only a few times in his life. Unconsciously and without his being able to avoid it, his memory is taken up with the image of Michelle Dubin entering his room (. . . entering *his* bedroom, where the atmosphere is thick with the smoke of the green Tuscan cigars ceaselessly smoked by "Doña Rosita," the serpent).

At that time, although he had already been named investigator for the CNRS, he was living in the University Residence Bures-Sud. His unalterable routine demanded that he go to bed at five in the morning and rise at twelve noon, after seven hours of sleep (and of arguments with the Kid). Afternoons, he went to his office in the laboratory of Theoretical Physics and High Energy. His room in the residence he thought of solely as an annex to his office, except that he slept in the former. [This was not the opinion, however, of Mickey.]

The cleaning woman in charge of his floor would have liked him to change his schedule so that she might make his bed and use the vacuum before noon. She was a bit older than Amary, rather attractive, and with the accent of a true Parisienne. Her name was Michelle Dubin. Every morning at eleven o'clock, thanks to her skeleton key, she entered the room with feigned innocence, went to the window, threw open the curtains all the way, and would then pretend to discover, in a show of confusion, that the occupant was still asleep in bed. She would run through a rehearsed apology in which all her complaints were incorporated: "Pardon me, I thought you were gone. It's so late. It's almost quarter past eleven, and since we take our lunch at twelve-thirty . . . Do you understand what I'm trying to tell you?"

Her tactics did not deceive Amary, but the woman made her point: she woke him up and hastened his leaving. One morning, tired of the game, he got out of bed when she entered and told her in a steady voice: "Every day you wake me up with the same trick. I want to tell you that this farce has ended for good. Now please leave."

At the end of a week, Michelle Dubin knocked at his door. It was six in the evening and Amary (with Mickey on his lap) was reading Calvin's *Institutes of the Christian Religion.*

"May I come in?"

"The room is already made up."

"I want to talk to you . . . Please let me come in." She entered the room with a decisive step. "May I sit down?"

Without waiting for a reply she installed herself on the edge of the bed. Amary turned a bit pale, went to the window, and pulled the curtains back.

"I must tell you something . . . important. Please sit down. There's a chair for you."

Amary obeyed her and placed his chair at a good distance away. It was too late to throw her out.

"I want your help."

"You want me to help you?"

"Let me explain. I speak to you not only as your cleaning woman but also in the name of three comrades. The four of us are provisionals, temporary help . . . for the past three years. That is, we have no rights to bonuses or retirement pay or to the pay raises the steady workers get. Besides, we can be put on the street whenever they feel like it."

"My business is physics."

Michelle didn't hear him or didn't wish to. "For two years we've been trying to make our case. We don't ask so very much. We just want to be like the others."

"Take your complaints to the administration."

"No. Everything depends on the others."

"Who are the others?"

"The union bosses. And they're heartless dues-mongers."

48

"What has the union got to do with it?"

"The union . . . I hope you understand me . . . is interested only in the steady workers. They couldn't care less about the rest of us. They won't even let us get a union card. In short, since the administration and the union are just using us, you might want to help us."

"I'm not the right person."

"Just consider my situation. I'm divorced, with two small daughters and my mother to take care of. And as for the allowance my husband was supposed to pay me according to the judge, I haven't seen so much as the envelope, nor will I ever see it. I don't make enough to live on from what I make working here. When I leave, I go to clean up in a couple of offices. You can't imagine what it is to go home at night and have to kiss my two dears in the dark so as not to wake them. Some nights my blood cries out. If they paid us what they pay the others here, four-fifty an hour more, I wouldn't have to do the offices."

Michelle had gotten herself so worked up that she was about to cry. But she was able to intuit that her tears would only have made her repellent in Amary's eyes, and perhaps even have aroused disgust.

"Why are you telling me all this?"

"You're not like the others."

"You don't know me."

"The other day when you scolded me about the curtains I realized that . . . well . . . that . . ."

"I didn't scold you."

"I mean I could see that you were not mean, like the others—Do you know what I'm trying to say?"

"They are my colleagues. Some of them are older, my elders."

"You're not like them, one can see that at a glance. You must help us."

Michelle had guessed something that none of his colleagues would have dared suppose: that Amary would take up the cause of some unknown part-time cleaning woman. For his part, without a twinge of sentimentality (Madame Dubin's domestic drama left him cold), Amary took on the problem as if it were a question of physics. With his habitual sense of order he began as if undertaking a mission. His first step was to consult the labor code, two union publications, and the administration rules, and he studied them thoroughly. Next he compared the declarations by the unions upholding the students and those upholding his colleagues. He looked over the manifestos issued by the diverse political entities at the university. All of them—though they were obviously directed in general at a university audience—gave themselves names liberally sprinkled with such sparkling designations as "worker," "labor," "proletarian," apart from the regulation clichés of "Marxist," "socialist," "Communist," or "revolutionary." Unfortunately, none of them contemplated the case of the only bona fide workers in that oasis of study. It was all new to him: he had no measure to encompass all the outrages which, with such grand style and sense of justice, were ritually "denounced," or the demands made that they "immediately cease," or the judgments issued as to their being "inadmissible and degrading." The proclamations bravely condemned the "Fascists," "Nazis," and "exploiters" who apparently pullulated with impunity within the ranks of the faculty. A text issued by the Dimitrov Faction caught his immediate attention: above the inevitable hammer and sickle at the bottom was blazoned a slogan which finally seemed to cover the case of the cleaning women. It read: FOR THE WORKERS' REVOLUTION. And, moreover: AGAINST THE REVISIONIST UNIONS, PARASITES OF THE WORKING CLASS.

Amary went to some pains to arrange an interview with Pierre Corneille, an experimental chemist with a brilliant academic record, at that moment secretary-general of the Dimitrov Faction. In the course of the very brief meeting granted him by this leader (it had about it the unmistakable aura of an *audience*), Amary was able merely to outline the case superficially. By way of his only reply, the leader agreed to receive him and Michelle on the following day, at the group's headquarters. He insisted, with a certain degree of solemnity, on the need for secrecy, because, as he put it, of "police hysteria," for "they are trying to destroy us." Amary went off in high satisfaction: Corneille was not, as he might have expected from his reading of the diverse posters and manifestos, a romantic and empty-headed radical chieftain, but a highly responsible organizer with his feet on the ground and, even more unexpected, one who did not suffer from verbosity. He had immediately understood, or so Amary believed, the essence of the problem, succinctly stated, and had proposed the ideal solution: a meeting with the victim in the presence of his committee.

He learned that Corneille was one of the most respected of the Marxist thinkers. His press releases and articles were sought after by the most circumspect newspapers in the world, including the Op Ed page of *The New York Times*. Even if, naturally enough, not everyone accepted his highly original ideas, the majority praised the subtlety of his analyses and the profundity of his reflections.

For its headquarters, the Dimitrov Faction availed itself of an elegant chalet on the outskirts of Fontenay-aux-Roses. An ample hall on the ground floor was well equipped to serve for the theoretical work of the group, and it was formally presided over by two portraits. Though at the time Amary was not versed in political matters, he had no difficulty in recognizing that the one on the right was Joseph Stalin. The one on the left he was unable to identify: a personage, also mustachioed, could be taken, if one were indulgent, for the head of some dark Sicilian enterprise, and inspired the confidence one would get from a dealer in used cars. The militants, most of them young, among whom he recognized various colleagues, were seated at desk chairs, in attitudes suggesting the nineteenth century. Corneille presided at a table raised on a platform under the two portraits, facing his recruits.

Amary was most struck by the similarity of their outfits: black hemp espadrilles, blue cotton pants, and blue Mao jacket-shirts buttoned to the neck. If it were not for the faces, he might be in Inner Mongolia. They all wore a red badge with yellow stars over their hearts; the badges sparkled so that for a moment they resembled rubies encrusted in gold. The badge was simply their Communist emblem. Corneille wore two.

Once Michelle and Amary succeeded in boxing themselves into the only available desk in the last row, Corneille identified the two he had invited "to serve as observers and witnesses." They were: "The worker Michelle Dubin and the intellectual worker Marc Amary." Next, as if the two no longer existed, he informed his people of the group's latest activities: with the use of portable ship's sirens and itching powder they had succeeded in "boycotting" a "revisionist" meeting organized by the "agents of socio-imperialism" in defense of Nicaragua. They had also been able, thanks to the programmed strategy of "entrism" (Amary understood the term to mean the same as infiltration), to penetrate the Union of the Book of Seine-Saint-Denis for the purpose of disarticulating it. Cornelle's obvious pleasure, near gloating, while he related these feats would have struck a frivolous observer as close to orgasmic. In truth, Corneille knew how to restrain himself, to hold back, so that he did not come all over himself with pleasure when his mouth welled up in rapture with the top cream and essence of his master Stalin and the maxims of his comrade Enver Hoxha (for such proved to be the other hero portrayed). The anthological knowledge of these two eminent heroes, these two Founding Fathers, proved so pertinent, and especially so vast, that the speaker could literally count on a bottomless well in which to drink and offer drink. Thanks to her own elementary powers of deduction, Michelle Dubin had already figured out that the dignitary who shared the presidential wall with Comrade Stalin was none other than Comrade Enver Hoxha, Secretary-General of the Albanian Communist Party, a humanist who had sacrificed himself for his people ever since 1945, when he had assumed the burden of Chief of State. Corneille professed a limitless admiration for this master—or, more exactly, the limits coincided with those of "scientific Marxism."

For his part, Amary was busy assimilating a lesson elegantly taught. Corneille was revealing the ideological bases of the proletarian revolution before he could get to the case of the cleaning women. The task ahead was glorious . . . but quite arduous: not only was it requisite to destroy Yankee imperialism and its paper tigers, the multinationals, but it was also necessary to crush Moscow's social fascists and its Cuban and Vietnamese mercenaries. The assembled comrades drank in the words of their rector with fervent attention, not to say devotion.

In Amary's view, the era's greatest renovator in mathematics was (along with Thom) a man named Bouteville, and that man, that very same man, was sitting in the hall at that moment, with eyes as big as saucers, taking in every word of the harangue.

The upshot was that Amary suddenly found himself confronted with a prodigious new universe and one that seemed wondrous rich—despite and even because of the manifest ideological extravagance. It struck him as coherent, and it was one he had never examined. The extravagant absurdities only served to demonstrate the depth of this new vision of the world, since the rigor of the system permitted such luxuries without destroying or affecting it. Amary proposed to look into the question of Marxism.

At one point Corneille appeared to be suffering an epileptic attack, such were his contortions. The militants contemplated him in a panic, but inasmuch as they were rightly terrified of him, no one dared move to help him. After a couple of long minutes the spasmodic gestures ceased and the leader wiped from his face all traces of the foaming spittle which had formed at his mouth. He then reassured his followers: "It was nothing of consequence. I merely suffered a petit-bourgeois temptation. I was forced to consider the *Antidühring* of Engels. I have now exorcised the thought."

After all, they seemed to think, he is a man like other men. They were confused. Were they wrong? Corneille now asked those present—by way of rekindling the ardor of the cell— to give an ovation to the comrades who had broken up the revisionist demonstration favoring a thirty-five-hour week. The clamor was likely to arouse the suspicion of the neighborhood's night watchmen. So the chief restrained the sonorous and vibrant ovation with a decisive gesture of his index finger, displaying the finesse of an orchestral conductor. They stopped short. But then they cheered the Albanian chieftain and comrade with a chant which gave evidence of their lack of poetic sensibility:

En-ver-Hox-ha!
En-ver-Hox-ha!

Another imperious gesture from the chief cut short the verse at the surname. Next he invited Michelle and Amary to sit next to him, on two stools. For quite different reasons the two had been seduced by Corneille's philippic, and in a certain manner they, too, could see in their imaginations the triumphant tomorrows, which, if not red, were at least rose-colored as far as the female workers were concerned.

"Comrade Dubin, present your case."

Michelle repeated what she had told Amary, detailing the tremendous injustice endured by the cleaning women. She told her tale with such emotion that tears came to her eyes. Corneille listened, breathing heavily, like a locomotive going up an incline, his head held between his hands, until he unexpectedly yelled: "You mean you want to earn zero, period, zero, zero five centimes an hour more?"

"It's not a question of zero, period, zero, zero five an hour more, but four francs fifty . . . and the right to retirement, and social security . . ."

Corneille had turned livid with fury. He thrust his finger at Michelle and howled: "You're no better than a reptile in the service of poisonous capitalism."

Luckily, he paused for a spell. Amary feared he might attack her. Surrounded by the faithful, he might have done so, but he took hold of himself and began to lecture her with much heat: "You're a traitor to your class. And you're willing to prostitute yourself for a wretched handful of change. Instead of doing your duty as a proletarian and working for the revolution, you busy yourself with filth, with the search for petty sums of money. You are a whited sepulcher. You serve the ends of monopoly capitalism. You are trying to deceive the Dimitrov Faction. Who sent you here? You've rehearsed your melodrama well. At what bourgeois police orders? Hyena and liar, deceitful crow. You're a parasite on the working class . . . !"

Destiny operates in impenetrable ways. For these strange manifestations of religious fervor, these rites, led Amary to "enter politics," as others, *mutatis mutandis,* enter religious orders. Michelle gained a certain notoriety as a "dissident" of the ferocious Dimitrov Faction (at the top of the union's blacklist, a fearsome position she had gained from a two-hour visit) and was allowed, out of fear on the part of her union, to qualify at a higher level and thus earn "the wretched handful of change" she sought to enable her to sup with her daughter every night.

Even in losing, Tarsis displays a certain harmony in his play, as if reenacting the ways of creation, of Genesis. From a certain point of view, he is. Now he takes the initiative and rivets Amary's error in place. His bishop, waiting in the refuge of c8 jumps to e6, whence he can espy the vagabond white queen and threaten her. Thus he underscores Amary's blunder in red, amplifies it, and undermines his rival's position.

Tarsis is convinced that Amary is involved in the abduction of the Soviet official Igor Isvoschikov. His suspicions admit

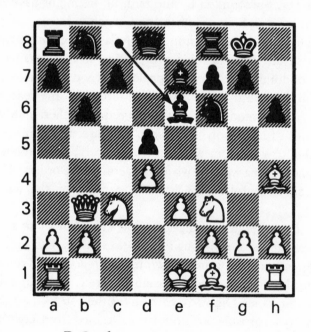

9. . . . Bc8-e6

no doubts, but fortunately he communicates them to no one.

Central to Tarsis's reasoning is the "incredible" nature of his opponent's setback in the fourth game. What the commentators saw as a howler or a simple oversight at best on the part of White, Tarsis saw as a deliberate loss: Amary wanted to lose—he *had* to lose—in order to justify the two delays he immediately solicited. He was granted a week's liberty—which he clearly employed to deprive the Russian official of his liberty. Tarsis intuited the following evolution of the drama: at seven-thirty in the evening Amary stops the clock and acknowledges his defeat; at eight he and his thugs arrive at his home at Meung-sur-Loire. A few hours later, Isvoschikov disappears: the police are still not able to say just when his sleep was interrupted. Amary has a week free to dispose of loose ends, including the best way to immobilize the Minister. He did not even have to defend his reasons for postponing play at the chessboard. "The useful idiots" of which Lenin spoke filled the bill. For example, the Yugoslav master Pantelic issued a declaration for UPI: "Such a resounding loss always results in a profound trauma. Amary requested two postponements in order to 'reconsider' the opening system which has suffered such a rude blow." (Chess players, like certain essayists, like to prefix any verb with "re-" even though the verb would serve just as well without it.) Tarsis is ready to demonstrate to anyone at any time and place that Amary has not changed anything in regard to his play.

Tarsis can smell out each and every error by Amary: not only does his opponent's pallor intensify on these rare occasions, but his odor changes as well, and so suddenly that he gives off a whiff of wilted geranium. And yet, after the "impropriety" he committed in the fourth game, neither his color nor his odor was in any way altered.

Amary appeared a week later with an exuberant air to play

the fifth game. His exuberance was not lessened because only Tarsis noticed it. The latter was busy reconstructing in his mind the "people's trial" to which the Soviet official would have been subjected. Tarsis pictured it as if he were sitting in the first row: Amary appropriating to himself the function of judge, legislator, and executioner as he presided over the farce; representing the judicial power as an intransigent magistrate, promulgating the law like the whole legislature, deciding the specific punishments to be meted out to the culprit; in sum, acting as the repressive arm of the executive to crush the prisoner.

No one would have taken his suspicions seriously had Tarsis voiced them, just as no one in the chess world gave any credence to the charges made against Tarsis himself in a British weekly, where he was credited with a past as a pimp in Barcelona. No one, naturally, lowered himself to the point of asking a single question about the ridiculous imputation. Such a bizarre accusation only Tarsis could have authenticated. He would have done so without blushing.

He had suffered a life change late one night or early one morning during one of the Wednesday-night/Thursday-morning sessions at the Principal Palacio. Destiny made use of the double life of his comrade Antoni Puig. That night the latter had gone to supper with his fiancée's parents. He had now become so taken with the girl that he had bought a rhyming dictionary in order to compose some verses to her along the lines of, and inspired by, "El Tren Expreso" of Don Ramón de Campoamor. Had it been known, such an activity would have been a great surprise to all those who knew him only as an unconditional enthusiast of Barcelona's whoredom. It was unthinkable. The foreman himself had issued a dire warning: *"A cada cerdo le llega su San Martín":* Every pig gets his ritual day of slaughter.

That night, Tarsis alone, without the company of his crony

in the pilgrimage of sexual surfeit, found a mate in the late-night film session known by the name of *"Las Golfas,"* the showing for she-bums. The film being exhibited on this occasion featured Esther Williams, who enthralled one of the most difficult audiences in the Christian West. That compact demoiselle emerging from the water, virginal and well rounded, was the compendium of all imaginable charms. And also of all unimaginable virtues for those whores and pimps who were not lacking in fonts of inspiration. Compared to the sordidness of their existence, they beheld the splendor of romantic adventure; instead of the griminess of their brothels, the lacquered sky of California; instead of their dirty little tucked-away rooms, a decor like a silver tea service; instead of the ill temper of their clients, the smile of a siren; instead of vice and sin, the perfumed virtue of a Hollywood star. Besides . . . she wasn't thin. And they were a generation which had assimilated the precepts preached by Spanish chocolatiers: far better to be fat, rich, hearty, easygoing, genial, than thin, poor, somber, ugly, and bitter. As an added benefit, the movie's story had nothing to do with the stories and scripts of her namesake, that other Williams, known as Tennessee, which this audience would have rejected as being morbid.

When Tarsis came into the theater, the film had already started amid a silence which was religious in nature: the Colombian baritone Carlos Ramírez, wondrously stuffed into an embroidered costume, was singing a love hymn to the belle Esther, audaciously evoking the beauty of her wrist (which she barely displayed), her ruby mouth, her dark tresses and pearl-like teeth. Again, these verses had nothing to do with those of Esther Williams's other namesake, those of William Carlos Williams, perhaps another reason that they captivated one and all.

But this romantic nonsense meant nothing to Tarsis. In fact, it led only to a sense of frustration, and with good reason.

He was looking for a *"pajillera,"* a hand artist who would help him out, and he looked the audience over carefully in the semidarkness. The most skillful and dextrous were already taken in by the goddess on the screen. Finally Tarsis sat down next to a dim form which he could identify in the darkness as feminine and blond. Ready for action, he unbuttoned his pants. These were times when the art of living was practiced with elementary elegance, even around the crotch: that is, there were no zippers, and Tarsis never could see the point of such an unfortunate invention, which only served to wrench one's pubic hair. He was limited to a mere fifteen pesetas but his strong powers of concentration allowed him to prolong nirvana until halfway through the film, as long as he was able to imagine himself submerged during the hot nights in an icy swimming pool at the North Pole.

If Tarsis had paid a bit of attention he would have noticed that the feminine figure to his right (though what difference did it make?) was actually *reading,* in the half-light she managed to utilize from off the screen, and even that she was reading *The War Against the Salamanders.* She was scarcely a lady of convenience at all. Far from it: she was a seventeen-year-old born in Sitges and named Nuria Roig. She was so wrapped up in her novel, which she had already read nineteen times, that she was not even aware of the salacious arrangement her neighbor had silently proposed. He finally made out her features, and given that her position was with her back to the screen so as the better to catch the reflected light, they could easily stare at each other. Tarsis decided to remain in his seat without any expectation of his neighbor rendering the expected comfort. But he refrained from speaking to her.

When the film ended they left the movie house together or, more precisely, they accompanied each other in total silence, walking up the Ramblas, Tarsis a couple of steps in front. When they reached the Plaza de Toros, Tarsis sat down on the ground against the wall and she fitted herself beside him, and they sat thus for more than a half hour, at the end of which period Nuria, her pretty head directly before Tarsis, told him that she loved him, according to the normal practice in romantic songs or prayers.

During the two months which followed that warm dawn, Nuria and Elias Tarsis lived like two corralled whelps, ready to escape at the first opportunity.

Nuria was a runaway, having escaped from her parents' house when she realized they had been transformed into "salamanders." First she robbed them of 28,000 pesetas. Tarsis calculated that he would have had to work for four years in his shop to amass such a sum.

Tarsis felt a strange attraction for Nuria, or so he thought. That is, he would never have acknowledged that he loved her. Perhaps he did not recognize such a sentiment. In any case, he could not do without her for a moment. He searched her eyes meditatively, touched her all over, stroked her hair, her eyebrows, held her wrists in his hands, tongued her mouth, drank her saliva, caressed her white, rounded, ever-so-smooth knees.

Fearing she might be recognized, Nuria dyed her hair black and dressed as an older woman. Elias bought himself a navy-blue suit and a striped tie and grew an impressive mustache. Every week they moved from one hotel to another. Thanks to a marriage license they had bought from one of the versatile smuggler-bootblacks at the Hotel Imperio for a thousand pesetas, they were able to pass as newlyweds. False identity papers cost them two thousand more each.

Except for the time they spent in bed, Tarsis passed his days consumed by jealousy. He was stricken with an unknown pain which made him shiver all over.

Nuria longed again for the first days, the days they spent locked in their room until they would begin to notice that the flowers the hotel management customarily bestowed on newlyweds had faded and were withering. And it was not merely because in those days (how many could there have been?) they revolved with the firmament or submerged themselves in each other as if they had been carried along by waves, but because now, every time they returned to the hotel, Nuria knew that Elias, beside himself, crazed, would begin to yell at her and even beat her, with as much revulsion as pain. If anyone had been following them, that person could not have been able to guess at the secret tension between them. Until the last moment, Elias seemed happy. But as soon as he closed the door, the blowup came.

"You spent over an hour looking at that guy with the sunglasses in the café. Right in front of me! You even had the nerve to turn around and smile at him at one point. I saw you. You can't deny it. You think I didn't notice what you did with your skirt? . . ."

Nuria knew there was nothing she could say to defend herself without making matters worse. Tarsis would throw her on the floor and sit on her, clamping her with his knees while he demanded she admit her fault, as if only such an admission might prevent him from dying of disgust. Giddy from sorrow more than from pain, Nuria would not know what to reply and would sob instead as she tried to understand the terrible torment she seemed to cause the man for whom she cared deeply. Tarsis would end up crying like a child himself and, entering her, would lick her tears and console her with infinite tenderness.

"You're my lovely werewolf," she would say.

"I'll never do it again. I'll never hit you again."

But the very next day Nuria would have to tell him for the thousandth time every detail of her life in Sitges before she knew him. He lay in ambush, waiting for some proof of her faithlessness, something that would show her incapacity for loving him. And thus he went on delving into her past, ceaselessly probing. She was forced to narrate in detail (but there were never enough of them) an episode, latent with burning threats to him, in which her fifteen-year-old cousin had kissed her on the cheek while they read a Jules Verne novel under the dining-room table. An almost forgotten event which happened two summers before had to be relived in a multiplicity of new lights, and broken down into fragments, all of them significant. The story had to be projected in slow motion, second by second: how? when? how many times? where had he placed his hand? where his knees? what part of him touched her? how did he touch her with his lips? what did she feel? ... Her entire past was an obscure carnal intrigue deliberately cloaked and disguised in innocence merely to deceive him. All the men she had ever known or even seen, with whom she had talked or argued, old or young, strangers or relatives, had betrayed him in the most depraved and perverted manner.

When he took up the chapter of his finding her at the disreputable Principal Palacio, his fury flared violently. And she, who felt that she cared for him more than she did for her own life, could only explain that she had gone there simply because she had not known where to go, especially since the hotels had all refused to let her have a room that night.

"You wanted to masturbate the first man that came your way."

"I didn't even know what that was, then."

"You're a cynical liar."

"It was you who taught me everything."

Tarsis, carried away with the pain of his self-imposed torture, would yell: "Tell me that you're mine, that you belong to me."

"You know that. I love you so."

"Why did you tell me that night, say to me, someone unknown, 'I love you.' "

Jealousy of himself was the most scabrous, the most salacious of twists: proof did not have to be sought.

"It seemed to me that I already loved you . . . I was so alone, so desperate. The words just came out."

"You would have gone with anyone, with anybody at all."

"I already loved you, but not like now."

"That's a lie. Tell the truth. You wanted to make a catch."

"It was only you I followed . . . I love you so . . . Don't make me suffer."

"You'll betray me just as you betrayed me the first time."

He found betrayal all around him, it besieged him. It was multiple but personal. The more all-encompassing and menacing, the less he could name it.

He would kiss her interminably, trembling all the while, afraid he would not get enough of her tongue, palate, teeth, all of which he probed with his own feverish tongue as he shivered. He wanted constantly to be touching her, to feel her skin under his hand, as if it was for the last time.

Sometimes, on the street, he would grab her, unable to control himself, push her into a doorway, tear at her under-clothes, and rub himself against her as if he had never done so before. Even on the Ramblas, he would begin to burn just from looking at her and would push her into an empty flower vendor's stall. Nuria would protest: "There are people around, they'll see us."

"Take it in your hand."

Nuria would have to obey.

"Tell me that you love me . . . Don't let go!"

"Of course I love you."

"Say it better."

"Don't yell, they'll hear us, people are passing by so close."

"I told you to tell me that you love me."

64

"You already know that."

"Tell me true."

"I love you."

"Not like that. Say it better or I'll bash your head."

He seemed so overcome with disquiet, so much in need of a declaration that could come from only her mouth, that Nuria, shaken and tearful, loved him more than ever, seeing him as a man she was saving from going over a precipice.

They would start kissing anew, but if Nuria were to whisper such a phrase as: "I love you madly," Tarsis would be derailed again, maddened, shrieking: "Don't be obscene, you fool!"

"But it's the truth."

Tarsis believed that everyone had always betrayed him. To begin with, death itself, when it carried off his father. Even if he was wrong, he was also right. He would sometimes look at Nuria as if he were staring into an abyss, convinced that a being so fragile, so white, so sweet—without whom he knew he could no longer get along, no matter how he tried—would someday treacherously sell him out, if she had not already done so.

Amary ponders for twenty-one minutes and could go on pondering much longer, for he is at a loss: perhaps it would be better to acknowledge his mistake and move the queen back (Q-c2). But after the incident of the pawn thrown into the audience by his rival, it would be the height of humiliation. And thus, just as if nothing had happened, he puts pressure on the center with the rook (10.Ra1-d1), assuring himself that an attack is the best defense. He is doubtless telling himself again: "So many times in my life, when it seemed that circumstances were against me, I have come out ahead in the end." He places his trust in his scientific vision.

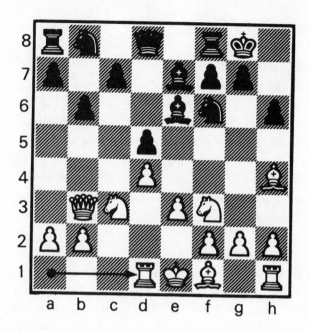

10. Ra1-d1

If Amary had been born in Salamanca at the height of the
Golden Age and if, to complicate matters, he had been an
atheist or an agnostic, only the faith of the Illuminati would
have led him to embrace Christianity. Scholastic arguments
would have made no impression on him, but he might well
have been swayed by the manner of thinking of those men
and women who, with the sublime María Cazalla at their head,
wandered through Castile in flight from the Inquisition. He
would scarcely have been dissuaded by their copulating with
jackasses crowned with thorns prior to repentance and prayer.
He would have been profoundly persuaded by the proposi-

tion that Jesus had come to redeem us of our sins and that therefore it was needful to offend God in the most bestial manner to permit the full realization of the divine sacrifice, and he would only thus have been transformed into a Christian.

Amary never did belong to the Dimitrov Faction, was never a card-carrying member of the organization, but merely a "sympathizer," a term difficult to attach to the character of the man. He was accepted by them, and they never pressured him to adopt the uniform of the sect. In any case, his native timidity would have made it impossible for him to disguise himself as an Oriental proletarian. Most surprising was that this incapacity did not arouse the suspicions of the faithful. This group, which devoted itself to sabotaging any revolutionary movement they labeled "revisionist," or breaking their strikes, and which fed on white rice so as to be like the heroes of the Long March, allowing themselves only one "banquet" a week in the University City's canteen, this group totally identified with its ideal of Marxist Leninism managed to arouse a fervent—and perhaps also morbid—fascination in Amary.

He gave himself over to reading Marxist books with such zeal and gusto that he almost forgot the practice of physics. He became so involved in this reading that he spent his nights at it, from sunset to sunup, and his days at it, too, from first light to last light, and thus, "from sleeping little and reading much," his brain might have dried up, as happened to the Ingenious Knight of La Mancha, who also lost his wit and his judgment. But instead, his brain, from the mulch of these books, ripened, flourished, flowered: or so he believed.

The opening sentence of the *Communist Manifesto,* "A specter is haunting Europe . . . ," spoke to his latent aggressiveness and to a certain bent toward suicide. Nevertheless, the polemic somewhat irritated him, because he considered it—O paradox!—"pointlessly aggressive." He was further irritated by the author's singular notion that the ambition of the bourgeoisie was centered on a desire to "dispose" of the wives and children of the proletariat. He entertained the suspicion—a repugnant one for him—that Marx was sexually obsessed [the Kid, on the other hand, gloated at the thought].

The reading of Marx's *Das Kapital,* however, filled him with enthusiasm. He felt a sense of plenitude, while at the same time a twinge of sorrow in the knowledge that the end of each page meant the inexorable approach of the end of the book and of the intense intellectual fruition every sentence furnished him: for he felt this monument to intelligence to be a unique and conclusive contribution, at the very least, to the development of science and of humanity. The fact that he should read, with the greatest naturalness, the four volumes of the treatise from beginning to end would naturally surprise (excepting the leaders or militants of the Communist Parties who would most naturally be surprised) those who did not know that when, at age fourteen, Amary had been given a two-volume dictionary as a prize, he had announced: "I shall read both volumes." (And so he did.)

It has always been said that the collapse of the Dimitrov Faction was caused by the *affaire Riboud.* Corneille, for his part, asserts that Amary himself brought it down through the tactics of "entrism" used so successfully by the group against its competitors.

Jacqueline Riboud was a young woman professor of English who boasted an enviable academic record, which had taken her from Khâgne to the Sorbonne, in the course of which she had displaced the number-one member of the faculty. It should have surprised no one, therefore, that her ample talent had led her to become a militant in the Dimitrov Faction. The unforeseen development was her sudden determination to quit the group.

The day Jacqueline announced her decision, it was presaged by a bad omen. Amary, who up to that moment had not allowed himself the least bit of commentary at these meetings, on this occasion, after a long harangue by Corneille, stood up and boldly declared (most irresponsibly, for he had only been with the group for a fortnight, and even then only as a "sympathizer"): "And why not proceed directly, as of now, to armed struggle, to terrorism?"

Corneille, turning pale, asked himself, *How dare this novice change everything around?* In actual fact, he was stupefied, paralyzed. To add to the confusion, three of the activists applauded. In the end, he came to his senses and chose to counter this piece of stupidity with . . . irony, a weapon he did not commonly use. And he did well to do so.

"I take note of the *frivolous* bourgeois haste of those who, *not* having the advantage of *being members of* the Dimitrov Faction, presuming on their standing as *sympathizers,* indulge in the most *superficial* and precipitous analysis of a subject which we have *already* studied in depth and which we have *already* brought to pertinent conclusion. We are not in a theater here. And we need only applaud chefs."

Corneille emphasized certain words with sarcasm and, if he had not controlled himself, would have cleared his throat and spit them out. He expected the three rebels who had applauded the troublemaker as if they were attending a theatrical performance to return quietly to the fold. But there is little doubt that the crack which the incident had opened in the perfect "democratic" discipline of the organization had lent wings to Jacqueline. It had also furnished her with a voice.

Later it was learned that Jacqueline had "shamelessly flirted" with Jaime Bellon, a known revisionist member of the PCE, the Spanish Communist Party, when they had met as they were pinning up their respective proclamations on the bulletin board at the law school; she had argued with him, displaying less animosity and heat than was proper or even necessary. She had shown so little enmity, in fact, that they continued the argument in bed or, rather, on a divan.

Corneille was all for settling arguments with "revisionists" on the basis of fisticuffs—provided he was not present himself. One legendary battle he always recalled with approval was the confrontation between the diminutive female Comrade Perlini and a gigantic Trotskyite, which she concluded by announcing, "I won't take the trouble to strike you!" Corneille was also wont to lecture the faithful by alluding to the exemplary conduct of some Japanese comrades of the Stalinist Beiheren group who, in the course of a "reflective" seminar which they had organized in a charming cabin at the foot of Mount Fuji, had surprised a pair of militants kissing each other. Following a summary "revolutionary" trial, during which the flustered lovebirds confessed they had been in love since the preceding day, the guilty couple were condemned to let themselves die in the snow, an act which they carried out with revolutionary stoicism. In commenting on this recollection, Corneille spoke in a premonitory fashion: "Here we would have liquidated them with a broom."

Jacqueline Riboud stood up to speak, but despite her experience as a teacher, which had prepared her to address the most difficult audiences with ease, she could only stammer: "Well, look here . . . the truth is . . . I'm leaving the group, I'm off . . . It's not that the organization seems wrong . . . but . . . how to put it? . . . it's not right for me. I'm going. That's it. That's all."

Corneille immediately understood the danger. A person could simply not enter and exit that organization as if it were a bus. With the utmost politeness, and concealing his deep concern, he begged Jacqueline to accompany him to the library to discuss the matter calmly and in private. Corneille's confidant and the group's treasurer, Christophe de Kerguelen, followed them, in response to an obscure signal from his chief.

De Kerguelen and Corneille soon managed to get Jacqueline into the cellar, where they bound her securely with a rope, and sealed her mouth with tape after having gagged her. Even if she had been a contortionist, she could have called for help only by rapping out her plea in Morse code.

Their mission accomplished, they rejoined the others in the main hall, where they found their people in ferment, if plainly muted. Corneille had calculated that the female Anglophile's outburst could have set back years of revolutionary discipline. Thanks to his understanding of mass psychology, he had come up with a brilliant countermeasure. Taking the bull by the horns, he explained in detail how the dissident enemy had been disarmed and immobilized. All was now quiet at the front, he explained.

And the "masses" were appropriately impressed. Everyone, even the least impassioned, applauded the leader's revolutionary ardor and spirit. They could not have been more pruriently enthusiastic if he had announced that he had swallowed her alive or bitten her to death. He thereupon announced: "Before we free her, assuming that we *can* free her one day, we must learn about the people she has talked to, and to whom she has given our plans, what police agency she's contacted . . . And, more than anything else, she must be able to assure us, and *convince* us that she will never betray us. The lives of our militants are at stake. And I am prepared to do *anything* to protect our group."

De Kerguelen ostentatiously handed Corneille a revolver, and the latter stuck it in a pocket of his pants. They were living such vivid moments! They felt they were participating at last in some way in *Ten Days That Shook the World* and the firing squad that eliminated the Tsar and his family. They intuited that they were about to participate in a crime that would unite them, to league them definitively, so that together (except for the reactionaries, who would be eliminated like the Tsar without mercy) they could build the most radiant future for all Humanity. Amary, too, felt drawn along by the surrounding euphoria and believed that in some manner he was collaborating, even if only as a spectator, in writing a page of History.

Leo Souness, his mouth dry with exultation, insisted that the prisoner must be made to "sing." To confess at once. And he grabbed a symbolic broom which was standing in a corner.

For nearly a week Jacqueline was submitted to appropriate torment. But what could she confess? She had not revealed the organization's "secret plans," not even to Bellon, the Spanish Communist. They hit her with their fists and beat her, and to express themselves better, they spit on her. In order to keep her from sleeping, they forced her to recite passages from Enver Hoxha. Leo Souness, with extreme revolutionary passion, insisted she sing the Internationale while he tried to force the broomstick up her backside. One fact was becoming clear: they would never be able to free her, for she was bound to inform on them, especially after their theories were so directly branded upon her.

The police, however, suddenly appeared and arrested the lot of them (except for Amary, who took cover beneath a pile of wood by the boiler). The police inspector couldn't make head or tail of the scene: in his repressive myopia he decided that these college creeps must have been playing at Sodom and Gomorrah in accord with the precepts of the Divine Marquis de Sade. Jacqueline didn't bother to set him straight. She was a woman of principle.

In fact, nothing much came of the group's arrest. Thanks to Corneille's bravura, all of them were released twenty-four hours later. The leader's fearlessness became clear later, when he bravely characterized the police as capitalist lackeys, persecutors of revolutionaries, and looters of homes.

Quite simply the Dimitrov Faction ended up beneficiaries of the detention: it showed everyone how dangerous they were. Inflated with pride, they read out the various manifestos which the country's intellectual luminaries had signed, demanding the end of police "provocation." The militants seemed ready to burst with self-satisfaction and smugness.

But their balloon quickly burst. Uneasiness, gossip, and complaints increased. Even Leo Souness's deviant behavior with the broom handle was the subject of reproach. Amary was instrumental in furnishing the coup de grace: one day he left without a word—along with the three people who had applauded out of turn. Amary, moreover, did not have to explain himself in the cellar. He left with an attitude of indifference, as if the Dimitrov Faction no longer existed. Four more members initiated a splinter movement, three quit in the middle of a cell meeting, whereupon the twenty-three mathematicians disappeared from the scene.

These inflexibly radical formations not only hallucinated about a monumental police interest in them (the "Marxist-Leninist left," savoring a future moment of exalted confrontation with the monomaniacal police, had prepared three decanters of sulphuric acid to overwhelm the class enemy), but even more, they dreamed of one day being able to count on a genuine worker in their ranks. At that moment in France there were only seven million workers—none of them available to these radical theoretical groups. To fill the vacuum, a lone old Spanish anarchist stonemason was ready to sacrifice himself. He was Ramón Espasa, and the theoretical radical organizations passed him from hand to hand. The game allowed the old libertarian to indulge his immoderate passion for verbosity.

When this Ramón Espasa told Corneille, "You'd better lock up the shop, you've shot your bolt," the latter understood for the first time that the working class was more discerning than he had imagined. Even if they were not very clever, they had clearer vision than he did.

Corneille remained alone in his luxurious chalet beneath the photographs of his mustachioed masters, left to meditate on the egotism and ingratitude of men, incapable as they are of recognizing and appreciating the sacrifices of their betters. Even in defeat, Corneille did not consider himself a nobody.

Amary provided the colophon. For reasons unknown, he summoned, in kingly fashion, the dethroned leader, who found himself in the presence of an ex-sympathizer who shuffled citations from Marx with utter precision and authority . . . But Amary also made reference to Khrushchev, and that was pure provocation, given Corneille's blind devotion to Stalin.

"I don't know how you dare bring up the name of the murderer of Beria, of the vandalizer of Stalin's work. I want you to know that the first Communist cell I founded was called the Lavrenty Pavlovich Beria unit."

Amary gazed at him with condescension (which only irritated Corneille still further), and began to digress: "Well, Stalin was more cultured than Brezhnev, for he was interested in science, he read the great Russian novelists, he spoke foreign languages and knew Latin . . ."

" '. . . knew Latin'? Is that what really interests you, the person who broke up my Dimitrov Faction, when you speak of the Little Father of the people of the world?"

Their adieus proceeded without rhyme or reason, or with a rhyming scheme so personal on Amary's part that it became indecipherable, and with a reasoning which unhinged Corneille.

"I've been reading Mao" (Amary confessed).

"Mao! . . . That reactionary!"

"There's a lot of juice there."

"Mao strikes you as succulent?"

"Yes, certainly. He wrote: 'Some terror is always necessary.' "

That series of probes and counters, that *Via Crucis,* ended very badly for Corneille, along the path of attenuated progress . . . for he metamorphosed into a mystic, to follow the doctrines of one of Buddha's nephews: Ananda Marga. And today, illuminated by a religious faith (whose fervor was as great as that accompanying the political convictions he formerly practiced), he prays for the rest of humanity. And he

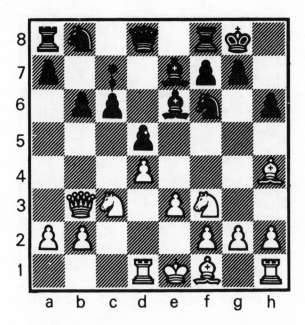

10. . . . c7-c6

iterates with a beatific (but energetic) smile: "I am like a truck on the highway: *Je roule pour vous.*" (And God save whoever gets in the way!)

Any confrontation with Amary is scarcely restful. For him, the chessboard is a barricade, a place where everything is decided, today his *raison d'être,* perhaps. There can be little doubt that he has established a categorical relation between the result of play and his own personal crusade.

For his grand purpose he must rid himself of ridiculous prejudices. Why not recognize his own faults and errors openly before the enemy? Self-criticism is the dialectic weapon of the revolutionary. (Moreover, Tarsis has played 10. . . . c7-c6,

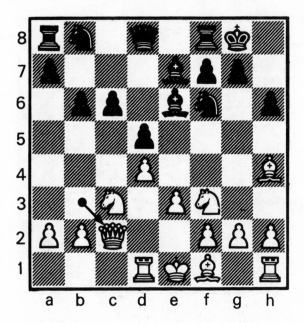

11. Qb3-c2

the conservative advance of a pawn with which he hopes to avoid a defensive counterattack.)

He therefore draws back the queen he had so ostentatiously advanced (11. Qb3-c2): he was acting in the manner of Ho Chi Minh at Dien Bien Phu. He had analyzed his error and, striving to avoid its repetition, imagined himself commanding Vietminh divisions. He consolidates his apparently modest positions: revolutionary warfare is not conducted for the gallery. The queen falls back, yes, but now she is able to dominate the column and, besides, to attack the e4 rampart . . . *Just let Tarsis become confident,* he tells himself, *as self-confident as the French colonialist forces facing General Giap.*

Over and above his martial allegories shines the rigorous light of his scientific providence. It is his best resource.

Tarsis is of the opinion that Amary, believing himself to be both the Napoleon and the Nero of terrorism, planned the kidnapping of Isvoschikov with the same strategy he employs in his chess moves. *It's quite obvious,* he feels.

In the course of his agitated honeymoon with Nuria Roig, the restless Elias Tarsis began to spend more and more time on chess, devoting an increasing amount of his days to it, although up to that point he had not so much as gone near a chessboard since his flight from Madrid. A leading chess master taught that "a threat proffered is worse than a threat executed." As for the girl, Tarsis apparently needed her with him, and so, each time he appeared in a circle of chess players on the outskirts of Barcelona, he brought her along. She was well aware of the dramatic overtones of the mystery play which her lover was staging and producing; her role seemed to be merely to sit near him and watch the game unfold. Her mute role, in short, called for silence, though she was allowed

77

to express satisfaction for the ever-happy outcome and the part played by her man. He, deliberately, never taught her to play the game. He did not wish to botch the drama. Nuria never told him that simply from watching the game intently she had managed to master the rules.

In the humble circles they frequented, generally housed in dilapidated surroundings, a kind of sweaty grime formed itself into a virile adobe which comforted the players and onlookers. They were always men. Still, the presence of that pretty seventeen-year-old did not disturb them at all—it simply made them restless. They looked at her, always stealthily, in a way habitual with chess players. In one sense they were all eyes, while Tarsis pretended that his eyes were clouded over.

At each place Tarsis would begin with an appetizer: a five-minute game with some member of the chorus, until he could uncover the best players. These he would then challenge to simultaneous play. Choosing White, he would confront various opponents at a time, each before his own board. The claque grouped itself around the action. Nuria would seat herself to the left of the player on the extreme right, in accordance with the libretto. She had to exercise great caution to make sure no one grazed her chair, let alone her back or her hair. She must not cross her legs, and her skirt must cover her knees. She was allowed to direct her gaze only at the center of the action or at Tarsis. In order to "concentrate better," Tarsis every so often would break away from the boards as if to see them in perspective. In this way he was better able to verify the position of his darling's hands, feet, knees, and eyes. The assemblage enjoyed these between-the-acts diversions.

Nuria played her part as protagonist with the utmost authenticity. Meanwhile, she mulled over Tarsis's disconcerting notions, or dreamed up plans to keep him happy, however unrealizable they might be. She kept herself in strictest check to avoid any provocation. Always, however, she could read in his face the presence of the phantoms of his imagination.

The mental equilibrium Tarsis sought to allay his anguish lay in finding the delicate balance between two clashing passions, the crisscrossing currents of sexual ecstasy and jealousy. Nuria must be able to seduce all the men in the world to prove she was the most desirable of forbidden fruits, but it anyone touched her, even grazed her, so much as looked at her, such a one might of course be able to seduce her, thus demolishing his furious and frightful fancy. He emerged from each circle of his torment in deep mourning. No sooner would he arrive back at their hotel than he would be plunged into a crisis of bitter jealousy.

He struggled to appropriate each moment of Nuria's past, fearing lest she had already betrayed him in her personal history. In this vain search she was forced to tell and retell endlessly how and why she had robbed her father of the 28,000 pesetas: at what time, what were her intentions, how did she happen to know where the safe was hidden and to know its combination, and how was it that she had not been seen or heard? She told him the truth: she had read *The War Against the Salamanders* eighteen times, and she was convinced she lived surrounded by these reasoning, efficient, viscous, slimy, and frightful creatures who dominated the world as well as her house. Her father was no more than a gigantic salamander who was gradually taking possession of her brain by means of his counsel and kisses.

Tarsis had no desire to read her book. He hated it and could surmise all the loathsome matter it contained. He did not think of it simply as a vile metaphor directed against the super-endowed, against exceptional people, but he felt threatened and insisted she tell him the whole story. Even when she was dead tired she had to answer each and every one of his endless questions: who was Captain Van Toch, when did he arrive at the lake, why did the salamanders torpedo a French cruiser, who was the chief, who taught him to read, did they know how to speak? If she answered that she would tell him all about it again the next day, Tarsis would blow up and demand to know what she was hiding. That pestilential book had influenced her more than he ever could. *I ought to burn it!* he thought.

Nuria was afraid of losing her stolen copy of the book, which she had "withdrawn" from the library at Sitges and which she had discovered was out of print and would not be reprinted by the publishers, Revista de Occidente (which had published it in their series "Exotic Novels" in 1945).

Tarsis was convinced that this book was the cause of all her troubles and of all his troubles with her. She would never have known that she could "withdraw" any object, such as money, if the book had not aroused her runaway passions. Then the robbery . . . The "descent into the abyss" was inevitable: the theft of the 28,000 pesetas, the need to run away from home, the eventual finding herself among the "she-bums," and finally her "making out" with the first man to come along, who proved to be himself. Now, Tarsis would have liked to have known her without her having been a runaway . . . but in full flight nevertheless; he would also have liked to have made her his mistress, without her being his paramour . . . while at the same time she could be herself. Tarsis had won the contest among the exceptional students, and only he understood his form of reasoning.

The book was liberally sprinkled with symbols indicating ownership: a circle enclosing a sloop, a radiant sun, and a label reading *Property of the Sitges Library.* All for the purpose of confusing the reader, but not the thief. The proof . . .

"Who got you to read this piece of depravity? Do you know the author, the translators, or what? Who is this Carmen

Diez de Oñate? What are these two lizards doing on the cover? They seem to be occupying the world. I'm a patient man, you've got to admit it, more than Job. But you've got to admit this book means more to you than I do. I've told you, and I'll tell you again: I'm going to burn it."

"Why haven't you done so already?"

Utterly distressed, one day Nuria lit a match and started her own book burning. As soon as the fire began to lick the cover, a furious Tarsis grabbed the book away from her and stamped out the flame, even though nothing had burned yet.

"I forbid you to touch any more matches!"

At the end of four months they calculated that they had spent 25,000 pesetas. They had only 3,000 left.

"I'm glad. It's better this way. I'll work in a shop again and we'll rent a garret. In the hotels everyone looks at you boldly."

Nuria had a most difficult time convincing Tarsis that she could go back to her father's office some night and "relieve" him of more money, the money they needed. She had kept the keys to the office and the safe and she remembered the lock's combination (30–10–30). Finally they set out for Sitges, and one night gained entrance to the empty office without any problem; she opened the outer door to the safe as simply as she had promised: the two keys still worked. But the handle in the center of the safe's disk didn't budge when she turned it with the combination she knew. Her father had changed it.

For Nuria this was a terrible blow. It meant that her father, more the *salamander* than ever, had suspected that she would return to rob him. Thus he deliberately was refusing to help her in her need, for he must have guessed that if she came again it would be because she would be up to her neck in trouble. And so he preferred to see her drown rather than let her rob him of his fortune. This was the cruelest blow she had ever received from her begetter. All of a sudden she was a little girl no longer. And never would be again, she knew. And Tarsis, relieved, concluded: "This means I no longer owe your father anything."

The old streetwise bootblack who had gotten them their false identity cards found them a garret for rent on Consejo de Ciento Street. The money remaining to the pair was rapidly disappearing, without any letup in sight. Nuria was in despair and racked her brains: she did not think she could stand seeing Tarsis working again as a laborer.

"It would be better if I found a job. I could be a telephone operator or a secretary or a clerk in a shop."

Tarsis became incensed at the idea that behind his back other men could look at her, talk to her, be around her, flirt with her, pay her compliments, touch her, caress her, drool over her, seduce her, win her heart; he imagined idylls and fascinating dissipations which ended with her in bed, "gone" on somebody, lost, wasted, turned into a sensual slave, an animal worn out under the weight of a lustful ladykiller.

Nevertheless, he accepted it as the most natural thing in the world when Nuria proposed the following solution: "I'll become a professional, and we can live on what I make."

It might even be said that, up to a certain point, his entrance into the craft of procurer served as a catharsis. If the Greeks managed to purify their passions by contemplating works of art, and most especially by watching a tragic drama, he managed to eliminate and almost uproot the mad jealousy which so perturbed him by means of his new roles as his woman's protector as well as her pimp. During the first stage, his work consisted mainly of observing and selecting and trailing her game.

Nuria took up her new profession with modesty and humility among the "she-bums" in the movie house. For five pesetas she would satiate and empty her "contact" by tactile groping. Seated in the last row, Tarsis would strive to combine film viewing with his mission as cynegeticist, as master of the hunt, for he must always be on the alert to point out her prey, her piece, to the huntress.

One night, on leaving the movie house, they met Manuela del Río, a woman from Granada who had spent twenty years in the profession, and whose bullyboy and swordsman was then lodged in the Carabanchel jail house awaiting trial. They became good friends, so much so that she moved in with them. The garret quickly became a garden: flowerpots transformed the balconies into garlanded arbors.

Together, Nuria and Manuela sailed out into the world, a universe which had as its axis the cabarets along the Sarria highway. They earned such sums with their bodies that they were appropriately called "ladies of fortune." Their specialty was a joint number tailored for older and more select clients who knew how to appreciate the imagination displayed by the Andaluz Manuela and the good disposition of the Catalan Nuria.

All the money she saved, Manuela sent by money order to her strong man; her gardening took her mind off the unfortunate Ministry of Justice restriction which precluded her visiting him because she was not his lawful wife. For her part, Nuria was enjoying a new Tarsis, a lover no longer consumed with jealousy. Every morning—at noon—Manuela would bring up three coffees and crullers, and the trio would take their breakfast in good spirits. Everything was milk and honey. Nuria forgot all about the salamanders.

The two nymphs did not begin their rounds until eight at night. They got themselves up in great style. Manuela showed Nuria how to perfume herself, to dress roguishly, and to fix her hair in accordance with her trade. At one in the morning they would come home in a taxi. The woman from Granada was friendly to all the night porters, with whom she joked, exaggerating her Andaluz accent, and whom she pleased by treating them as if they were gentlemen. No one could have called her a "woman of licentious life."

Tarsis no longer plagued Nuria with questions. He never cared to know what went on behind his back, nor was he interested. On the other hand, the work the pair engaged in was no big deal. In general, Manuela took care of massages from the back while her helper extinguished the fire in the main shaft from the front. The boldest number in their act was when they did the "omelet": the two of them, stark naked, would wind themselves around each other, mutually kiss and caress, all to the accompaniment of moans of satisfaction. They were forever fearful that they would burst out laughing. They managed, however, to hold their laughter until the voyeur-aesthete had gone. And had already paid. Moreover, many men hired them merely so as to tell them their misfortunes. In such cases, the she-confessors officiated from a chair drawn up at some distance from the penitent; and they would not comfort him with so much as a kiss. One of these men always brought a suitcase full of clothes to dress the ladies in masquerade: it was one of his manias.

Tarsis gave himself over to chess intently and spent his days in front of the board studying games played by Fischer, Morphy, and Steinitz. Nuria had the impression that he was still not happy; she was well aware that it was she who now had to assume all the responsibilities which he formerly had taken on with such impetuosity. The money simply piled up in a box . . . as if he did not see it. It was she who bought him shirts, suits, and shoes. The fact that with her body and her work she was able to keep her man in some luxury filled her with a rare pride. In addition, she bought him books on chess, and an ivory chess set—which, incidentally, he never used.

This fairy tale ended without warning.

One morning Manuela surprised them in some hectic activity in bed; she boldly drew back the sheets and reacted to the inviting situation by indecently massaging and stroking Tarsis's back. Nuria, beside herself with pleasure, was carried away by her lover's renewed and frenetic excitation.

Early the next morning, at the habitual hour of one-thirty, coming home in the company of Manuela, Nuria found a note from Tarsis:

> I was not born to be a pimp. I do not want to accept living at the expense of anyone and especially not of a woman. Do not look for me. Go back to your parents. There are people who say they love someone so that when the objects of their love awake from their dreams they will be more wretched than ever they might have been. Study, as you wanted before you met me. Take your final examinations. Forget these months. They were an inferno. I ask God to forgive me for the grave wrong I have done you.

And Nuria again saw hundreds, thousands, millions of slimy, horrible salamanders all around her.

Tarsis jumps the unassailable rampart at the center: (11. . . . . Ktf6-e4). Amary had protected the bulwark with his last move, nevertheless Tarsis forces the position. He carries out the move in order to demonstrate to his rival that nothing is inaccessible to him, Tarsis . . . He soon realizes that it was the best possible move. His instincts never deceive him. So he thinks.

Naked instinct is perhaps Tarsis's most fruitful asset, and it is thanks to a sharp sensibility that for him time is not the

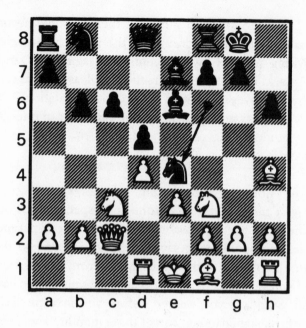

11. .... Ktf6-e4

immutable drip-drop which Amary measures like the robot
he is. For Tarsis, a game of chess unfolds during a certain
given period, as in the ceremonious stages involved in dis-
pensing death in a bullfight: he lives this condensed period
of time, which to him is sacred and magical, as if it were the
ritual expression of a myth. His use of time is creative and
not merely repetitive.

It is his instinct that tells Tarsis that Amary is behind the
abduction of the Soviet leader. There are concrete proofs as
well, to his mind. Every time he reads one of the communiqués issued by the Comité Communiste International he
reads between the lines and deciphers the imprint, the stigma
of his enemy. Each communiqué is numbered, thereby sig-
naling Amary's hand: his "systematization." And systematically the communiqués reach the editorial offices of the press

every Tuesday and Saturday, and the Polaroids arrive on Thursday: the three days of tournament play. On the preceding days, Monday and Friday, days on which there is no play, Amary must compose the texts, and on Wednesdays the photo is taken. All done systematically, as is obvious. Tarsis finds it suprising that no one has noticed all this, just as he is surprised that the police have not questioned Amary as a suspect. What he does not know is that they have already done so.

Tarsis is sure that Amary never studies the board in the manner of a chess player who feels emotion, who suffers, who takes pleasure, who, in short, "plays," but that, instead, he looks at the board like a bureaucrat putting a five-year plan into operation (this comparison would have more than pleased Amary had he known of it), using the same method he used in abducting Isvoschikov.

One thing was certain and that was that Amary analyzed the position with the same will and talent he employed in studying Marxism, after his conversion, that is, following his illumination. (One is struck by the turns and twists followed by destiny in carrying out certain conversions. If those of St. Paul or St. Augustine captivate us because they were replete with a certain pageantry, those of Claudel and Faizant, for example, are astonishingly pedestrian in their triviality. Amary's, now, came about at the hands of a domestic servant.)

He read all the texts from beginning to end: the works of Marx, Engels, Lenin, Stalin, Gramsci, Mao Tse-tung, Suslov, Togliatti, Thälmann, Pieck, Althausser, Lefebvre, Lukács, and Rosa Luxemburg. Going back to the sources, he steeped himself in the writings of Plato, Thomas More, Campanella, Messler, Mably; and he didn't miss a comma of Fourier or of Owen. He also passed the blacklist through his hoop: beginning with Trotsky, back to Bakunin, Liebknecht, Proudhon, Lassalle, and including Castioradis, Daix, Morin, and

Garaudy. He learned Russian and managed to get some notion of Czech, Polish, Hungarian, Rumanian, and Albanian. The language he quickly mastered was Bulgarian, thanks to which he was able to read George Dimitrov without skipping a page.

He told himself that anyone who did not take a position regarding Marxism could no longer be taken seriously. He was fascinated that the only terrorist theory to be found in his milieu was in one of its intellectual satellites. Above all, he was won over by the "apparatus of the Party," with its purges, its self-criticism, and its labor camps. And its strict discipline.

He had made up his mind: he, too, would wage war . . . but without hatred, alongside the oppressed and those who fight for justice. Suddenly he saw physics to be . . . so indigent! Marxism, *that* was science. Science.

He told himself, *I am a Communist, I am a part of the Party of the Poor.* It was the sort of resolution to be made in secret, by way of vigil over his personal struggle.

A reef lay in his way. According to Marx, class-consciousness is achieved, that is, one becomes class-conscious, becomes a revolutionary materialist, because of the practice (praxis) of exploitation, insofar as one is a victim of it. But he was not one of the "exploited": he had, then, become a materialist thanks to ideological election. Was he not, by embracing materialism out of pure idealism, provoking an absurd short circuit?

The recollection of his past eased his mind. His birth placed him on the level of the exploited even though he had not come into the world at the bottom of a mine shaft. For he first saw the light in a far worse place. In point of fact, proletarian mothers are not in the habit of delivering their offspring in mine shafts.

He had been born in New Delhi, where his father was

posted as commercial attaché to the Swiss legation. It was on the occasion of a visit by a Mexican team to compete in a local grass-hockey tournament. When the Mexican team won, the Mexican embassy gave a ball for diplomats and players in a grand park situated on the outskirts of the capital. The Amarys accepted their invitation. The luxurious Occidental villa's only concession to native folklore was the presence of outhouses: at the far end of the park, concealed behind the shrubbery, stood three squalid toilets, already awash, replete with filth, despite which the diplomatic corps—or body—"disembodied" itself there with shameful sacrifice. At the door of the squalid kiosk was a native guard sitting on his heels; in one hand he carried a damp napkin (once white), in the other a dented bowl to collect tips, which appeared to be equally grimy.

While the orchestra was attacking the Mexican song *"Amapola"* for the third time, Amary's pregnant mother was seized with furious pains, which she took to indicate a need to evacuate. It was nothing extraordinary, given the effects on all recently arrived members of the diplomatic corps of the change in diet: it was known to them all as "Shiva's revenge." Without telling anyone, she rushed hell-bent for the latrine, and there she did what she thought necessary: she pushed as hard as she could, and out came the young Amary: he fell plumb into the accumulation of excrement.

Seven years later, in Tokyo, on the occasion of another party given in aid of victims of tuberculosis (this disease was still fashionable in diplomatic circles), Amary's mother drank almost an entire bottle of Fernet Branca which an Irish colleague of her husband's had brought from Bari. Amary's father had to use all his wiles to get his wife home and into bed. The effort wore him out and he fell into a sleep as comatose as hers. However, she was not as overpowered as she appeared, and instead of sleeping off her overindulgence, she got up, staggered around, and eventually made her way into the boy's bedroom. There she was inspired to relate to him the narrative of his unusual birth.

There was no way of telling what effect his mother's drunken comings and goings had on her son. What happened, in any case, is that he began to put on pounds: fat on his cheeks, his thighs, and his belly. In a short time he was so stuffed that all the protuberances seemed to join into one. He was good-looking in a sense, but he went from looking like a chubby angel on a church altarpiece to being a fleshy roly-poly, and finally to being simply obese. He didn't fit in his skin. In his heart the Kid wanted to die, without committing suicide, to die of indigestion, to explode in the toilet. This ambition, which Rimbaud might not have condemned, was Amary's secret, his innermost secret. It was the first of a series.

He went through infancy and adolescence and even his first years as a researcher without yielding up a pound and without paying the slightest attention to the outlandish jests of his peers, especially of the official jokers, for whom he was an "unstitched mattress," or "potted jelly," or even a "barrel bung." He didn't so much as hear their jibes.

But once he took up political reading, he began to lose weight. And when he launched into his systematic study of the Marxist masters, he soon became visibly thinner. His colleagues' questions seemed on the tip of everyone's tongues.

"Are you on a hunger strike?"

"You're scarcely the same man, almost unrecognizable!"

"Watch out for your health!"

"What the devil is the matter? Have you found a girl?"

He had found something better: a revolutionary destiny which demanded a more "common" figure. He laid his plans meticulously, and carried them out punctually. Every day he limited himself to 600 calories. And when he reached the weight he had set for himself, 120 pounds, to cover his height of just under five feet six inches, he decided that for the rest of his life he would limit himself to 900 calories a day. [The Others, with the Kid at their head, opposed the diet and attempted to boycott it every chance they could get.]

In all truth, Marc Amary was obese when his mother died. Cécile Amary passed away two months before her son could finish his baccalaureate. Her last days were hair-raisingly painful, and were not made easier by the delirium agitating her until the end. At death's door, she prevailed on her son to lay her out for burial, using her New Delhi sari as a winding sheet. Her reasoning was frightful: ". . . with the sari I was wearing when I shat you out . . ."

It was the second—and last—time his mother described his descent into the world. But this time she used a word he had never heard from her before.

This was three days after the burial when Amary's father appeared. The long and tiring journey from Manila, involving three changes of plane, affected him more than did the death of his wife. He wore no mourning of any sort, not so much as a sign. But he did feel a knot in his throat when the doctor informed him of the serious suspicions that it was his son who had murdered the one who had once been the woman of his dreams, his betrothed, his promised one, his sweetheart, and his wife. Nevertheless, he took up residence, temporarily, in his former home. For two nights. On the second night he discovered a list in his older son's handwriting stuck in the telephone book: it was headed *My Enemies*. His name was on the list. In fact, it was in second place. He tried to sleep, but he felt a cloud lowering over him; suddenly, unexpectedly, he found himself standing in front of a mirror, crying his heart out.

The next morning, father and sons shared breakfast in the kitchen. While Marc Amary stuck his head in Willem Einthoven's book on electrocardiography, his father conversed with the younger son, Gabriel.

"Do you need more money?"

"I don't believe Marc has any problems. He takes care of all money matters."

"If you need more . . . The price of everything has gone up. Do you have enough to pay for school?"

"School is free."

"Tell me, haven't I written you often enough?"

"Yes, yes . . . Why do you ask? What's wrong?"

"Your mother . . . I loved her very much. One day you'll understand that it's impossible to live with one and the same woman all your life . . . especially . . . when she's crazy."

"I don't blame you for anything."

"Let me kiss you, my son."

And his father kissed him with such emotion that he upset the lad. Marc raised his eyes for a moment from his book and contemplated the scene with repugnance. But he was like a stone statue, like the stone-dead Commendatore in *Don Giovanni*. And he didn't move a muscle even when his brother suddenly said: "Mother's last words were to tell Marc that he had been born in a toilet."

"Why, yes, that's true. I'd completely forgotten . . ."

Gabriel recalled what Marc had said to him one day: "Adults lack any integrity, any courage or honesty." But that wasn't right, either. His father had simply forgotten the incident; it had been erased from his memory, sunken into oblivion, without his noticing it; he hadn't put it behind him, nor had he deliberately erased it. He didn't have an elephant's memory, his amnesia simply meant that his subconscious had taken over.

"I did everything I could for her."

"You don't need to justify yourself."

"When the director of the sanatorium informed me that

92

she wanted to take her meals with a hog, I authorized it—and the purchase of the hog."

Gabriel remembered the dialogues, the duets, the person-to-person talks between his mother and her pig (she called the beast "my little piglet" and "my treasure"). Marc's behavior during breakfast had irritated his father, but he did not dare to ask him to stop reading or venture to address him. He finally did so, indirectly, through his brother:

"Marc has always been distant, inaccessible. He has never shown any feelings. Do you remember when he was a boy in Caracas and he staged a hunger strike to force us to 'strangle' one of the maids, whom he accused of *pawing* him in the bath? He was only six years old. We had to fire her and hang a marionette in the pantry before we could get him to drink a glass of milk. Young as you were, you can't have forgotten it."

"That was all kid stuff."

"Exactly. That Kid's stuff. You remember, he insisted we talk about him in the third person. And he himself would say, 'The Kid wants to go out.' Or, 'The Kid has swallowed Cécile's string of pearls.' And then we had to wait until he passed them normally, in his stool."

"Mama has just now died, and we see you only once in a while . . . couldn't we simply get along? Marc couldn't have treated her any better."

"What are you trying to say? . . . I couldn't live with her. Your mother spent her days staring into space from the time she began to entertain those ridiculous suspicions. And then she'd get up in the middle of the night and lie down in the garden beside the railing."

"It would be better to forget all that."

"It's very easy for you two to forget. But what about me? You've never thought about your father's position. Do you know what your mother did to . . . *her?* She lay in wait, crept up on her, cut off her braids, and then scratched up her face."

"She asked us to pray . . . She thought you'd come back."

"How was I going to come back? Life with her was a hell."

"I suppose you know that every Sunday we'd go bicycling over to see her. When she saw us she'd say, 'Are you really my children? You're so tall! You look all tired out. You'd better go to bed.' And she'd always end by asking, 'Is there something I can do for you?' "

"The sanatorium director wrote to tell me that she ate on the floor with her hog, so that she could be like him, and that she petitioned the priest to bless her urine and transform it into holy water . . . In the end she forgot everything else and kept only one obsession, and that had to do with a supposed African cat, which had already devoured her own mother, according to her; she wanted us to prevent it from harming her little piglet. She would ask us to hunt it down."

Marc suddenly and brusquely put an end to the conversation: "Let's shut the family album once and for all."

In order to carry out a breakthrough (12. Bh4xe7), Amary consumes almost a quarter of an hour, thereby demonstrating that he must utilize all his energies to carry out the reconquest he envisages.

He has taken a Tarsis bishop as if it were a viper which might bite him . . . or as if it were his rival's finger . . . or his phallus, as Professor Fine would have put it.

It might be said that Tarsis felt Amary touch his very being. He surveys him with a certain disgust mixed with curiosity: the gesture his opponent has just made in taking his piece has, once again, struck him as almost familiar, something nearly recognizable, something from out of the past. It's as if he could name it, has it on the tip of his tongue, but he cannot quite. Ever since the beginning of the match he has been unable to unearth the original memory of this evocation.

Tarsis turns and openly stares at his opponent's escort: a chauffeur and two bodyguards. The three are sitting in the first row of the hall, impassively, never taking their eyes off the chessboard, though none of them can play the game. "What does Amary need that trio of thugs for, a pack of dressed-up hypocrites . . . ?" The International Federation, following the recent abuses and scandals in the world matches, has issued orders prohibiting contenders for the title from accepting any help in making their analyses of postponed games or in the preparation of upcoming ones. The excesses committed by so-called assistants during the latest contests had transformed individual championship matches into contests between teams. But the Federation has not forbidden "second officials" being present in the company of the players.

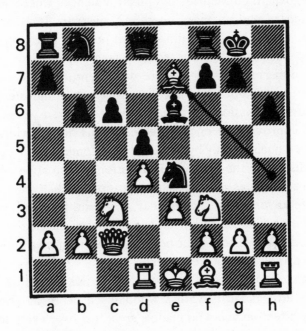

12. Bh4xe7

Tarsis is boastful of the fact that he needs no help from anyone. *Amary's three followers, in spite of their pedantic college-boy airs, are a trio of simple fanatics,* he thinks. He visualizes them in the company of their leader the night the Soviet official was abducted, driving the car and then cooperating night after night in the "scientific" questioning and torture of Isvoschikov in the cellar of the chalet which Amary had purchased in Meung-sur-Loire . . . only to turn it into a People's Prison.

Tarsis left Barcelona precipitously a scant two hours after writing the letter to Nuria.

He took a circuitous route which led him from Barcelona to Segovia, then Madrid, and finally Valencia, where he took lodgings in a house on the beach at Malvarrosa. It was a family *pensión* next to a large tumbledown house in the process of being systematically battered by a gang of youngsters: it was a headquarters for the Frente de Juventudes, the Falange youth movement. And the battering was administered by express permission of the authorities or, even worse, with their approval and encouragement. This house, which had escaped burning only by miracle, had belonged to the Spanish novelist with the greatest international reputation, Blasco Ibáñez, who, as an added provocation, had been a leftist before anyone else. To this day, in Spain, he is still paying for the original sin of having been famous, and neither Hollywood nor the apocalyptic horsemen could improve his image: in fact, they only made it worse.

The *pensión* where Tarsis was staying was owned by a vigorous little old lady with a wooden leg, who ran about in every direction and who made a great fuss over every insipid remark uttered by her granddaughter, a silly madcap. The housework was done unobtrusively by a maid called Soledad Galdós, a tall blue-eyed blonde who was so imperturbable and boasted a glance so mysteriously calm that she was thought to be Swedish. As a result of this presumed identity, the other three male boarders—an accountant and two ink-stained wretches from the local paper factory—dreamed of seducing her. The truth was that she had been born in a rural village in Teruel province and was Spanish on all eight sides. She never meant to look at anyone in a mysterious way, but simply with reserve, and when she ran across one of the swains on her way to bed, she would look at him with a certain disdain.

In Valencia, Tarsis worked for a time in the machine shop of the paper company. And he became a novice to the Jesuits.

At that time in the Society of Jesus, young postulants who had not yet entered the seminary called each other *"agapito,"* as did their spiritual directors. These novices continued working at their trades, those they had taken up before they felt a vocation. They were all prodigal in their visits to the altar and in their Latinisms: their offerings "To the Greater glory of God" were heard as one word, as if it were German, *"admajoremgloriamdei."* They were also distinguished by chastity, which they practiced with all the flaming torment of the disciples of the Marquis de Sade devoting themselves to pornography. To minister to this chastity and avoid accidents, they counted on St. Aloysius Gonzaga and St. Stanislaus Kotzka and a large scapular which at critical moments brushed against the most elevated part of their spur. Confronted with nocturnal emissions they were, nevertheless, naked as babes; still, in general, they didn't count such slips . . .

The word *"agapito,"* according to the teachers of doctrine, was to be explained as follows: there are two forms of love, that which God feels for men and that which men feel for their Creator. The first is infinite; the second possesses no such sublime amplitude and is, therefore, the love of the *"agape"*—the lowly love feast among the primitive Christians—and therefore a plebeian, vulgar love if it be compared to the higher love, but still majestic enough and full of hope if it is compared to the quite ordinary relationship between everyday human beings and the Supreme Maker . . . Thus, the origin of the nickname *"agapito"* to denote a zealous aspirant to the Jesuit order.

During the course of his soul's navigation, which Tarsis undertook with much zeal, his spiritual director was one Father Benito Bertomeu, S.J., a close friend of Father Gregorio, E.P., of the San Antón school. The two had been friends from their student days in the diocesan seminary; as soon as he was ordained and able to say Mass, Father Gregorio opted for the E.P., transforming himself into a Piarist Father or member of the Scuole Pie; Benito Bertomeu joined the Jesuits a few years later, as a "Father" (the Jesuits know God's designs are impenetrable). They maintained excellent relations despite the natural worldly competitiveness of the two orders (in fact, the Jesuits considered their Piarist brothers to be no better than yokels, while the latter were convinced that Jesuits were more stubborn than cloves of garlic). So when Tarsis appeared before Father Gregorio intending to don the habit of a Piarist penitent for the rest of his life, the priest told him: "It would be an act of madness for you to hide your talent in an order such as ours. The Society of Jesus is the right place for a young man of such endowments as yourself. Now, I have a friend . . ."

Though he was no Jesuit or even a seminarian at the time of that first visit to Father Gregorio, Tarsis had already employed one of the weapons used by St. Ignatius: mental restraint, limitation. On escaping from Barcelona, wallowing in remorse and ready to retire from the world forever, from its show and vanities, his first visit had not been to Father Gregorio. Now it was difficult to confess the misunderstanding he had run into at Segovia.

When he had finished writing the note to Nuria, he had understood clearly enough that if he wanted peace he could find it only by completely reversing his course, a course which had eventuated in his becoming a pimp. There must be total emendation, a definitive change, and he felt a need to embrace the way of poverty, silence, penitence, and chastity.

He had gone to a Trappist monastery near Segovia one day, under the impression that it would be much like joining the Spanish Foreign Legion. It would simply be enough, he thought, to shave his head, sleep five hours a night in a coffin with a stone for pillow, work in the fields from sunup to sundown, and open his mouth only to murmur, *"Morir Habemus."* Such a program would be good for him. Or for anybody else.

He was received by a monk who was both inquisitive and distant (the last was fortunate, for he stank to heaven; *They also don't bathe,* thought Tarsis). He asked more questions than a police inspector. At length, after a long hour of scrutiny, during which Tarsis had squirmed with shame while he recounted his life and miracles in Barcelona, as his inquisitor seemed to require, the friar smiled (beatifically!) and read out his sentence: "You are unable to live alone. You must have friends."

"But, as I've said, I had two friends, two . . . female friends."

"You must change your life around. The step you have taken is positive, but not sufficient. You must pray, do penance so that God may help you. Lead a pious life for twelve months and come back to see us then."

Father Benito, on the other hand, had won him over from the first moment. More than a priest and a Father, he was like a smiling and sly old grandfather who might have been a father to his father. He had spent nearly twenty years as village priest at Vitigudino, until, in his fortieth year, while he was engaged in spiritual exercises at Salamanca, he felt, for the second time, the call to his vocation. The Holy Spirit had inspired him with the belief that he would best serve the fight against evil by entering the Jesuit Order. Highly intelligent, he was also sweet-toothed, a failing which endeared him to Tarsis, to whom he would make a present of half a dozen pastries, most often Heavenly Custards, whenever he received the envelope with his meager pay.

Every afternoon, at the end of his workday, Tarsis would take two trolley cars, which brought him, one after the other, to the center of Valencia, after passing the port area and the dry riverbed of the Turia. His confessor would be expecting him and it would be hard to tell which of the two was waiting more impatiently. Sundays they spent together, in company with the five other *agapitos* Valencia boasted during that year of drought. They would set out for the suburbs to catechize strayed souls (in time, these strays began to move to tonier neighborhoods).

Father Benito was confused and even a little frightened by the tender love he felt for his *agapito*. Was this feeling not turning into a personal friendship? The boy's past quite simply scared him: a young man who had lived in Barcelona as he had lived and had tortured another boy—would he not be capable of some further and awful mischief? At the same time, thanks to Tarsis, the priest was part of an adventure of the type that took place before the Nationalist Crusade swept away such horrors.

In order to become a machine operator in the Malvarrosa factory, Tarsis dispensed with all mental reservations and decided on an enormous lie. Later, his spiritual director absolved him of the sin without assigning any penance, except for a symbolic *Ave Maria*.

At the time Tarsis arrived in Valencia, the factory's management had decided to build a plant to convert the chaff from the region's plentiful rice supply, a byproduct totally useless until then, into paper paste. Such a sophisticated operation was not to be entrusted to the indolent natives of Valencia, who were, as all the world knows, most adept at making such useless things as tambourines. The management spared no cost and, thinking big, engaged four Italian engineers. These enlightened beings, who trod like occupiers of a conquered region, which in a certain sense they were, were instinctively distrustful of the capacity for work of the natives, whom they saw turning out not only tambourines but earthen wine jugs . . . Such people would not be able to stand up to a modern machine; an Italian machine, for instance. The four Italians went about with cameras and telephoto lenses at the ready to surprise the locals, who, ignoring the new maxim of "Work is Freedom," would take a siesta on top of the barns. It should be said that the afternoons were long and the sun punishing.

The Italian engineer who interviewed a group in search of work, among them Tarsis, asked: "Is there a machine operator among you?"

Tarsis was not aware that in the scale of things the machine operator was the best paid because of his skilled work. He simply liked the job title. He thought it might involve working in the company kitchen and that he would learn in a jiffy. And so he announced that he was the very thing they were looking for.

"But are you a machine apprentice or an advanced apprentice?"

He knew the answer to that. Like the other handful of applicants, he knew well enough the highest category to which one might aspire. And so he asserted: "Yes, I'm a first-class operator."

"Where have you worked before?"

"In Prat de Llobregat. My parents moved to Valencia, and I had to come along."

"I won't ask you for credentials. I already know how you manufacture them here. But you'll have to prove you can do the job. You will copy a piece from this plan," and he unfurled a diagram on the table. "But if you make a blunder, you'll be put to sweeping up the electrical shop, to learn the consequences of lying. I'll give you two days. When you're finished, come see me."

Once he had looked at the drawing, Tarsis felt faint. It was a complicated draftsman's sketch with endless lines and measurements. He studied it closely, but in the end he was unable to make any sense of it at all. Miraculously, an old hand in the shop, Pascual Mayoral, took pity on him and helped him get started on the enigma. Then, thanks to the skill at close work he had developed in the jewelry shop, he began to make progress, always under the guidance of Mayoral, who stayed his hand whenever he was on the point of blundering.

The Italian engineer accepted the work, contracted him, and said: "Valencia is not the same as Prat de Llobregat, where you worked before. Valencia is a pest hole. Watch out for the whores."

Tarsis could only smile. What else could he do?

Sundays, the six *agapitos* would set up a film projector in the course of proselytizing the suburbs. It was not exactly "the movies," which was something more modern. They would set up the projector wherever they could, in some room or other in the *barrio,* and "project" the film—always something pious—against a bare wall. Since the "picture" was silent and lacked subtitles, it was Tarsis's job to give the commentary. He was witty about it, and Father Benito would chuckle the while. Unbeknownst to the latter, much of the improvisation (now censured) Tarsis had first head at the *"Las Golfas"* sessions at the movie house. The priest thought the boy's humor inspired: "You will be a fine Jesuit, one with an open and generous heart, as well intentioned as our founder, and like St. Francis Xavier."

Despite the secrecy Tarsis maintained, on the advice of his spiritual director, at the factory and at his *pensión,* he was certain that the maid there knew of his religious calling. Every morning when he returned from Mass at seven-thirty, she had his coffee and toast ready for him. And one morning, when he had not left at the usual time, she knocked at his door and said:

"There are only fifteen minutes left before Mass."

Father Benito hoped that Tarsis would not be content to be simply a lay brother. He was annoyed that Tarsis had made clear his admiration for Santa Teresita del Niño Jesus, who, "without having taken major orders, had attained sainthood."

"You must become a priest. You must not disdain the gifts God has bestowed on you. You must celebrate the mystery of the Eucharist. You will hear confession."

"*I* should hear confessions?"

"The tombstone of your vocation has been laid over your past."

In Father Benito's eyes, Tarsis would be his successor, his heir, his son . . . his spiritual son. The younger man would carry out all the tasks he had not been able to carry out himself due to the fact that he had joined the order so late in life. He pictured Tarsis as a missionary in Japan or teaching at the Sorbonne, as Provincial of the order or a founder of monasteries, and finally perhaps even a minor saint. When the good Father spoke to him so glowingly of his future, Tarsis felt as content as when he had sat with his own father under the apple tree in the garden at Céret. He even thought he might not be surprised if one day, speaking with the same unforgettable accent as his father and with the same tranquillity, Father Benito were to say: "Priests are merely parasites who live from feeding spiritual alfalfa to Christ's sheep."

At last Tarsis takes Amary's bishop with his queen (12. ... Qd8xe7), just as all the spectators had expected for the past ten minutes. No other move was possible. He had been spending all his time in his quarters, no one any the wiser as to whether he had in fact been analyzing his position. After finishing the move, he looks at the board as if relishing what he has done. He had already cleared the decks for action when he installed his knight at e4, and after the obligatory pause following the last two moves, he is set to destroy his rival.

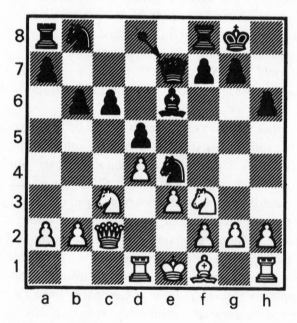

12. ... Qd8xe7

Contrary to what the press holds to be the case, Tarsis is convinced that Isvoschikov is collaborating with his kidnappers: the "revolutionary trial" is unfolding without any complications; the Minister accuses himself, confessing and revealing everything he knows . . . without Amary and his gang touching a hair of his head. The ecchymosis or contusion around his right eye which appears in the Polaroid photos is merely the result of an accident, according to his own testimony: when his abductors first awakened him, they applied the gag with such precipitation that damage was done.

At the age of seventy-one, a man like Isvoschikov, accustomed to the opulent living of a member of the Soviet *nomenklatura* (the luxurious residences, the disciplined chauffeurs, all manner of reverences, attention, and special considerations, the servants who prepare the best food, the male and female nurses who attend to the punctual administration of his medicines, the doctors who watch his blood pressure and his rate of sedimentation and his pulse, the obedient subordinates), comes apart upon falling into the hands of a robot like Amary. Or so thinks Tarsis. In short, the higher-up official, the superior, protected and served by hundreds of subordinates, neither knows how nor is able to live on his own. And Tarsis further assumes that Isvoschikov has read and given credence to all the accounts of how men of his caste (whether rulers or millionaires) have behaved when abducted and has believed, along with the press and public opinion, that the captives have always faced up to their captors with dignity, not only facing up to the "revolutionary trial" but also facing up to and confronting their executioners. He imagines the first hour of captivity as if he had lived it himself: Isvoschikov, gagged in the car that took him from Paris to Meung-sur-Loire, fuming and "fit to be tied," impatient to deal with these impertinent nobodies who think they are so many Al Capones. The pain in his face from the initial blow only increased his anger. But then, when they reached the chalet . . . not a one of them so much as looked at him or addressed him with a single word . . . Amary forced him to descend to the cellar and made him sit on the wet earth, the floor. He was chained to the wall, and finally given a bucket for his toilet. Amary had already decided, thinks Tarsis, on the required tactic, based on the chess norm "The threat is worse than the execution of the threat." Isvoschikov is the ideal prisoner: disoriented now and with no previous experience in meeting any violence not purely brutal. And so Amary left his prisoner locked in his solitude. He counted on fear provoking diarrhea and forcing him to use the bucket interminably. Amary sought not only humiliation but a gangrene of the reflexes. Twenty-four hours were enough. And then Amary appeared in the cellar, cold and calculating, with a metallic apparatus in his hands; from it hung three electrodes. He plugged it into a socket and an almost inaudible hum emanated from the box.

Isvoschikov, who might have been able to face up to a violent confrontation with his kidnappers, was totally disarmed (with no nurses or aides-de-camp at his disposal). He was alone as never before, a prey to fear, terror, and finally panic. Tarsis was sure that, following years of well-being and security, the threats now hanging over him would have made him lose every notion of dignity and even of identity. He would have revealed and "confessed" everything and anything that Amary and his gang demanded without any need to bring the electrodes into play . . . (And such items might have been merely a theatrical device.)

All through his adolescence, Amary conscientiously wrote out a series of notations. He burned them at the end of his first year at the university. One of these notations, written two weeks after he had finished off his mother, was couched in the following language:

MEMORANDUM (CÉCILE)

Eleven years old. An episode: the three of us on our knees.

Before that: Cécile dances, goes out alone. Tuberculosis. Sanatorium in the Pyrenees. Father meets her there. Idyll. "Romantic"—according to Cécile. They exchange letters. In secret. Before her death, Cécile shows me a packet of letters. She tells me: "Your father loved me. He loved Humanity. He loved everyone." They married. I was born (excrement). Gabriel was born. She says: "Your father was a true diplomat. He lived for Switzerland."

Until I was six: Father shy, plays with Gabriel and me. We take walks together. He pretends to adore his children. An irrational relationship. A game.

The Kid appears, then Mickey, then Doña Rosita, the snake, and Teresa. Later, the Others.

Father: the respectable person of the two. Mother: the worthless role: runs the house, deals with servants. Father: travels, returns with gifts. Cécile: scolds. Father: smiles.

First point: Father does not answer questions (on life, death, sex, view of the world). *Wants* to appear shy. Was impotent. I don't ask Cécile.

Second point: Father and Cécile, nothing in common. They do not understand one another. Cécile is content to be "wife to a diplomat." Astrology. Danish literature. Novels. Poetry. Goethe and Schiller. The main point: security. Ideal: a nineteenth-century marriage. Father:

Switzerland. 1914 war: killing. He says he is an anarchist. They quarrel: over Carole (civil servant).

Third point: The adults I know are weaklings, cowards, and immoral as well. They feel no compassion, only rancor, which accumulates in silence. Cécile: The orders she gives as housewife.

An episode: Cécile says: "Something dreadful has happened. Get on your knees." Gabriel laughs to himself. Then he cries. And she prays. We pray. She invents prayers. Against "the bad woman" (Carole). I already knew about it. I had rummaged and found the letters before she did. Carole calls Father "my little bear."

Father does not come home at night. When he does show up: a ruckus. Cécile strikes him. Plates fly. Chairs, too. The end always the same: an attempt at reconciliation. Father does not dare to make the break. Cécile: requires abandoning. Father: patient. At last he makes the break. I am glad. At that time I admire Carole, the "bad woman": I still do not know her.

Cécile sees the neighbors as people who steal her silverware. One more degree of mental confusion. She is taken off to the madhouse. Visits. She attempts to get close to us, sits me on her knees, caresses me. She's mad.

Gabriel and I are finally alone. I ask myself: Do we live to eat, work, and sleep? Only that? Is there another, hidden reason. Sex? But sex is linked to procreation.

What the Kid likes, always a good deal: bread and butter and chocolate-shavings. Tomatoes. Boiled potatoes with hard-boiled eggs and mayonnaise. Pastry. Bacon. The Kid insists on stuffing himself.

I study: science: the Great Unification.

Father does not show up. He pays monthly. Sometimes he forgets the rent. He apologizes by mail.

Cécile returns home three times. Cured: according to the doctors.

The first time: She maintains that the neighbors send out inimical rays. They attack her internal organs. She curses them. A violent incident. They lock her up again.

The second time: She maintains that Gabriel and I take away her sexual energy. She attacks the striking garbage collectors with an ax: they are trying "to rot her guts." Return to the madhouse.

Third: Death.

Cécile abominates my studies. Science corrupts. I should also not be a diplomat. There are bad women. I should engage in the scrap-iron trade.

I wrote Carole. Motive: because she was the person who had liberated Father. I admired her without a reason. Carole did not answer. I placed a copy of the letter under a sheet of blotting paper. I marked a cross for each day that passed. At the end of two months I burned the letter. Then I met Carole. She was decolleté. A social climber. Disillusion. She advised me to read Amiel. She made me sick.

Thefts: I stole twelve fishing hooks. For Gabriel. Using strategy. A humiliation: not for having stolen, but for having stolen badly. Two years later I stole a khaki-colored sweater. That I stole well. I have not stolen again.

The death of Cécile.

She arrived home with an open wound on her thigh. I gathered some pieces of horse manure. The Kid insisted on it. I fermented them in petri dishes. I covered them with agar. The tetanus bacteria grew and multiplied. Tested positive. Chicken broth and sugar as nutriment. They continued to multiply. When there were enough, I put them through a filter. Only the tetanus bacteria remained. I applied them to Cécile's wound (when the Kid told me to). A long death throes. She said: "I shat you." She died.

The Master.

Another one of the writings that Amary burned bore the title:

WORLD YOUTH CHESS CHAMPIONSHIP
REPORT

I won the Swiss Junior Championship. I was fourteen. Qualified for the World Championship automatically. The National Selector: Alain Mayot. Infatuated with the second boy classified, Paul Shirley. Intellectually. Sexually?

Mayot announced: "The World Championship is a great opportunity . . . Amary is unknown . . . he has won only one championship match. Shirley has won three . . . and he's twenty . . . the best junior player in Switzerland for years . . . Amary is too young. A match between Shirley and Amary is called for . . . Let the best man win . . . and on to the World Championship."

The adults—displaying neither honor nor valor—accepted. I protested. A letter to the federation. Published in the *Gazette de Lausanne*. It reads: ". . . This decision is an outrage . . . I must prepare for the World Youth Championship . . . without the loss of time involved in any other match . . ." And I affirmed: "Money from patrons like Monsieur Mayot are a help only to professional gamblers. Mediocre patrons strive to be full-fledged bosses."

Match against Shirley in Lucerne. The mayor summons me. I've written a letter to the press. Inelegant. I am watched. He doesn't want a scandal. The adults make common cause. I won. Every game. I am classified for the World Youth Championship. Final ceremony. The press. I said what I thought. I was disqualified. Shirley goes to the world match. I was suspended for two years. No play. Goodbye to chess. Science. The Great Unification.

The Master.

Though years have passed and Alain Mayot is no longer national selector (he continues to belong to the federal committee), chess circles still recall the episode that has passed into legend as the "Lucerne scandal." The most common version now current regarding what Amary said before the assembled press corps seems almost too novelistic. According to this version, he had declared, amid the silence and stupor of the assembly: "I will tell you a joke. Monsieur Alain Mayot owned a parrot which had ceased to talk and was languishing away. He went to a veterinarian, who proposed an infallible remedy: 'Tell your parrot some charming stories, regale it with pleasantries.' By the end of the month the parrot died. The veterinarian asked: 'Didn't you follow my advice?' 'I did,' answered Monsieur Mayot, 'I told him I was a splendid person. That everything I do is done for love of chess. And that I like women.' The veterinarian replied: 'No wonder he died. You administered a dose fit for an elephant.' "

What Amary did not know is that after the two years' suspension he was put on the federation's blacklist. And that Mayot's wrath was almost enough to destroy his own meticulously prepared life project, for which the world Championship was only a base. He would never be able to contest the title if he did not first win the Swiss crown, the point of departure and of access to the cycle of zonal and interzonal tourneys.

Amary accepts Tarsis's challenge and takes his knight (13. Ktc3xe4). One of the game's analysts immediately tells the newsmen that the Swiss champion shows signs of nervous stress, and at a crucial moment, too, which is worse. If he had accepted the fact that he has already lost the initiative, he would have been satisfied with a tie after 13. Bf1-d3. But he is bent on winning, going on the attack and destroying his rival's king-side, which he finds unprotected following the knight's disappearance. He had no mind for defense: he must win the match and forge the apotheosis he foresees. The struggle is revolutionary, that is, scientific, and he is opposed by an enemy relying on absurd means. If he concentrates

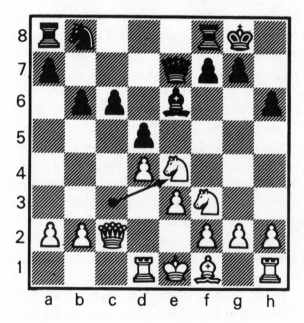

13. Ktc3xe4

fully, he tells himself, victory cannot elude him. He plays only to win, and he is convinced that he will commit no more indiscretions.

But he has just committed another. The second one of the game.

Amary was thrown off balance because the sciatic nerve of the position (e4) had been ever so lightly grazed. Tarsis tells himself that he is the only human being who knows how to find his rival's faults and exploit them. Who else, if not he, would have thought to reconnoiter the residence which Amary had purchased at Meung-sur-Loire? One day, taking advantage of a rest period on which no play was scheduled, between the seventeenth and eighteenth games, he went to the very place where he was sure the Russian was sequestered. Unfortunately, the mansion was surrounded by a wall nearly ten feet high, which made closer inspection impossible. The two-story house lay in the middle of a well-tended park. Gendarmes watched the residence from five strategic points: at the entrance to the park and from its four corners. And they were armed and equipped with walkie-talkies. Tarsis could not but admire his enemy's ruse: demanding police protection on the pretext that he feared for his life! And then to ask that four motorcycle policemen either precede or follow him on each one of his sallies! It was a typical chess maneuver for purposes of deception. Thanks to it, he would place himself outside the circle of suspects. Who would accuse him of kidnapping the Soviet Minister, now that he was protected by the police day and night, automatically under surveillance; that is, automatically beyond suspicion? But Amary managed to get around the self-imposed vigilance and carry out the abduction of Isvoschikov. Tarsis needed to know only how Amary had managed to elude his guard one night without the gendarmes seeing him. He had considered a multitude of hypotheses, when the solution was furnished him by a civil servant working in the property office of the municipal government of Meung-sur-Loire.

"The whole region is undercut, sieved like a Gruyère cheese, with underground tunnels, paths, mines, and secret passages, some of them leading all the way to Orléans. Some of these corridors and passages date as far back as the Middle Ages, their purpose being to afford escape routes for the owners of ancestral homes in case of *force majeure*. During the French Revolution not a few of the nobles escaped the guillotine thanks to these escape routes. Some thirty years ago the security services asked that they all be sealed off; they were quite dangerous; frequent cave-ins had sometimes occasioned casualties. It could be assumed that the majority of proprietors had filled in their tunnels.

But not the owner of the mansion which Amary had bought: he was a highly original character, a sculptor with anarchic tendencies who did not like to be told what to do with his property.

It had been through one of those tunnels that Amary and his followers had made their way on the night of the abduction, and brought back a gagged Isvoschikov a couple of hours later, Tarsis assumed. Thus had they evaded the police assigned to their protection and turned them into their best negative witnesses.

A hair shirt almost did Tarsis in, almost prevented him from obtaining his passport into the seminary. At the same time, his talent for religious agitation nearly led to a schism in the Society of Jesus.

It was the time of the slogan "Oran is Spanish"—a claim made for the Spanish city in North Africa. And if rice chaff could not successfully be converted into paper paste without the help of colonizing Italian engineers, Spain nevertheless could give lessons to anyone in the area of hair shirt manufacture. Spain held the cathedra, the Distinguished Chair of Hair Shirt Studies. The sun never set on this empire. The Spanish hair shirt, highly crafted, handmade with great care by cloistered monks, was an export item to the Philippines and the Marianas by way of the province of Castellón de la Plana north of Valencia. This national industry—like beggary—did not require the slightest help from Italian overlords or engineers. This was in an epoch in which the fine arts, despite their patriotic fervor, were more notable for monotony than for imagination. And the Spanish hair shirt was truly outstanding, a model of form and figure. Examples existed in all sizes and shapes, for all tastes, with or without pious ornamentation of wire or rope, with spikes or tacks, to fit the leg or the waist, baroque and complicated or simple but efficient. Their production was informed with a sense of possibilities, of respect for the farfetched in special tastes and even manias: no one could say there was nothing for him, no one was left disappointed.

Except for Tarsis. He could not stand the instruments. The very sight of them provoked nausea and put his teeth on edge. He addressed Father Benito point-blank: "I won't wear one."

And this despite the fact that the model which his spiritual director proffered him with such piety and affection was embroidered. At first sight it resembled a wide bracelet—for the thigh—composed of a series of metallic semicircles which gave it the look of an avant-garde sculpture. The key detail which transformed this jewel into a form of hair shirt or instrument for mortification was provided by the sharp points attached to the rings: thanks to them, the artistic bracelet was outfitted with ninety-two pricks, which, once attached to the thigh, drew blood. Today one would say that only the most

dedicated masochists would be happy with such an adorn-
ment. In those days, in the eyes of the other *agapitos,* the
psychopath was Tarsis when he rejected the honor of wearing
it. For Father Benito the gift of the cilice represented the
colophon to a period brilliantly lived through by his protégé.
The cilice was the symbol of his entry into the company of
the elect. The dialogue began thus: "Today is the day of the
Most Immaculate Conception. And I can tell you the joyful
news. Beginning *today* you are allowed to wear the cilice.
Here you have it."

Tarsis had seen the ones the other elected *agapitos* wore
and had regarded them with repugnance. With no attempt at
kindness he replied: "I will never wear any such prison device.
I can't stand pain, in any case."

"But, my son, do you realize what you are saying? You
cannot reject it. It's an honor. Not all *agapitos* have the right
to wear it *yet.* It will help you suppress all temptations against
purity."

It was Father Benito who did not realize what he was
saying. There is no denying the virtues possessed by the hair
shirt, but there is one which can hardly be mentioned: it does
not inhibit the male organ. On the contrary, any *agapito* could
have instructed the forgetful old ecclesiastic about his early
morning *Via Crucis.* In short, these long-suffering youths
would put on their sacrificial instruments in the morning and
wear them through the Mass. On returning, they would take
them off. But meanwhile, during the course of the Mass—
and, most curiously, precisely at the moment of the Elevation
of the Host, for reasons utterly unknown—they were prey
to a rigidity of such potency that many had to loosen the
buttons on their flies. As if that was not enough, later they
suffered a bitter kind of hangover which was vulgarly alluded
to as a "reheating of the eggs." Even the most noble adventures have their complications.

Father Benito had to make use of all his reserves to overcome the quandary. He was blinded by passion. He kept telling himself that the rebellion shown by Tarsis was simply the fruit of the damage done him in Barcelona, from which he was not yet fully healed. He did not dare ask himself if Tarsis would ever heal. For the moment he announced that he would report to his superiors—as he was in duty bound to do—"later on." This phrase was one of his most handy mental reservations.

Meanwhile, Tarsis pursued his devotions with the same zeal (but without the consolation of the cilice). In the mornings he would hear Mass in the chapel of the Sanatorium of Tubercular, Scrofulous, and Rachitic Girls. This full-bodied name was displayed on the beach at Malvarrosa, without any noticeable upset on the part of the bathers. In those days, of course, it was not surprising to see people walk into the water and swim in shorts and t-shirts. The girls themselves were not disconcerted to be named in the sign, since it was merely descriptive, and they might even have felt some pride at being alluded to at all. For his part, Tarsis was accustomed to such descriptive epithets: he had discovered a similar inscription not far from the San Antón school, which proudly stated, at the very portals of the Convent of the Teresian Mothers: HOLY SISTERHOOD OF YOUNG LADIES DOWN ON THEIR FORTUNE. Nowadays young ladies no longer even get down on their luck. Meanwhile, a similar fate has befallen the Holy Brotherhoods and Sisterhoods themselves.

Tarsis stood out in that gynaeceum of tubercular girls, that women's Gymnasium of nuns and unfortunates. For obvious reason he was at war with the officiating priest, although he kept his peace. With the girls he maintained equally silent relations, but with a romatic tinge. He pondered his luck in choosing the Society of Jesus: otherwise he would have fallen in love with the lot of them. Especially with those who had difficulty in making their way to the altar. He took Communion in their midst, most fervently, and even without the spur of a cilice, he found he could not prevent happening to him what happened to the other *agapitos,* and his turgidity caused a swelling in what should have been his little slave.

He always managed to impose his will-to-chastity. And when he returned to his quarters after Mass, he managed to avoid fixing any undue attention on Soledad, who awaited him in the kitchen with her offering of breakfast coffee, as silent as the sick girls in chapel. He had not yet taken the four vows of his order (discipline, poverty, chastity, and obedience to the Pope), but he already practiced them rigorously. The fourth vow—obedience to the Pope—caused him annoyance. Why had the Society of Jesus imposed on itself this unprecedented and inane obligation, which no other order had taken upon itself? Were the relations with the Sovereign Pontiff so dubious? Would the Jesuits be likely, in the absence of this vow, to ridicule the Papal Encyclicals, or bite the Holy Father's behind? The Jesuits could easily have done their duty normally: perhaps false laughter suited them.

Never had Tarsis felt himself so fortunate, blessed, happy, and radiant. Not even in his father's company at nightfall in Céret, on the banks of the arroyo. The days, the weeks, the months passed in exaltation while he awaited the longed-for coronation of his efforts: entrance into the seminary. Parallel to his interior life, which was governed by constant piety and devotion, went an increasingly saintly life in the world. He became fired by his apostleship, and now he evangelized his fellow workers with such energy that the managment began to think the worst: that his religiosity was a cover, only a slight cover, for political militancy. He exercised his talents as a social agitator with such fervor that he might often do so mounted atop a rice-chaff haystack, as if he felt himself to be "in the highest." He urged his comrades to undertake spiritual exercises at the Jesuit House in Sagunto. It was an absurd endeavor—and was crowned with the success common to many absurd endeavors. In that epoch, the religiosity of the factory workers reached a measure approximating absolute zero. Before Tarsis ever got to Valencia, the figures of Christ which had presided over the workshops of Spain for the elevation of spirit among the masses had begun to disappear without much notice. After this period of elimination, there came a time of substitution, when the missing religious figures were replaced by full-color photos of U.S. amazons. It might have been said that in some of the laboring beehives a reverential cult was now rendered, as had been the case at *"Las golfas,"* to Esther Williams in a bathing suit. When the factory chaplain realized that he would be unable to cathecize six hundred sinners who dreamed only of the breasts and flesh bustle of the California Valkyrie, he sank into melancholy with infinite patience. He fully realized that he was no more than a decorative figure put there by the victors in the Nationalist Crusade. His only solace he found in the lap of a young woman belonging to Catholic Action who was, as well as a consolation to him, in charge of the Office of the Sick and Injured. She was most scandalized by the lack of purity on the part of her colleagues: on occasion she came upon the spoor of their activities: account books whose punched holes in their wide, soft leather backs had been *violated.* The chaplain and the girl spent their days together in mourning, and their nights all in one stretch.

In this wasteland abandoned by the hand of God, the counterproductive mission undertaken by Tarsis to lead his comrades to a Jesuit house for spiritual exercises had an unexpected outcome. He had made a sound choice and there was a bit of good luck, for it turned out that the legislature had unanimously (in a manner of speaking, for in those days the "opposition" or even the "minority" was only a phrase to be bantered about) voted a decree which authorized all the nation's workers to engage in week-long spiritual exercises, without loss of wage or employment. As if that was not enough, management was obligated to pay all expenses: costs of lodging as well as those of the priests. The factory owners were forced to accept Tarsis's plans for a retreat without a murmur.

At first the workers did not appear convinced, and even seemed to imagine that only milksops could go in for such novenas. But in the end, the more venturesome decided to try the week without work so graciously offered them. They came back delighted! They gave detailed accounts of how they had eaten like pigs, slept like logs, read some Westerns, and lived like occupying troops in splendid rooms in three-star hotels (with time and progress, hotels have come to boast six stars and soon some will boast ten; we can hope that the same measure will not prevail in the army).

According to those who returned from the retreat, it was not a Jesuit house they had gone to but the Promised Land.

"And what about the spiritual exercises?"

"That's the least of it . . . And why not make the most of it? Just so long as one's body holds out!"

"You mean they don't make you carry a cross on your back all day?"

"Not a bit of it! A priest comes along and tells you all about hell . . . and God this, and the Virgin that . . . but always in a nice way. An interesting type. I didn't always fall asleep."

Another witness, more given to fantasizing, told about his week in the following way: "I had a fabulous time! They treated us like kings! And Pedro, the clown, the one who works on the winding machines, spent his time whispering in church and telling randy stories. We split our pants laughing. On the last day he showed up at solemn High Mass with a kiss he'd painted with lipstick on his chest."

It became a stampede: the entire factory signed up to go. There was a waiting list until the end of the year. There were some who wanted to go again. As regards the firm itself, the movement involved such a mad and expensive displacement that the management appealed to the state-run vertical union and, finally, to the Minister of Labor in Madrid to stop the bloodletting. To no avail, for those Sancho Panzas had run up against the Church.

The new program represented a bonanza for the Society of Jesus, according to the gossips, and they were not all wrong. For the Jesuit House at Sagunto devoted to spiritual exercises, which before Hurricane Tarsis struck the beach at Malvarrosa had remained closed half the year due to lack of clientele, was now posting a NO VACANCY sign at all times. The news quickly reached the ears of those at the top of the order . . . and thereupon occurred the row that nearly caused a schism in the society.

The Provincial Directors of Madrid and Barcelona each desired to enlist the new preacher in his command. Tarsis did not have the gift of ubiquity. Madrid affirmed that the boy's family, his tutoress, in any case, lived in the capital of Spain. Barcelona held to the present moment: Tarsis had chosen Valencia for his domicile, a provincial capital which formed part of the Church province of Tarragona.

Tarsis himself was to resolve the conflict with one of his infamous flights.

Tarsis takes Amary's knight (13. . . . d5xe4), and it is assumed that he cannot lose and has Amary cut off: the pawn he sacrifices will only choke his opponent.

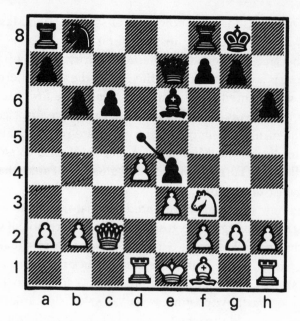

13. .... d5xe4

He gazes at the board with concentration and satisfaction . . . when suddenly, there among the pieces, he makes out a phrase, as if it were floating on the surface of a lake: YOU WILL LOSE.

And he recalls, while that hallucination gradually dissipates, how one day in Barcelona, after Nuria had kissed the palm of his hand, he had been seized with an access of heat, a strange sudden fever, and that when she withdrew her lips, a cockroach had sprung out of the center of his palm and on its shell was written the word SOLITUDE.

Tarsis is overcome with the fear that the entire variation he has played will allow his rival to execute a successful trap. Would there not exist some theoretical study written up in one of those exhaustive Yugoslav encyclopaedias which would give the key to a "demolition" of his opening? Looking at the board, one finds it all so easy . . . too easy. Has not Amary already prepared, at his mansion at Meung, a refutation of his play? Is the hallucination he just suffered a proof of weariness or a premonition? Or both at the same time?

For Amary, physics and chess demand the same concentration—and the same solitude. At the moment, he certainly neither feels nor sees anything outside the perfect square of the chessboard.

He had always lived alone, even at the height of his political militancy, and he is incapable of establishing a normal relationship with another person, and yet he had set himself the task of resolving the problem of the Great Unification. For that purpose he would have to establish a relationship among all the forces, actions, and interactions in the universe.

[Marc Amary hated the Kid. He knew he would have to put up with him as soon as he returned to his quarters. He was not bothered by the fact that the Kid addressed him as the Master: none of them had ever called him by any other name. The Kid simply infuriated him, and he often ended by hurling insults and calling him a murderer, and a matricide into the bargain. And of course he was dead right.

For example, the Kid did not like the Master to play chess. Whenever the latter set himself to analyze a game, the former would place himself precisely behind his neck and would regard him with disgust. The Master could not see him, but he felt his breath and his disdain . . .

Chess upset the Kid, and that was because he knew he was incapable of learning to move the pieces. The Kid only knew how to play hide-and-seek, hopscotch, and heads-or-tails. His playmate was Mickey, who was a cheater and a gambler.

Mickey was a small rubber mouse barely two inches tall; the Kid could not sleep without him; the Master thought he was old enough to sleep alone. Mickey was always smiling, his feet sticking out and his arms outstretched, as if he thought he was about to be embraced. His pants and his tongue were red, his socks were green, and his gloves and his face were white, while his snout, like his enormous ears, was black. His disposition was so peculiar that the Master never could figure him out.

The Kid took advantage of the situation whenever he could manage it. For instance, he himself had grown stout, and he therefore imposed obesity on the Others (except, of course, on Mickey) through the years; it never bothered him that the Master dragged his more than two hundred pounds to the institute and the university without any shame about it; he was made to eat, sometimes to the point of nausea, all the butter, bacon, and eggs covered with mayonnaise that were forced on him.

Despite everything, the Kid knew that he had overawed the Master in insisting on hanging the maid and murdering the mother, and he made the most of these feats. He was totally irresponsible and, in addition, had compromised the Master by the matricide.

In their frequent discussions, the Kid threatened the Master by saying he would call on *"Him."* Naturally *He* was always at the Kid's side anyway, and the Master knew it. *He* never took sides, but that fact did not make *Him* any the less present in all matters. *He* might not be actually "present," as the term is generally understood. Neither the Kid nor the Master would have been able to specify what *His* opinions might be, or what *His* voice said or what *His* powers were. *He* was an ever-present threat and that was enough.

Mickey intervened whenever the Kid and the Master entered into polemics, and he would recount a bad joke in a falsetto voice which made the Master's nostrils flare. Nevertheless, all the accidents suffered by Mickey in the course of his existence were always repaired by the Master under the pretext that the Kid was so clumsy. He even glued on his head when it was knocked off. But the Kid laughed at him for doing so: "A man of science like you pasting on the head of a little rubber mouse . . . Ha, ha . . ."

Mickey also annoyed him during the operation with his out-of-tune voice (the doll, peculiarly, was capable of talking even while decapitated). Like all mice, he was obscene, and he spent his days telling blue stories; he even ventured to paw the other's Cowper's glands, something totally unacceptable to a man who could not stand even to be tickled. The Kid let himself be fondled, though, but then he had no principles or dignity, or any morality.

Mickey knew *Him* better than anyone else did, almost as well as the "Three Condors." Whenever he allowed himself to reveal some secret concerning his intimate knowledge of *Him,* the other two, the Kid and the Master, would listen impatiently. One day the latter insisted: "You must tell us at least where he sleeps."

"Why, with us, in bed!"

He had raised his voice to such a high pitch that they couldn't tell if he was jesting or revealing a secret. Nevertheless, from then on the Master left some room in bed, on his right. The Kid slept to his left and Mickey between the two of them. The Others did not, of course, have any right to sleep with them at all.

On the sly Mickey and the Kid traded secrets. The Master could not make out what they said in whispers, but they always laughed when they mentioned Madrid.

The Kid refused to become a Marxist, and he offered no explanation. He was simply headstrong. What he said by way of explanation drove the Master wild. He simply asserted:

"The Kid does not want to be a Marxist." And that was all. Mickey, on the other hand, embraced the idea with enthusiasm. But just when the Master was feeling the most satisfied with his convert, the little mouse hit him with an old chestnut: "I'm a Marxist, all right, Groucho tendency, and a Leninist, Lennon tendency."

The Master stepped on him viciously, but the little fellow was unbelievably resilient in spite of his small size.

The Master would have liked it best if they had all shown an interest in physics, or at least if the Kid and Mickey had. With infinite patience he explained his work to them. They would listen to him open-mouthed. Perhaps they did not even hear him.

"Einstein postulated a theory relative to gravity in which space, time, and matter are the same mathematical and physical objective. The theory I am seeking would unify all the forces of nature. Do you understand?"

Invariably the Kid answered: "Seriously?" As if it might be a joke.

In his ventriloquist's voice, Mickey would inquire, as if he had understood everything: "When you realize your objective, you will be like God before Creation?"

"You can forget God."

Mickey's commerce with God on a quotidian basis set the Master on edge: Mickey was an obvious racist, or at least he discriminated openly, which was only natural in mice. And then he would make matters worse: "We mice are quite mystical. There are many hermits among us."

"Come down from the heavens and put your feet—your four paws—solidly on earth. I'm explaining to you that I'm on the point of unifying gravitation, electromagnetism and its interactions, strong as well as weak. Do you understand me?"

That postscript, "Do you understand me?," was no less aggressive than the Kid's eternal reply: "Seriously?"

Fuming, the Master cut him off: "The only one playing the fool here is you."

"You're jealous ever since I did in Cécile. You talk big when you don't need me, but when you do, it's cap in hand . . ."

"Assassin!"

"It was you who prepared the tetanus," the Kid answered insolently.

Mickey always intervened at the most tense moments: "That's true. I'm a witness. You collected the horse manure."

"You shut up!" And he yelled at the Kid: "You insisted I make up the preparation. And now you dare recall it to me! I'll kill you!"

"If you kill me, you'll die."

The Master had to yield to the evidence. "The only time I'm happy is when I get out of here and leave you all behind. What a relief!"

Like most mice, Mickey possessed the talents of a diplomat: "You were telling us about physics. It was very interesting. Please go on. The Great Unification is fascinating."

The Master took the bait: "The Great Unification will trace the relationship between the greatest present energies with the infinitely small, like those which gluon might possess . . ."

"You've never told us about that," lied the mouse.

"Of course I have."

"Tell us again."

"For the last time: in the atom there is a nucleus composed of protons and neutrons. The proton contains three quarks. These quarks are united by a gluon, a gluing; a glue, in short."

With a know-it-all air, the Kid interjected: "That's false. You speak of particles you've never seen. I'm certain of that."

Conciliatory, Mickey interposed: "Don't keep interrupting. Please go on."

"The truth is that the Kid is right: no one has ever seen these particles or is likely ever to see them, and it isn't possible to imagine an electronic microscope which will allow one to see them. All of us investigators are waiting for the moment when the proton can be disintegrated."

"And who will achieve that?" Mickey asked.

The Master was always pleased to come to the moment when he could overawe them with an image of the eternal: "The investigator who desires to behold this phenomenon will consider the possibility of achieving it. Consequently he will sit down in a chair and wait various billions of trillions of centuries."

One time the Kid interrupted him most vulgarly. "All this sounds like something you'd tell Teresa later to turn her on!"

The mere mention of Teresa was enough to cause trouble. She was the "worst kind of vixen," according to the Master, who kept her locked in a basement cupboard, and they were all forbidden to talk to her. Mickey and the Kid, however, were fond of her and they consoled her on the sly; they had even managed to let her sleep with them, at their feet on the rug.

The Master's antipathy toward Teresa was altogether irrational. He called her "whore" because of an incident which had embarrassed him one night in New York. While he slept, Teresa, the Kid, and Mickey managed to elude the guards and make their way into the United Nations building, and there, in a deserted General Assembly Hall, Teresa took off her clothes and did an erotic pantomime on the Secretary-General's table.

The trip to New York, which the Master had organized to give a lecture at N.Y.U., had begun badly. He had told the Kid to buy a collective ticket for them all, but the latter, as brazenly independent as ever, had bought an individual ticket, on which they all, nevertheless, got to the United States. During the flight the Master, swallowing his ire, had said nothing, so as to prevent a scene. But once the door to their New York hotel room was closed, he flew at Mickey, pale with rage: "I forbid you to indulge in any cheating which might be discovered! I'm a state functionary! They could throw me out because of you!"

To avoid any further disasters, the Master did not take any more trips until the interzonal competition.

Mickey would return to the charge: "Then who the devil is ever going to witness this famous disintegration of the atom?"

It was a rarity for the Master to let an opportunity to expound on his theme slip by: "It might be achieved if the PP machine reached the necessary luminosity. What can be asserted is that the LEP, the subterranean apparatus being built between Switzerland and France, will bring it about. And on that day we will reach to the smallest while we analyze energies of 10^{16}, infinitely superior to all those studied today, and which will be the basis of the Great Unification. Unknown energies of fifteen orders of magnitude exist: it's what science calls the 'desert.' "

And the Kid interrupted: ". . . So it's a 'desert' . . . you can tell that to somebody else. All you want is to get into Teresa."

"You're plainly cracked."

"That's why you allow her to sleep at your feet on the rug . . . so you can leap on her like a tiger as soon as we take off our clothes. You want to seduce her with this story about the 'desert.' "

"I neither can nor want to seduce her. And she understands nothing about physics."

Once again Mickey threw fuel on the fire: "Do you expect me to explain it to her?"

"I won't talk to you again."

At such a juncture, the Master would closet himself in the

bathroom with El Loco, who was kept behind the toilet bowl, so that neither the Kid nor Mickey nor *He* nor Teresa could find him. It was the Master's own secret. He could speak easily there, and if once in a while they argued, the talk never degenerated. They held each other in mutual respect. Though the Master was convinced that El Loco knew *Him;* thus he shielded him even more than he did all the others. El Loco never made reference to *Him,* not even when the Master attacked him. But he could summon *Him* whenever he wanted to, and this was a fact the Master did not ignore. The threat *He* represented was even more disquieting.

Luckily, the Master told himself, none of them, after the terrible trip to New York, accompanies me when I go out now. What a hell it would be to have to put up with them

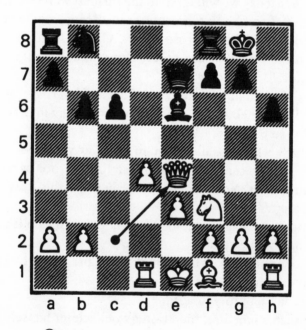

14. Qc2xe4

in physics laboratories or at political meetings or during chess matches.]

Amary plays 14. Qc2xe4, and immediately Tarsis begins to sing to himself, keeping the words and music, however feverish, strictly *sotto voce*. In fact, he is in such a hurry to think that the idea he is endeavoring to hold on to escapes him like a bubble, in between his analysis of position, the words of the inner song, and his terrible urge to urinate. It all comes down to a phrase in the end: "Amary has abandoned his queen-side, and he's about to be left toothless."

Though it is true that talk is prohibited during play, in unofficial contests the players spend their time muttering incoherent phrases to themselves *ad infinitum*. Morphy, for example, would obstinately proclaim, a thousand and one times, in French: *"Implantera la bannière de Castille sur les murs de Madrid, au cri de 'Ville gagnée,' et le petit roi s'en ira tout penaud."* González would intone war chants, and Benet, on the point of winning, would roar: "Thus ends the story of an arrow which marred."

With the help of his refrain, Tarsis strives to overcome the uncertainty which rattles him more than ever, now that he can imagine himself at the gates of victory.

Tarsis had most memorably heard the song he was now humming on the night of the flood in Valencia. The madcap granddaughter of the landlady of the guest house where he was staying was singing it like a lunatic.

The day had begun on a most auspicious note—and it

ended in the most unexpected manner as regards the Jesuit order, or at least for the Provincial General of the province of Tarragona. As day dawned, Tarsis had received a visit, in the form of an apparition, from the Virgin Mary. Then he put in his eight hours as a machine operator at the paper factory. Next he went to see his spiritual director. And finally, after a dramatically decisive night, he made his way out the city's carriage gate—en route to the French frontier.

Even though the apparition of the Virgin had moved him so deeply that he was reduced to tears merely by its recollection, he did not speak of the event to Father Benito. Would it not be a sin of pride to claim to have seen the Virgin? Would it not be to lay a claim to sainthood, with the additional danger of being called mad or, even worse, vainglorious? What proofs could he offer? On some other occasions the virgin had mantled herself in a miracle, or had asked for the construction of a basilica; or, even more telling, she would make three or four apocalyptic prophecies, something to impress even the most barefaced iconoclast. This time, the Virgin, like Tarsis, played a silent role (and with no subtitles). Father Benito would believe him or pretend to believe him, but would he not actually be convinced he was a presumptuous pretender? Only the saints or the blessed receive such graces from heaven, Tarsis knew. But he was wrong.

And yet he had not concealed any of his previous adventures from his spiritual director: not the Madrid days with a French slave, nor his activity as a pimp in Barcelona, nor his failure at Segovia. He had not even kept back his early morning prurience at the sight of the little sick girls at Mass. But the prodigy of the apparition was a different matter altogether. Would he be acting treacherously against the Society of Jesus? No. Or against the Virgin? Not that either. The Virgin had smiled at him without asking for anything in return. Of course some people would think he was asleep and dreaming when he claimed he saw her.

In that epoch, on the Iberian peninsula, the Virgin appeared only to shepherds and shepherdesses. It's not surprising she is seen so seldom now, given the gradual disappearance of that trade. And who would now believe that she had appeared to a machine operator in a city "pushing toward a million inhabitants before the end of the century"? Tarsis was pleased she had not asked him to build a hermitage . . . on some shore where at dawn the beach could be seen littered with sleeping condoms resembling vintage snail slugs.

When he arrived at Malvarrosa that night, after having spent the afternoon with his spiritual director, he found the streets inundated, submerged under water which reached his knees as he walked on, and soon reached his crotch as he went toward the *pensión*. The night was made all the more sinister by a failure in the electricity supply. The power failure was no great surprise: there were no Italian engineers connected with the electricity company, and all the equipment seemed made of wrapping paper, so that the slightest rain brought on a blackout. When he heard the popular song the madcap granddaughter was singing, he recognized her voice at once: her name was Angelita and she was singing a song called *"Angelitos Negros."* For the first time he was amused by her antics. The turmoil was a big adveture for Angelita: the inundation, the blackout, lighting the candles, it was all a blessing from heaven. Her grandmother, the landlady, was so beside herself that in her comings and goings she attempted, for no good reason, to pull out the "crab" from the fuse box—with such bad luck that she pulled out half the electricity meter. Now the "crab," like the hair shirt, was a masterpiece of popular craftsmanship in the entire nation. Moreover, it had the virtue of forging links of communal solidarity, nowadays to be seen only in films from Bulgaria. Whenever the company meter man appeared in the distance, the word ran from door to door, and Doña Rita would normally have time to carefully remove the "crab's" feet from the meter before the inquisitor arrived. Nothing much has been written about this ingenious kilowatt thief, an authentic marvel of national talent. But that night Doña Rita blew it. Tarsis was not even aware of the constriction his destiny was undergoing: the day had begun with an apparition and ended in black darkness.

Doña Rita explained: "You won't be able to get to your room. The garden is covered by more than three feet of water."

His bedroom, at the end of the garden, had probably been the gardener's room in better times; that is, in the great days "before the civil war." This expression, "before the war," was the equivalent of *"la belle époque"* for the French: it suggested that the country's only goal was to return to the past.

Tarsis was on the point of jumping in and swimming the rest of the way, across the whole garden, in search of a holy image he kept, a favorite one of the Virgin. Had he done so, and breasted the flood, she might possibly have saved him from the temptation which lay in store.

"Imagine the state of your mattress and the sheets!"

Dōna Rita went on lamenting, but Tarsis, due to a contradictory egocentrism based on devotion to the Virgin, did not care a fig whether or not his bed was to show up the next day, or two days hence, or at the end of a week, covered in mud. He was thinking only of his holy image, his sacred picture.

"Soledad has put a mattress in the attic, on top of a rug on the floor. It's so hot you won't need any covers. But, in any case, there's a pile of blankets on the landing."

She was right about the heat. Everyone was sweating. As for the attic, Tarsis hadn't even known that the house had one. As he went up the stairs to it, he could hear the lowing coming from her-grandmother's-little-treasure, Angelita. She was singing *"Angelitos Negros."*

When he had gone about a dozen steps up, Doña Rita informed him: "Soledad will sleep in the attic with you. There's no place else. My jewel and I will occupy her room. The four rooms downstairs are inundated. We'll sell our lives dear!"

A trio of office workers had prudently opted to stay at the factory. They parapeted themselves behind a large carafe of red wine, and set about turning the archive rooms into Sodom and Gomorrah: the soft-leather account books suffered the assaults of those great fencers upon their pliant backsides during this memorable orgy.

Doña Rita had armed Tarsis with a candle as his only viaticum. Reaching the heights, he said his prayers, blew out the flame, and beatifically summoned the apparition once again.

It had been at six-thirty that morning, just as he got up to go to Mass, that the Virgin had appeared in all her radiance, atop a cloud, adorned with a halo of dazzling incandescence. Her face was that of a most serene and beautiful being. She held a veil against her breast with the hands of a dove of the Holy Ghost. She smiled on Tarsis and gazed on him fixedly, as if to say, "You are my favorite son and all my hopes are placed in you." As he recalled the infinite joy he had experienced, the tears welled in his eyes. He could not have said how long the apparition lasted, for the time elapsed was the quintessence of time between infinity and the moment. He had felt splendor and ecstasy, the light of creation, a halo around paradise and the splendor of angels. The Virgin seemed to conduct him through the heavens, sweetly aloft, gliding between heaven and earth. And nevertheless, she remained immobile and equidistant. She was wafted from one end of the firmament to the other in an instant, without ever for a moment shifting her eyes from his. He sensed that he was gold and silver, sphere and tree, sun and moon, understanding and love. Drops of rain and flame seemed to emanate from his pores, as the Virgin continued to gaze on him, and his very soul burned with ardor. When a convulsion shook him he let himself go easily, as if he were dissolving in her grandeur; between light and light she left only a soft smile behind. She seemed to disappear, and he wanted to pray, but his lips and his mind could enunciate only "Hail Mary."

An hour later, when he had returned to his workbench after taking Communion in the chapel, one of the numerous holy pictures in his missal fell to the ground. It was the very image that had appeared to him: the Immaculate Conception by the painter Murillo just as he had seen her . . . only the angels had been missing.

He had again grown so engrossed and exalted by the memory that he was not even aware that Soledad had lain down beside him. When he realized what had happened, he drew back his leg, which was grazing her, as if she had been a dangerous snake, and he exclaimed: "You've gotten into my bed!"

"Don't make a fuss. There's no other place. But if I bother you, I'll go sleep on the stairs."

His eyes had grown accustomed to the dark, and now he saw what he had not noticed before in the light of the candle: the attic was filled with trunks, suitcases, furniture, and the two mattresses on the floor had been placed side by side in the small space that was left. Soledad's bed and his were joined together immutably. She was dressed in a chemise, but he wore only underpants, since his pajamas were in his bedroom; they were Spanish-style underpants, to be sure, halfway down his legs, with a useful central aperture; a true national jewel, a product of native ingenuity (like Spanish stew with chick-peas, and resulting from the same circumstances), lately replaced by the ridiculous "slip," formed by two isoceles triangles, multicolored or multistriped, or even monochrome, but always loud and brash, which squeeze the noble parts of a man, who perforce wears them to prove his modernity: small wonder the impotence and even sterility of a sex which was once alarmingly virile.

Restless, uneasy, Tarsis was on tenterhooks. With his heart in his mouth, he felt time stand still, as if it did not care to advance.

"Can't you sleep?"

"Can you tell?"

"I can hear you breathing and your heartbeats."

"I drank too much coffee," Tarsis lied.

"It's so hot! And changing beds, and the flood . . . Are you nervous?"

"A bit . . . And you?"

"No, I'm not."

Soledad was like a pool of peace and ease. She had always managed to keep herself calm in a boardinghouse where the deviltry of the granddaughter and the grandmother's impatience led to constant turmoil.

Unable to settle down or sleep, Tarsis and Soledad spent the night talking. When the first light of dawn could be seen, they went on talking, their heads close together and their bodies separated, as if they had decided to place a sword between them, following one of the commands courtly love demanded.

Tarsis had been initially surprised when, at the beginning, Soledad had inquired, and he had confessed his vocation.

"Why do you go to Mass every morning?"

"I'm going to be a Jesuit."

It was a secret known only to Father Benito, to his superiors and the other *agapitos*. His spiritual director had asked him to keep it completely to himself, and he had just revealed it . . . to the *maid*. But it seemed that he breathed easily through his new wound. They spoke with animation . . . of religion.

"You believe, of course?" asked Soledad.

"Yes, thanks be to God."

"The insects do, too. Religion is a recollection of one of our former lives. Before we were humans we were parasites, silkworms, flies, caterpillars, bees. Sheep are quite different. Man was never a sheep, or a goat, nor ever will be . . ."

It never even passed through his mind that Soledad might be mad. It was obvious that she was not.

"My uncle was a shepherd. I spent two years with him," she went on. "We used to watch insects, and we noticed that they, too, believe in resurrection. Larvae, like the souls in purgatory, have a subterranean life. Live insects can feed the larva, just as believers can help the dead by praying for them. Then they emerge from the earth, sometimes with wings, like butterflies. That's like the Ascension."

"And the Immaculate Conception! Are you going to tell me that there are Virgin Marys among the spiders?"

"My uncle thought a lot about virginity. He used to experiment with his little boxes. The insects can also have virgin mothers. Some of them are born without any help from a father."

Soledad said that she often dreamed of her uncle: the two of them together were like two insects as large as cows. He would show her his wings, his antennae, his paws, his pincers, his eyes made up of thousands of eyes, his shell, and his stingers. And she would touch them, each one of his members, in fascination.

Tarsis interrupted her suddenly: "Did you sleep beside him? Like tonight, with me?"

"Every night. He would stretch out on his stomach and I would get on top of him. I'd keep him warm, rubbing my body against his."

"How old were you then?"

"If what you want to know is if he came, I'll tell you. We did it like scorpions."

"I don't understand . . ."

"I'd put my mouth against his neck and squeeze his bottom with my hands. He'd come on the goatskin which we slept on. Then he'd move over and I'd spread his liquid on me."

"Don't you believe in anything? Not even in God?"

"I'm closer to a bee, an ant, a termite, a flea, a mosquito, a locust, to a vine louse, than I am to God. And though you might not believe it, a firefly has given me more light than God has."

"You don't speak like a maid."

"My uncle taught me everything I know. From the names of the stars to a dragonfly's changes. Unfortunately he died, and I had to come to Valencia and take up service."

Soledad did not believe in sin. But she was forcing him to sin. Mentally. And with desire. So that Tarsis suddenly decided not to see Father Benito again. He would not be able to confess his night with Soledad.

"I can't return to the order. Tomorrow I'll go to France. I won't become a Jesuit."

"If you go to France . . . I'll go with you. May I?"

For the first time in the game, Tarsis checks Amary's king: 14. . . . Qe7-b4 + . He thus penetrates the unguarded queen-side, *just as I penetrated his abduction plans,* he tells himself.

The leftist press, the extreme-left press, continues to sustain the thesis that the abductors of Soviet Minister Isvoschikov are "irresponsible elements from within the working-class movement." Tarsis is surprised they are not called "Fascists." Perhaps the leftist journalists read between the lines, as he

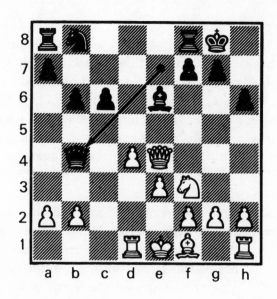

14. ... Qe7-b4 +

does, and discern the reasoning process of the authentic Communist in the dispatches from the "Comité Communiste International." Meanwhile, the radical press accuses the government of pusillanimity and the "bourgeois" police of being deliberately inefficient. A giant mass demonstration is called for the Place de la Bastille to demand of the authorities, "the objective accomplices of the kidnappers," the "immediate liberation" of the Soviet Minister. For its part, the Soviet government threatens to break diplomatic relations with France if the French government does not rescue Comrade Isvoschikov, that "great friend of the French people and of peace." In the corridors of the United Nations it is openly acknowledged that relations between the two blocs are strained and that the results are unpredictable. The most perspicacious

Kremlinologists assert that the security of the Politburo is, over and above all petty division, a matter of prime importance to each one of them, for their lives are at stake. They cannot accept a fatal precedent.

Tarsis is convinced that Amary has foreseen this cosmic dramatization of the abduction. And that he rejoices in it.

Tarsis's sudden flight aborted the mini-schism in the Society of Jesus. Would the order not easily have weathered the storm? All around them there were examples of fragmentation: there was an "authentic" Spanish Falange, and another which was just itself; and a Basque ETA "M" and another "PM"; "historical" socialists, and others unhistoried; Communists labeled "renovated" and others unrenovated; and there was a government "in plenum" and one that was unadulterated. The Society of Jesus would have stood to win if they simply divided into "S.J." and "S.J. (N)" for example. The faithful could have opted for Nazarenes or for the "orthodox," and the Society would have gained an unexpectedly modern tone.

Amary had found it a matter of the utmost simplicity to orientate himself in the labyrinth of current revolutionary formations (PTI, PCMLF, CCJD, PGC, PCF, PCMLF, HN, FR, LCR, CSFM, etc., etc.). It was ever so easy, for he knew how to distinguish the tributaries from the subtributaries, the trunks from the branches, the shortcuts from the bifurcations, the submultiples from the subdivisions, the fractions from the fissions, the sections from the committees. (In his own house, in private, his relations with the Others had accustomed him to think and proceed subtly.)

Perhaps, Amary told himself, the high incidence and plethora of intellectuals and the absence of proletarians in these revolutionary "workers' " organizations was due in part to the perplexity of the ordinary common mortal in the face of these apparently endless and trackless hieroglyphics.

The first elements of the group which Amary formed were constituted by the three dissidents from the Dimitrov Faction: Christophe de Kerguelen, John Hermes, and Jacques Delpy. Much later, they were joined by Claude Delacour.

De Kerguelen, a well-mannered aristocrat, a man incapable of talking with his mouth full or of putting his elbows on the table, had been Jacqueline Riboud's most implacable tormentor. Implacable but elegant. He was already an investigator for the Molecular Biology Laboratory of the CNRS when he finally understood something he had been hearing all his life without wanting to listen: it was the old adventure, proposed this time by the voice of Corneille: "If you desire to be perfect, sell what you own and follow me."

And he did so. He followed Corneille and joined the Dimitrov Faction, after resigning "definitively" from the CNRS, thus losing his state doctorate and his salary. He gave everything, biblically speaking, to the poor, that is, to the revolution, through Corneille as intermediary. When the latter took up transcendental meditation, in the manner of a Rumanian Minister of State, de Kerguelen was so disconsolate and downcast that he decided to commit suicide by masturbation. It was his second attempt. He had developed a taste for it. Since he had been tubercular in the past, he decided that it was the best form of hara-kiri, given the precarious state of his health. The truth was that he was trying to kill two birds with one stone, because Corneille, following his conversion to the doctrines of Buddha's nephew, Ananda Marga, now conceived of salvation as attainable only through chastity, so that de Kerguelen was intent on making mock of his former idol. But he presumed too much. At his age, death by masturbation was a form of death not attainable even by putting in overtime.

When he was eighteen, in the Sanatorium of Bouffémont, the account of his first suicide attempt was published by André Breton in one of the first issues of *La Brèche (action surréaliste)*, illustrated by two drawings from the pen of René Magritte (who at that time was a nobody). The narrative boasted suspense and denouement: his attempt to die by masturbation (he had begun early) developed well: he was wounded in action and, for lack of ammunition, was able to produce only a few drops of blood, until, at death's door, when the ultimate death rattle was upon him, the sick-bay doorway was illuminated by . . . a new nurse. He was infatuated . . . and his fire was slaked. André Breton was "fascinated" by the poetic short circuit: he compared the author to Baudelaire and Vaché.

On leaving the sanatorium, he took up residence in the convalescent center at Sceaux, and he was admitted to the Surrealist gatherings which took place between six and seven-thirty in the evening (it would have been considered a terrible *faux pax* to have shown up a minute late) at the café called La Promenade de Venus. André Breton found society's high jinks amusing: he called them "poetical charades," and the players "exquisite cadavers" and "the one in the other." He was a most refined Frenchman, Breton, but his pleasures were scarcely green. One day he suggested that each character discussed be alluded to by the animal which most poetically symbolized him (Rimbaud was the "Phoenix," Victor Hugo the "Lion of Judah," Van Gogh the "Starfish," and so on). It was de Kerguelen's role to portray St. Just allegorically. Inasmuch as he was not yet well versed in the Surrealist saints, he lightly proposed, as his symbolic animal, the rat.

Excommunication from the group had been ordered for less. Breton limited himself to a look of furious amazement, as if he were searching for hair on an egg. De Kerguelen smiled a rabbit's smile by way of protection. But Breton, after laconic denunciation, thought he had discovered an absurd secret: "You've come to spy on our group!"

But simplemindedly the neophyte answered: "To spy . . . but on what?"

The Surrealist movement, like all the most powerful literary and artistic movements of the epoch, had established points in common with the proletarian politicals. And not only a shared fanaticism. Surrealism was a rough school (but necessary) for de Kerguelen and for his future revolutionary militancy. And it was both formative and a step to maturity. At the end of that period he was ready to take a vow of obedience . . . to the first Cause that came along.

As preliminary to acceptance in his group, Amary insisted that de Kerguelen return to the Molecular Biology Laboratory. Like Breton, Amary was afraid that the uninitiated might stick their vulgar noses into his arena. In addition, breaking with his own past of noisily militant and infantile leftism, he demanded that all his comrades act normally: he wanted no self-indulgent loafers.

Less demanding than the Surrealists, the CNRS once again took him in, despite his resounding abdication and the three intervening years of escapades. So that he was able, in a double action, to join the clandestine committee of the underground movement.

Amary was well aware that the epoch of loudmouthed revolutionary groups short on actions had passed into history. To the latrine of History. They had been the childhood diseases of Communism. A new day was dawning, and the new men would help accelerate it: the capitals of the capitalist world covered endless space, every mile of which could be converted into a front line where they would wage war on the bourgeoisie by means of urban terrorism. At the head of his militant hordes Amary put on the bravest of appearances. [Thus compensating for the moment when he would arrive home and have to face the sarcasm of the Kid and the Others.]

Those leftist groups so thoroughly despised by Amary had been brought into being at the hand of a butcher. If history as it was narrated by the PCF itself (the French Communist Party) was to be believed, it began in Albacete, where André Marty, in order to indoctrinate its experts, created the French Communist Marxist-Leninist Movement: the MCF (ML). Only those totally devoid of religious perspicacity could confuse it with the Union of Communist Marxist-Leninist Students: UEC (ML). The former were pro-Chinese, and the second allies of Althausser. In order to fool the police and rival factions, the former, in their turn, were also friends and allies of Althausser (although less so) and the latter just as pro-Chinese as their rivals (or more so). The passion Althausser inspired in these people was not surprising. He was a philosopher who could write, for example: "The banners of the revolution unfurl and wave in the void." (In general, the common people cannot achieve this feat in the void.) When the two tendencies were on the point of coming to blows because of a question of interpretation of the NEP, the New Economic Policy, they suddenly decided it would be more revolutionary to join forces and form one party, to declare a fusion. The consortium thus established was named the PCF (ML), and since they were still pregnant, they gave birth to L'Humanité Nouvelle. And this only served to irritate Althausser and General De Gaulle. The former abandoned them to their fate, though they sometimes paid court to each other in private; the latter placed them outside the law, "dissolving them by decree." Meanwhile, they had married rich: and the Chinese handed over a few thousand dollars by way of dowry. In the middle of the honeymoon, De Gaulle's low blow sent them reeling. So now they decided to split up again: the

Gauche Proletaire and the PC (ML) F. The astuteness of the second group consisted in their simply sliding the F (for Français) all the way from the center to the extreme right. The "Proletarians" achieved the memorable feat of proclaiming themselves Maoists . . . but anti-Marxists! In order to divulge the glad tidings they created La Cause du Peuple. Naturally, "Cause" did not mean what the French dictionary states: "case" or "trial" or "criminal process." Then the PC (ML) F, so as to let no moss grow on them, in their turn split in two. But retaining their sense of humor, the two groups, the recently born and their rivals, continued to sport the same designation and initials: PC (ML) F. The confusion thus created was so great that they were now differentiated in progressive circles by the not very edifying titles of the "old" and the "young." In view of this mix-up, each of the antagonistic organizations, with a great sense of responsibility, founded a publication of its own to give vent to its cries: there was *Front Rouge* and *L'Humanité Rouge.* The fact that they both settled on *Rouge,* Red, did not deceive the experts, who knew how to measure the abyss which separated *Front* from *Humanité,* between Front and Humanity, a measure of the distance between the two parties. The Chinese, ever ostentatious, threw the baby out with the bathwater and gave another two thousand dollars to the Humanity group.

Nevertheless, it was not a rosy path they trod, for there suddenly loomed on the horizon the menace of Le Proletaire-Ligne Rouge. Now the "Rouge" or "Red" in the title was added only so they might stab the other two organizations with "Red" in their appellations in a more subtle manner: the real intent of this new section was to "unmask" the "revisionists"; that is, mock and parody them. The same idea had already given rise to the CCJS (Comité Communiste Joseph Staline) and the CCGD (Comité Communiste George Dimitrov). These two organizations declared war on all other left groups, but fought among themselves like Guelfs and Ghibellines. It must be admitted that they both wanted to renew old hostilities by creating the first *petit groupe compact*. The fertility of the revolutionary imagination did not stop there, and only a voluminous new *Almanach de Gotha* would be able to encompass the infinity of groups and grouplets which were ideated in that Land of Promise. The Trotskyists deserve a separate chapter: they aided the workers' cause with innumerable formations, which ranged from the LCR (Ligue Communiste Revolutionnaire) to the AJS (Alliance des Jeunes pour le Socialisme). And we should not forget groups like Socialisme et Barbarie, and the "Spontaneists," the Anarchists, the Structuralists. Amary hated the last and considered them no better than dogs who had no respect for Lenin or other apostles, for they had permitted themselves a joke at the expense of one of his groups, calling them the "Kids."

Lenin himself had told his collaborators: "Watch out for your nervous systems." Left grouplets resembled coalitions of spoiled children and exhibitionists who had certainly not understood Mao when he said, "History must be seen in the larger scope, not in the smaller."

When Amary spoke to his supporters, he constructed formulas with mathematical rigor. He would say, for example: "First, the people who now govern cannot do so as they did before Marx. Second: The governed cannot continue living as they did in the past. Conclusion: The revolution will be brought about only by historical, social, and economic reality on a grand scale." Or; "A. In the Soviet Union today only the armaments industry works. B. When the U.S.S.R. conquers the world and the problems of defense are obviated, problems of consumer supply can be resolved. Thus, whatever our view of the revisionism existing in the Kremlin, we must help the Soviet Union sweep away the last vestiges of the feudal past, capitalist society."

De Kerguelen would listen to him open-mouthed: "Are we Don Quixotes?"

Amary corrected him: "Don Quixote attacked windmills in the belief they were giants. The revolutionary attacks precise objectives. We are not altruists but realists."

[And he would go off to sleep with the Others.]

Amary does not play Rd1-d2, which would consolidate his defense (but thereby also give Tarsis the initiative); he chooses the more aggressive move: 15. Ktf3-d2. *The indispensable move,* he tells himself, *which will lead me to victory.* Tarsis can amuse himself eating up the pawns on the queenside: when he awakens from his delusion, he will find himself in a trap which will lead to the checking of his king. *Now I'm sure to win,* thinks Amary. *My attack is unstoppable.*

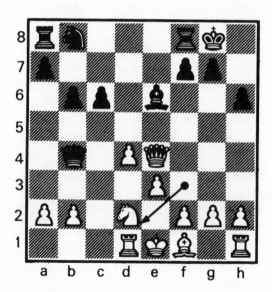

15. Ktf3-d2

My attack is unstoppable, so Tarsis also tells himself as he takes the pawn in b2 with his queen (15. . . . Qb4xb2). He is convinced that he will win, for he has destroyed Amary's queen-side and he knows how to paralyze his rival's counterattack. *He can resign now.*

Soledad decided to set out for France for the same reasons that caused Santa Teresa to leave Spain when she was nine: *"Para conquistar gloria."* To achieve Glory.

In Soledad's time, quite a few Spaniards crossed the frontier, with a flower in their mouths, dreaming of paradise. In the first place, they were convinced that France was full of Frenchwomen. They were right, but the trouble was that these ladies all spoke French and were not overwhelmed by the charms of the incomprehensible Spaniards. This could not have been foreseen, and so the wretchedness of exile had

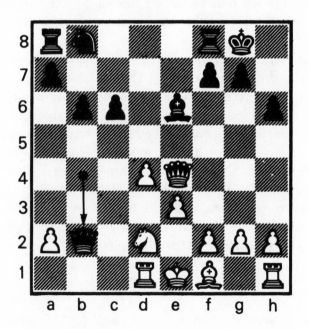

15. . . . Qb4xb2

to be endured to the full. They experienced trying to say things and not knowing how to, like overgrown babies placed by destiny at the foot of the Tower of Babel. Thus, playing a kind of blindman's buff and orientating themselves like octopuses, they began to learn someone else's language and customs, while they continued to practice their own, constructing along the way a homemade emotional pocket-Spain where they could take refuge, even when they lived in, say, Saint-Quentin (in the province of east Picardy).

Tarsis was crossing the frontier for another reason: he wanted to elude his past (once again), to take flight and put a good distance between himself and the Society of Jesus. Nevertheless, he missed it painfully almost at once. The pious life can count on one great advantage: it is quite cheap to lead. With the savings he had been able to accumulate, he had enough not only to pay for the trip but also for the fee the contrabandist would charge him to get him across the border.

Once on the train, the pair began to use the familiar *tu* to each other for the first time. Though he was near falling asleep, Tarsis recalled the *agapitos* and Father Benito with the same nostalgia with which he often remembered his own father. Was he not about to betray the happiest impulse of his life? He clenched his fists to avoid being overcome. He was recalling Father Benito with a hitherto unknown fervor.

Some time later Father Benito told the Provincial: "If Tarsis were to return and prostrate himself on his knees at my feet as he did the first day, I would greet him with joy, and even if he had committed the worst sins, I would move heaven and earth to see him a Jesuit. If necessary, I would ask for a dispensation from the General of the Order or from the Pope himself."

The Provincial offered scant consolation: "We live in a valley of tears."

Worn out by his sleepless night Tarsis was beginning to doze and was soon gripped in the deep sleep of an early morning nap. And he dreamed:

I am standing by the side of a wide river. On the opposite bank a man is calling me: "Come, come," urging me to swim across the small body of water. As I gaze on him, he reminds me of "my French slave" at the College of San Antón.

The stream is infested with fish. In their fury they strike their heads out of the water and look at "my slave" as if importuning him. The latter takes out a baby he was carrying in an enormous cradle and throws the baby into the water. The fish devour it. A bloodstain spreads on the surface. And then the fish begin to clamor again for their ration, and "my slave" throws them another baby, and another bloodstain covers the water. Once again the fish begin begging for more, sticking their heads out of the water. "The slave" whispers something incomprehensible to them and then shrieks at me in a commanding voice: "Come here, once and for all!"

I watch him strip off my clothes and . . . I enter the water to be devoured.

Tarsis awoke with a start. Nuria was gazing at him, her face so close she seemed to want to stroke his face with hers. The rattle of the train and the dazzle of the lights cradled twin desires. For Soledad was gazing at him, too, and he made her out in detail through his half daze.

Her breasts were round and at the same time tapering to points. But when he drew near, he could see they were crowned with two small spheres. He could see through Soledad's clothes: her breasts were the color of ivory and of pomegranates, and also green and blue, and then white again, like her belly. They beckoned him, as did the lips between her legs. He wondered if he was not sleeping with his eyes open.

Soledad questioned him at length about his life, and Tarsis told her everything, bit by bit, sketching out a self-portrait. He began to feel beaten, a lesser man, and felt sorry for himself—to the point where he began to discover the tenderness of self-pity. Soledad became particularly interested in knowing all about Nuria, and so he had to describe her face and its form, the color of her hair, the shape of her lips. He also had to reveal how and where he had been born, where he had lived, and all his studies.

She gazed at him without blinking: "And what if you don't find work in France?"

"There are never enough milling-machine operators. It's my trade."

"But you don't have any papers to prove it."

"In any case, I'll do something."

"I can work, anyway . . . You don't need diplomas to become a maid, and in France they earn a lot. The two of us can live on what I make."

Tarsis replied to this idea with a resounding: "No!"

"If you want . . . I can do what Nuria did."

"Be quiet . . ." And he changed the subject: "I've been dreaming, you know."

I dreamed I was beside a river from which giant chickens kept emerging, each so enormous that I was only as large as one of its claws. From the other bank Father Benito was feeding them agapitos, *who were snatched up in an instant. I wanted to run away so as not to be fed to the fish, and I started running even though the priest commanded me in a loud voice to stop. I tripped on an oar and fell flat. And I could suddenly see the gigantic beaks of the fowl coming at me, ready to eat me up.*

He wondered if he was giving a good account and true of his dream. While he was telling it to her, he was thinking of something quite different: he was speculating on placing calipers on her belly and drawing ever more concentric circles around her omphalos or her heart or her thighs while the river fish swam between her legs.

No ceremony of any kind accompanied the arrest of Tarsis

by the military police at the Puigcerdá border. He was trapped like a helpless sparrow. Soledad, however, decided to add spice to the proceedings: the ex-shepherdess, the image of serenity, flared up like a rebellious runaway. She fought like a she-devil to free him from the menacing guards. People congregated around them, voicing their support for her; but all their help was moral, and their force and impact was expended through their mouths. Tarsis took part in the drama, all of it centered around him, as if he were only one more witness to a distant event.

He was still not very clear about his situation when the Civil Guards left him in the hands of a captain of the Signal Corps.

"What are you doing here, man? What's your business on the frontier? What's your scheme?"

The captain addressed him colloquially with the familiar *tu* and so he understood at once that he was in the presence of a "comrade," that is, a member or adept of the Falange-Española-Tradicionalista-y-de-las-Juntas-de-Ofensiva-Nacional-Sindicalista, the association or party also known as FET y de las JONS. (All this would have brought consolation to Lacan, who never, however, showed any interest in this theme in relation to his theories.) In short, a member or sympathizer of the Spanish Falange, the proto-Fascist organization. This humanist minority dreamed that the majority of Spaniards—Volterian and nihilist—would be put on the right path, brought to reason by the use of colloquial and familiar address. It didn't work. At the time. In a few years, and after they had fallen into disgrace, they would witness a generalized and much more ample colloquialism of the very opposite kind from the one they had advocated with such meager success.

Tarsis opted for an ambiguous attitude as a precaution: "I can't see that I've done anything wrong."

The captain did not appreciate the attempt at ambiguity and fetched him a cuff that knocked Tarsis off his chair: "Don't try to be smart with me."

The captain was a man of talents, but not in the field of psychology. Tarsis decided to pull himself together and argue with all the composure available: "I simply can't stand pain. It's useless to hit me. I'll confess to whatever you want. If necessary, I'll say I killed my father."

Without taking his eyes off him, the captain yelled: "Guards!"

Two soldiers appeared. The captain pointed to the arrested man and gave an order: "Incommunicado!"

A few minutes later, Tarsis understood the meaning of the word. Without any undue force, he was put into a dungeon of a type which those who do not fear to reveal their ignorance of history might call "medieval." Despite the absence of light, he soon made out that his new abode was a low-ceilinged den slightly longer than it was wide. Half the box's space was taken up by a narrow stone bench, which he knew was his bed-to-be. At one end there was a hole, which he took to be the toilet. Since he could not stand without hitting his head against the ceiling or stretch out unless his legs were cut off at the knees, he lay drawn up into a ball. It was a posture to match his state of mind. He spent the night with cramps in both his posture and his belly, his face screwed up in discomfort.

The next morning, the iron door swung open. A stout heavy man came in carrying an aluminum plate; Tarsis saw only a piece of bread and a spoon.

"Breakfast."

Tarsis smiled as he announced: "I can't eat a thing."

He could not have swallowed a wafer. Anguish held him by the throat and squeezed.

"Make an effort . . . Don't give in. There are worse places in the world."

154

"I really can't."

The voluminous guard sat himself down on the stone bench next to Tarsis and, with infinite patience and sweetness, like a mother with her infant, fed him spoonfuls from a previously unseen dish.

"Don't give up . . . Everything passes, some day or another. Now eat . . . It's worse if you don't have anything in your belly."

Tarsis was incommunicado for only five days. He managed to eke out a note to Father Benito in the margins of the newspaper pages they gave him for toilet paper:

> *Reverend Father: I dreamed that I was beside a river. As I walked along I noticed a lion in the water. He was following me near the riverbank and eyeing me threateningly. Whenever I stopped, he halted. I knew he would eat me if I went in the water. When I reached a bridge, the Father Provincial called to me from the opposite shore and asked me to swim toward him. I took off my clothes and waded into the water. I saw the lion hurling himself toward me . . .*

But Tarsis had been unable to dream ever since landing in his dungeon. He kept going over and over his situation so continually that he had no time. He had recounted in his letter what he had dreamed just after getting on the train, the dream he had told Soledad in a slightly different version. At the end he added a phrase indirectly inspired by his fellow traveler: "Am I a prisoner or am I a termite?"

Once set down, that question caused him to throw the entire account into the toilet hole.

At the end of the five days of incarceration, he learned he was classified as a deserter. He was dispatched to the disciplinary battalion of a work camp in the Pyrenees, in the province of Navarre.

His outfit was made up of four companies of one hundred prisoners each, under the command of captains and sergeants. The food ration was meager, but the work took their minds off the hunger pains. Twelve hours a day. At night the cold in the barracks was so intense that they slept with their boots on and their caps on their heads; they used the straw pallets as covering. Their teeth chattered in their mouths all night long, and they were turned into icicles, even though they had stopped up all the cracks in the barrack walls with a mash they concocted from pine-tree bark. Their quarters were like ice boxes.

The work consisted of hacking at rock and pulverizing the granite which surrounded the camp. Tarsis took pains, along with his fellow prisoners, to avoid injury from flying stone chips: they all wore wire glasses covered with a metallic web.

They were always so hungry they could have eaten the wooden beams, and certainly would not have spurned them if offered. Tarsis became as strong as an ox. It could not be said that the work suited him, but he carried it out conscientiously. Of course, those who did not work as well as the chiefs thought they should, who did not put their backs into it with the proper spirit, were brought about with a handful of blows or, if they acted up, were made to run outside around the barracks at night, with sacks weighing forty pounds tied to their backs.

Whenever Tarsis was able to think coherently, he wondered, for instance, at the curious fact that the men whom the jailers called deserters, condemned soldiers, thieves, or criminals should be taught to handle explosives. They were all required to fill cartridges with powder, to prepare the percussion caps and the waterproof cloth tube to be used as detonators in the holes previously dug in the rock. Chiseling the holes was the hardest part and sometimes took a couple of days.

Gradually Tarsis became accustomed to life in the camp. As he told himself, *Man is a creature of habit.* He was in charge of the crowbars, long metal bars with claws at their ends, and he worked them with some dexterity. After making an opening, he would insert a wooden or metal wedge to help force the rock to split as he worked on it with a mallet.

The best moment in the day was provided by the imaginative cook at breakfast. He was some kind of aesthete and had managed to invent a source of succulence. He boiled twenty-five quarts of water with malt in cauldrons to which he added his special touch, a dry branch previously singed in the fire: it added a roasted taste, such as is found in Italian coffee, so that the breakfast gained a flavor more pleasing to the prisoners. Another source of culinary delight was to be found in the cans of red lard made from hog grease seasoned with pepper. Sometimes the prisoners would sneak into the barracks and would share a can with as much communal comradeship as milligrams of cocaine are shared in Berkeley.

The slaves would join forces and console each other at the most discouraging moments. When Tarsis collapsed after a month of hard labor and seemed to have lost his mind as he endlessly mumbled, "What will become of me," like a broken record, a comrade from Cádiz brought him around with a series of tricks. He bent a coin with his tongue and lifted a chair with his teeth, and that raised Tarsis's spirits and drove away the blues. Tarsis also gained satisfaction from the fact that he no longer finished the day with bleeding hands; they had hardened.

"And now you'll see: you'll be able to break rocks with your bare hands," his fellow prisoners told him.

Amary moves 16. Bf1-d3. *I'm going to blow his world apart*, thinks Tarsis. *I'm going to pulverize the eighth wonder of the world, which Amary thinks he's built, since he takes himself for a master builder.*

For his part Amary is ready to oppose the rational architecture of his position to the Flamboyant Gothic of Tarsis. His move lays the foundations for castling, with all his pieces harmoniously joined and conjugated, while his rival is busy fabricating useless costly moldings king-side. He feels he is on solid ground, while Tarsis is building on shifting sand. When Amary raises his eyes, he observes that his aides have been surrounded by plainclothes police who are watching his men intently. But they cannot be policemen, he thinks, for no one could consider him or his men suspects. But perhaps

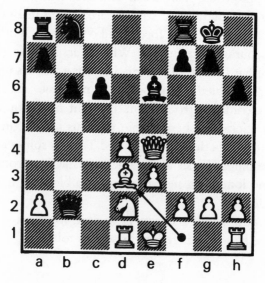

16. Bf1-d3

the newcomers are agents of the secret police, anticipating his victory and preparing to furnish him protection.

Closeted in his rest area, Tarsis has been studying Amary's play. He had already foreseen his reaction a few moves back as he thought over the possibilities. Still, he wants to make sure that his intuition has not deceived him. He starts to play and moves 16. ... g7-g6, with the mortal threat of 17. ... Be6-f5. He tells himself that his adversary's position is so bad that it is painful to look at.

The hall is filling up with police. *At last!* thinks Tarsis. *It was high time! They must have discovered the tunnels under his house.*

The police have not even thought of the tunnels yet. And yet, since the end of the first week, they have considered Amary and his "aides" possible suspects, not because of their present activities, of which they are ignorant, but because of their past as sympathizers of "revolutionary groups."

Amary's first intricate revolutionary mission was to convert himself into a businessman without doing too much violence to himself. A revolution is easier to make when there are resources at hand. Lenin had held much the same view, for he clearly stated that money is the nerve end of warfare. Thanks to this decision, Amary and his committee soon were able to boast a stout purse and to forget the puerile and romantic views of political activism. Weapons could be bought with ready cash. Perhaps Amary had other reasons for wanting to get rich, and they weighed in the balance: he was anxious to buy another residence, away from the Others.

[In all truth, these characters were becoming an ever greater nuisance. Mickey and the Kid longed for the past; the isolation imposed upon them by the Master was getting tedious

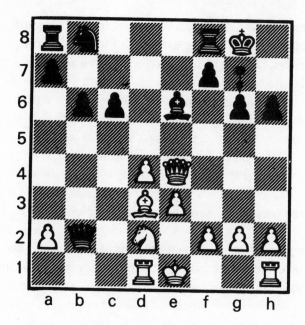

16. ... g7-g6

and hateful, and Mickey demanded the right to participate in committee discussions.

"How do you know that I've created a committee," asked a fearful Master.

"I've read the papers you leave around on your desk," answered a bold Mickey.

"I've forbidden you, a thousand times, to stick your nose into my business and my documents."

"I have a snout, not a nose."

That was the kind of correction the Master could not abide. He was the voice of reason and he could not abide a rubber mouse not much larger than a couple of walnuts telling him what was what in the presence of the Others.

As if the first indiscretion hadn't been enough, the Kid added sarcastically: "To convert political activities into capital and interest is in the nature of party trickery. I have nothing to do with any party. Amary *dixit.*"

To hear his own words used as a basis for ridicule by the Kid was a form of martyrdom.

"I've had enough of you all."

Mickey tried to calm him down: "The Kid is sad. Ever since the death of Cécile he feels abandoned, all alone."

"Ever since he killed her, you mean."

"No need to be peevish. Everyone has to die some day . . . The Kid would simply like to meet your friends. We're always alone in this house. I'm afraid he'll have a break-down . . . If he is aggressive, it's because he's losing his mind."

"He's trying to destroy everything I do."

The Master was right about that. The Kid was bent on undermining all the Master's projects, especially his revolutionary ones. Whenever an important political council was scheduled, the Kid spent the night trying to upset the Master, interrupting his sleep in the hope that he would wreck the meeting. If the Master refused to be drawn into any provocation and kept as silent as the tomb, then Teresa would appear in his bed and soon begin to give vent to sexual sounds, as if dirty deeds were taking place. The Master was repelled by such repugnant spectacles and would go off to sleep in the toilet.

"I'm going to sleep *alone,* in the toilet."

In the toilet, El Loco would console him, waxing eloquent about his enthusiasms: gliders and waterfalls. The Master thought that neither Mickey nor Teresa nor the Kid knew of his friend's existence. What he didn't know was that as soon as he locked himself in the toilet, Doña Rosita would spy on him from the heating pipes, and since she was a gossip, everything was related to the other three.

The Master despised Doña Rosita, whom he did not bother even to salute. She was not allowed to sleep in the same bed with them. She was a snake who drugged herself smoking green Tuscany cigars, and according to the Master, she had instructed the Kid in the arts of autoeroticism. (This was not factually true, since it was the Kid who had taught the snake how to masturbate by using a catheter coupled to a screwdriver.) In payment for these vices Doña Rosita was locked in an empty radiator; the tap was never opened lest she be boiled in hot water. But in truth the snake was not bothered by water, even if it was boiling; she was armored and could circulate in the pipes around the house smoking her horrible evil-smelling cigars.

After a night spent sleeping with his head in the toilet bowl, with no more comfort than some words from El Loco, the Master would wake in a devilish humor.

And the Kid would renew his taunts: "Did you sleep well, *all alone?*"

"I can't stand it any longer."

"Why don't you take us to New York again?"

"I've had enough."

The Master was convinced that he needed two houses: one in which he could lock up the Others and to which he would repair for sleeping (he did not dare to put an end to this obligation definitively in fear of the reprisals *He* might take) and a second place where he could spend most of his free time and where he could meet with his comrades.]

Amary devoted himself to business for the sake of the committee, Comandante Menoyo, and the Garcías of the Workers' Autonomous Front (the WAF).

The latter group maintained fraternal ties with Amary's committee (which kept in the shadows) through the offices of a liaison: Christophe de Kerguelen. The four Garcías (Luis, Juan, Jaime, and Antonio) were united, not only by a common surname and identical doctorates from the Sorbonne, but also by a joint project to build a guerrilla movement in the province of Granada on the slopes of the Sierra Nevada. The ingenious plan proposed to initiate operations by swallowing half the province, thanks to a military base in the foothills of Mulhacén Peak. They planned to gobble up a chunk of Andalucia, and as final promise, they dreamed of a great celebration in the capital of Spain, after a triumphant military march through La Mancha. The fact that the four leaders were every one of them emaciated specimens in physique added even more spice to the venture. They had even dreamed of what they called *couverture aerienne* (which one of them called "an aerial blanket"): during their epic march they visualized being supplied regularly from the air by a commercial airliner, which would take off from a beach south of Agades and would drop both food and ammunition. This project had won the support of certain authorities in Castro's Cuba, who had promised, through the mediation of Comandante Menoyo, some arms and funds for the insurgents; for this purpose a subscription drive had been organized called "Un peso para España" (a Cuban dollar for Spain).

Given Amary's passion for silence and secrecy, the only mission he entrusted to de Kerguelen as liaison was to conceal the activities of the Comité as much as possible from the Garcías and, at the same time, to gather all pertinent information about the organization of the terrorist group. He established working relations with Comandante Menoyo, who impressed him most favorably for his talents and courage. He was the very man, one of Fidel Castro's intimates, who was eventually to inform them of the true state and result of the Comité's first initiatives in the struggle to defeat capitalism. The Comité was systematically sending to Havana (and accessorially to Moscow), by ordinary mail, the most confidential and secret documents relating to French research, especially that involving the neutron bomb, atomic submarines, and intercontinental rockets. Amary wanted to know how the revolution, the Triumphant Revolution, was using such explosive material. On his last trip back to the "Free World," Menoyo was depressed to find that it was rotting in the offices of State Security in Havana, awaiting to be deciphered, someday, by the best East German sleuths. For the moment, they were assumed to be counterrevolutionary messages, instructions from the CIA in complex cipher. The regime's paranoia disturbed Menoyo, who proposed to clarify the matter. He must have attempted to do so, with such bad luck that from that day on he has been busy with pick and shovel in a concentration camp on the Isle of Pines.

On that final trip back to Cuba, Menoyo transmitted to the Garcías a message he had received from Fidel: "If they want arms and money they will have to spend some months in a Cuban Army training camp in the province of Oriente under the direction of the Russian Colonel Wadim Kotschergine of the KGB." A bit of sound advice from a wise man, but it was not something the Garcías could appreciate. They could not even understand it: they were prepared to tear up paving stones with their teeth, but not to receive lessons from anybody. Their plans did not call for them to act the part of novices to anyone anywhere, but instead to march on Madrid covered with blood, sweat, and beards, at the head of a column of jeeps seized from the enemy, and to enter the city to the sound of the Internationale at high pitch, after having forced the dictator to hurry his ass to the mists of Andorra and his ministers to start life again as lice in Paraguay.

This setback did not give the four chieftains pause. But the advice was not altogether in vain, for they got the message in their own way. Because of their slight constitutions, their very lack of weight, they had unfortunately been rejected as army recruits and had not done their compulsory military service. That is to say, they had not touched a weapon in the course of their studious lives. Since they were, however, clairvoyant, they began to frequent every street festival in their neighborhoods, so as to use the shooting galleries always set up at these carnivals. They spent half their salaries and learned a lot. They fired away in furious fusillades at dozens of clay pipes and numberless plastic ducks swimming between one tinsel star and another, implacably shooting them down as hateful representatives of Big Capital.

But they needed money for what they called the "armed infrastructure" (the plane and some artillery). Jaime García had the solution. He knew that not far from Perdiguera, in the province of Zaragoza, there was a factory whose pay-master came and went from Zaragoza every Friday with the payroll for the factory's workers. The war plans were meticulously drawn up. They would lay an ambush at a turn in the road, they would stop him, rob him, and, only *then,* shoot him.

They carried out the ambuscade according to plan, most stealthily. They were ready to exult when they heard the hum of the paymaster's motorcycle. With their big hearts bursting in their tiny bodies, they stopped the rider, waving the two pistols they had managed to "requisition." When the pay-master got off his motorcycle they were unexpectedly as-tounded to discover he was a cripple. He came toward them with his game leg dragging and they were suddenly rendered impotent.

Without so much as discussing the matter, they decided to leave him alone. They had been ready to kill a hundred field marshals, but the sight of a poor crippled man utterly disarmed them, affecting, as it did, their sentimentality. They let him go scot-free.

And now they had to beat it back to France in Juan's Renault. But a few miles from Candanchú, they got into a skid that almost landed them in an abyss. They had been through so much! And the highway was such a tight place, and all the Fascist police would be looking for them—or so they imagined! One of the car's wheels hung over the precipice. They got out to push it back on the road and did so with such concentration that they never noticed the approach of two Good Samaritans—who turned out to be a pair of Civil Guards. They immediately offered to help. The four Garcías bethought themselves of the two revolvers and the General Staff maps of Granada Province they had in their possession, tucked into the glove compartment. Each man doing his bit as if they were jointly giving birth (the four terrorists and the two Civil Guards), they managed to rescue the Renault from the void. And so the four Garcías went on to reach a safe harbor in France (through the port of Somport) safe and sound.

The "FAT" brought its exemplary history to a close in Madrid a few weeks later. The Garcías, rather than speak out of a window in France, decided to wage ideological war in Madrid itself. They showed up in the Faculty of Sciences building, where in a mere two days they made themselves notorious, and even gained a recruit, a new militant for the group: Eulalia del Rosal García. On the day they set up a duplicating machine in their apartment in the Rosales section, they placed Eulalia as sentry at the doorway. Her mission was to pull on a cord if the police showed up. Within a matter of hours, growing bored, the neo-militant hailed a girlfriend passing by on her way to swim at El Lago, and they both went off. Shortly afterward, the four Garcías were being received, with scant courtesy, by Commissioner Yague of Security. (The commissioner, however, made up for everything by kissing the hand of Antonio's mama, who had come to beg him to be compassionate with her son.) Since the police had much to talk about with the Garcías, their host held them for a couple of weeks before sending them on to the Salesas station en route to Carabanchel prison.

The four Garcías found that the bravura they would have

displayed in their triumphant tour of Granada was not a qual-
ity they could easily make use of as they confronted, rather
bloodily, their wardens. They began by standing up like heroes
and ended singing like canaries. So much so, that even Christophe de Kerguelen was singled out and described in detail.
All the information ended up with the French police, who
from that time on kept a close eye on every member of
Amary's Comité. Why should it be surprising that he might
be considered one of many suspects in the Isvoschikov kidnapping?

Amary never knew, moreover, that for years past he had
figured on the blacklist at the Direction Centrale de Ren-
seignements and of the SDECE of the Ministry of the French
Army. To his mind, the adventure in which the Garcías had
indulged themselves was something fit only for a band of
paranoid cretins. He spoke as an expert. Still, since every
evil produces some compensation, he was also enlightened,
once and for all, by the perception that the "armed struggle"
is not a matter of improvisation. His first revolutionary act,
therefore, would be to gather money for the cause.

For the next couple of years the Comité lined its pockets
with funds. Business ventures grew up like mushrooms, almost more rewarding for him than physics. Every morning
he began by reading the capitalist press. He called it "more
reliable." The *Wall Street Journal,* the Paris edition of the
Herald Tribune, and the *Financial Times* became his bedside
reading matter. He bought land at low prices with his first
funds, and sold it whenever favorable; he speculated in gold
and platinum, modestly at first, and then by the ingot. He
bought in Paris and sold in Zurich, or vice versa, thanks to
his "professional" trips to the CERN in Geneva. At the
end of the day he would listen to American radio sta-
tions to ascertain how the market was "breathing" in New
York. He could spend hours reading stock-market quota-

tions as if they were a collection of the thousand best poems.

Amary put such passion into the search for the Golden Calf that the group's militants sometimes thought that he had been completely devoured by it. At the end of two years, with more money than an overseas investor, he would stop his chariot, safely invest his pile . . . and live off the income! His treasure was spitting out doubloons! He had only to let the money make money, like fairy gold.

In fact it was a war chest. And had no other end and purpose than to serve the cause of revolution.

Tarsis believes that to play chess is to enter into the realm of order, the secret and inexplicable calligraphy of precision. For Amary, on the other hand, everything in chess can be explained: each problem has its rational solution, and so he moves his queen (17. Qe4-f4) as he tells himself that an analysis of the lessons of history is always instructive. His chess piece at the vital center position is dominating the board and attacking one of the ramparts of the adversary's defense: h6. Tarsis believes that the most decisive results come about after much useless planning and that in history, moreover, the most lofty endeavors may be the result of chance and the most mediocre causes may provoke the most fabulous effects.

Tarsis plays 17. . . . Kg8-g7. For a quarter of an hour he has weighed the two ways of protecting his parapet: h6. At length he discards King-h7. He decides by intuition . . . after long reflection. He thinks he is recalling certain moments before his birth . . . and that his intuition comes from a knowledge gained before he came into the world.

Amary is convinced that the encounter between himself and Tarsis represents a historic and apocalyptic combat between Good and Evil, between the Proletarian and the Bour-

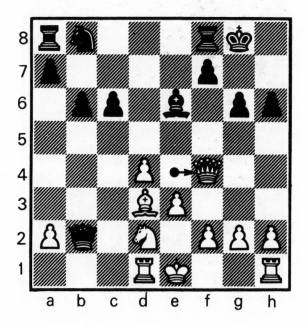

17. Qe4-f4

geois (the bourgeoisie represented by the workman Tarsis and the proletariat by himself).

This world chess championship match in reality opposes precision allied to intelligence against grace crowned by talent (reason vis-à-vis the mystery). When Fischer learned that his rival Spassky had declared, "Chess is like life," he corrected the statement to "Chess is life."

Korchnoi and Karpov, the two players who for years competed for the crown which the federation usurped from the American genius Fischer, each wrote books, years later; two different books with the same Fischerian title: *Chess Is My Life.* The history of chess is most exemplary in its own way: in the sixteenth century the Castilian monk Ruy López de Sigura reigned, and he was the inventor of the Spanish game,

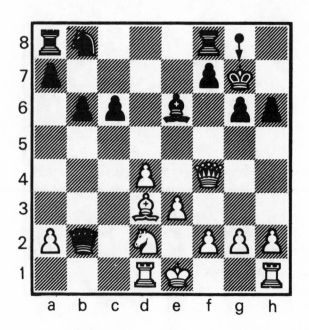

17. . . . . Kg8-g7

with the most audacious and daring attack, like that of the Conquistadores, while in the same epoch the southern Italian Giochino Greco exemplified the Italian Renaissance. The French Revolution of 1789 was preceded by Philidor, the French player who discovered that "the pawns are the soul of chess," thereby guillotining anterior monarchic dogmas based on the omnipotence of the king and queen. In the epoch of Romanticism, the German Anderssen played to win with splendor; the games bore the names of sonnets ("the immortal," "the eternally young," etc.) and prizes for Beauty flourished. Lasker, like Freud, adduced the importance of psychology early in the century. Alekhine, moving between his roots and exile, traveled the world with his cat, Chess, illustrating the painful road of expatriation . . . But the real confrontation between dissidence and power culminated in the encounter between Korchnoi and Karpov. Fischer, the solitary, anticipated today's spiritual renaissance, and the blind mullahs of the bureaucracy wrested his crown from him to underline the fact that his kingdom could not be of this world. Why should it be surprising that now the man of science is locked in combat with the man of intuition?

Tarsis spent weeks trying to imagine how Amary and his aides could have broken into Isvoschikov's residence in Paris, evading the police in the process. He rejected the possibility of their getting in by air with a helicopter or the idea of their having been able to bribe the Soviet or French guards. For days he pondered how anyone could get into the quarters of a Russian Minister invited and protected by the government of France without anybody intervening. It was an enigma, and he proposed to solve it.

On the far-off day when Tarsis received his first package in the labor-camp barracks he was in no state to undertake enigmas. His reaction was one of the usual puzzlement, even stupefaction, for nothing was clear to him at the time, and he did not even venture to ask who the sender might be.

He was so brutalized by the work that he thought of nothing. He had no time. There was no point in his work and no reward, and he was consumed by it. The thought of rebellion did not cross his mind, nor did the idea of escape. It was difficult, working around the clock and with no period of idleness to join two thoughts together. If he had been compelled to work eight hours a day instead of twelve, he might have realized that his life was being used up like that of a mule, or if he had been analyzing "weak reactions" in some laboratory, it is possible that he would have been deeply moved by all the injustices committed in the world, especially in such places as the one where he spent his days. Perhaps this is the reason that from the days of the peasant revolts in Spain to the feats of Comandante Zero in Nicaragua all insurgents have always belonged to the well-to-do classes, for they can see injustice clearly from the best seats in the stands, from the front row in the bullring. More power to them.

Besides, the first package could not have been more enigmatic. (If he had sharpened his ears he could have heard an echo of Puccini's *Tosca* coming from inside it.) When he opened it at last, he was staggered to find dozens of medicine bottles, dozens of pills, two thermometers, and two lemons. He kept mum—and threw the entire contents down a ravine. He would have loved to have stuck the lemons between two slices of bark and eaten them, peels, seeds, and all. He was convinced that somebody was trying to poison him with herbs camouflaged as medicine.

Nevertheless, a rumor ran through the barracks that "someone" had taken an interest in him. Most odd. Here he was tucked away at the farthest remove, because the authorities believed in the adage "Travel broadens the mind," so that they systematically sent the prisoners to places as far as possible from their original home. Since he was nominally from Valencia, they had sent him to the northern part of Navarre, a northern province in itself, while those from the north were sent as far south as possible. The authorities had their reasons; for one thing, they thus avoided the ugly spectacle of wives and mothers moaning at the prison gates. Inside the barracks the voice of rumor now ascended from the lower ranks to the higher-ups, so that one morning a captain said to Tarsis: "It seems that someone has asked the colonel to swap places with you."

This officer was a man who didn't mind breaking one of the central taboos of prison: Don't increase a prisoner's despair by harping on the theme of freedom, for "ears that hear nothing—a heart that expects nothing." And so now Tarsis despaired. He felt something like an air bubble travel between his mind and his heart. He tried to drown out the news, but the bubble was like a bit of mercury. And the rocks around him seemed more stern and unbreakable, the hammers heavier, the work unbearable.

Packages rained upon him like manna, sometimes two a week, thus topping the regulation limit. The contents had been assembled under the supervision of someone more concerned with balanced diet than appearance and who knew the value of each calorie: the sweet counteracted the salty, bacon the dry figs, the whole aiming at health and not looks. Tarsis thought that Father Benito and the *agapitos* had not forgotten him. He was right, but mere remembrance is a different matter from a package of sweet butter from Soria. In the end he learned *two* women had proposed some sort of exchange to get him out. Rumor had it that the commanding officer had sent them away with their songs unsung. But the truth was that the officer had in fact talked to them quite kindly: "Look here, ladies, it's as if you were to ask the operating surgeon to switch patients."

The troubles now afflicting Tarsis were not a matter of serious disease, neither typhus, say, nor yellow fever, but simple depression. The packages had only served to clip his imaginary wings. He began to have mock nightmares, aborted visions. He might awake to find the moon sinking into one of his boots while the mechanism of a clock would resound in his chest and a mad dwarf ran around inside his skull with a fifty-pound sack on its back. A voice could be heard intoning, "The moon is sinking into one of your boots while the clock's ticktock . . ." The amenities to be found in psychiatric hospitals were absent, and he was being transformed into a psychoanalytical case history.

Then one day he was taken to a spot near the French frontier. He was supposed to pick rock in a place as remote as the one where Christ cried out thrice.

He did not see the smuggler until he was upon him. He took him to be a warder dressed in civilian clothes. And he followed him obediently. He had learned discipline in the labor camp; he was as fearful of the whip as an animal. His submission, as normal now to him as a callus, proved most propitious. He followed the smuggler across the French frontier and soon found himself in Saint-Jean-Pied-de-Port. Nuria and Soledad were awaiting him. They had spent weeks making up packages and bribing jailers.

During the trip to Nice, Tarsis began to awaken slowly, like an invalid who finds, when he tries to take the first steps after a long illness, that his legs will not respond. In his case his reflexes weren't working. At each step of the way he was afraid he would find himself back in the barracks after this brief interlude.

Nuria and Soledad were brimming with happiness, most of all because they could imagine how happy Tarsis must be. But the truth was that he felt none of it. And he thought to ask no questions. More important things came to mind: for example, he wondered whether on his return to camp he would be punished and made to carry a heavy sack of stones. He could even hear the captain's orders: "Third brigade, fall in!" He could "hear" the captain. And Tarsis made excuses: "Captain, I have this air bubble running from my heart to my head and my head to my heart, and it's as heavy as steel. When I'm down it bangs my head fit to break it."

"What's the trouble?" asked Nuria.

"Don't you feel well?" inquired Soledad.

When he looked at them, Tarsis felt the bubble traveling inside him turn to air and nothing more; it scarcely existed.

Nuria wanted to let him know how she had lived in his absence. It had been so long for her. But the moment had not yet arrived to speak of it. Her father had talked of her "adventure," after she had gone home: of course he knew nothing of the beds she'd slept in, or the money paid to get her there: "My daughter made a little mistake . . . a youthful slip . . . I'm convinced that it was good for her development. She made her mother cry, cry tears of blood, but I knew all along that this misfortune would help her grow up. And there you see her, her final exam passed without a hitch. She's just written a small dissertation on Puccini's *Tosca,* and it has astounded her teachers. She's immunized forever. I can leave my safe wide open anytime . . ."

And so Nuria was able to operate at will. She sharpened her nails this time, and instead of going for half, she left her father bare.

After Tarsis was arrested, Soledad was able to track her down. The two of them joined forces to free him. His rescue proved far harder than fleecing the father, even though now they were two pretty women moving against one object. First they paid the toll fee to the commandant of the labor camp, each one on her own and each in her own personal way. Their conversations with the colonel revolved around their life's purpose: "You must let him out."

"The two of you are mad. You're going to get me in big trouble!"

"You can see to it that he gets out if you want."

"I'm doing everything you ask me to do, and more. I saw to it that he got the medicine and even the two packages a week . . . And he was a deserter!"

"What kind of deserter could he be!"

"He was escaping to France without having done his military service. You're both marvelous girls, but you can't ask for the impossible."

But after three months, deliberately playing the fool, the good colonel didn't know he was doing a new production of *Tosca*—and in the valley of Roncesvalles.

Soledad went on the offensive, launching a frontal attack with fixed bayonet: "You put him on the frontier tomorrow or this little business between us is over with."

"I haven't got the authority to do it."

Standing in his undershorts, he was put on the defensive, and his own sword had to be sheathed and was rendered useless. It grew faint and limp. If it had known that it was taking part in the last act of an opera, it might not have refused to play its role so cravenly.

"Soledad, please don't insist so. I can't; that should be evident."

"Well then, your orderly can suck you off."

No quarter was given in this battle. Every strategy was employed; man-to-man combat was the order of the day. Low language, the lowest form of address, and low reprisals were in order. It was more degrading than the battle of Guadalajara in the Civil War—without the presence of any Italians to do the dirty work. The colonel raised the white flag, "Nobody has ever treated me like this."

But Soledad was prepared to give no quarter, and charged ahead: "Listen to me carefully. You set Tarsis free tomorrow or I go to the police and swear that I've seen you committing indecencies with Nuria."

The conflict grew red hot following this unexpected attack from the rear. In this stage of siege the colonel thought of his wife—a saint—and of his children, with whom he appeared in a photograph taken on the day the Head of State had bestowed on them the title of Family with Numerous Offspring. For the moment he sought to fall back strategically: "I'll request that he be sent to the infirmary for a rest. I can't do any more."

"That's worse than nothing. I'll tell the police that you tried to rape Nuria behind Holy Ghost Hill."

He lowered his head and his beak, bent his knee, and begged for mercy. He surrendered his arms and furled his banners. But the hog in his heart, which the two ladies had been feeding with the choicest slops (to best ensure its continued endurance), grunted most endearingly. "But tell me you'll pay me a visit from time to time. The two of you together!"

With contagious enthusiasm, Soledad lied: "Of course, handsome!"

The colonel did not know Puccini's *Tosca,* which unfortunately is not taught in the courses on strategy in the military academies. But he might have gotten the idea. For their part, Nuria and Soledad knew that Scarpia wanted to get next to Tosca without having to free Cavaradossi, and they knew that she was trying to free her lover without lying down with the warder. Due to a lack of negotiations, Tosca stabbed Scarpia in the belief that he had *already* freed Cavaradossi, while in fact Scarpia was getting ready to know Tosca in a biblical way, having *already* given the order to have the prisoner shot. Everyone thought themselves clever in their own way, but in the end Tosca had to throw herself into the Tiber River. What else could she do? Minimum concessions on the part of all would have saved three lives. Many wars could be avoided if the lesson were pondered. "Less sieges of cities and more Puccini" was Soledad's slogan.

But Tarsis, en route to Nice, was not up to celestial music.

Amary, who has no idea of how to sing a Gregorian chant, opts for a fusilier's march and presses the attack. He moves 18. h2-h4.

As far as Tarsis is concerned, Amary sings out of tune, and what is worse, he is following the beat set up in his previous movements. What was needed was a pause, a silence, a fermata, and not an andante without counterpoint. Enough of impromptus and capriccios! The moment for polyphony has come.

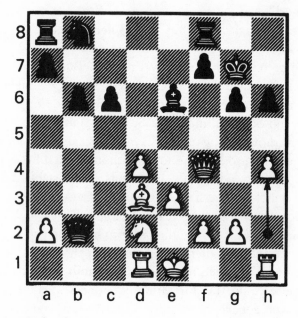

18. h2-h4

Tarsis is of the opinion that Amary is now faced with a *fait accompli,* that he has no options left: he can fuss about, or fall back and pretend that his flight is a galloping attack. Tarsis moves 18. . . . Ktb8-d7, keeping control of the two black squares at his center (e5 and f6). He has choked off the white counteroffensive. Still, Amary is confident of his attack and the tactical possibilities created by the mobility of his king-side. He could win, and rapidly: the entire unstable equilibrium of his rival's construction could come down at the least inexactness. *Black's play lacks grounding,* he thinks.

One article's title aroused his interest: "Melody in the Cat-acombs." In it Jean Michel Sanders recounted his under-ground odyssey:

> I raise the lid of the sewer without anyone seeing me—and nevertheless I am only a few dozen feet from the National Assembly. I then descend five sets of stairs until I find a platform leading to the main sewage chan-nels; it also leads to a spiral stone staircase which takes me to the subterranean passageways . . . Underground Paris is endowed with a network of nearly three hundred miles of catacombs and tunnels where one can walk— if one is not afraid of the oppressive silence—with the help of only a lantern or flashlight. Many of the tunnels are walled up by the authorities. But it is comparatively easy to demolish the barriers, which were apparently hastily built. A municipal decree dated 1955 prohibited all access to them, for they led to the cellars of many of the old houses of Paris.

Tarsis at length understands how Isvoschikov was ab-ducted, and he assumes that Amary and his followers made their way into the Marigny Palace (residence of foreign guests

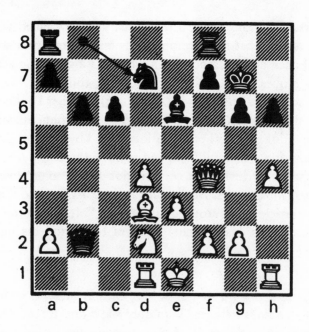

18. . . . Ktb8-d7

of the President of the Republic) through an underground tunnel leading to its cellar. He is surprised that he had not thought of it before. But then three days later an article in *France-Soir* shows him his error. On the night of the abduction, eight Soviet police changed guard at the very door of the minister's quarters and, moreover, all the adjoining rooms on the floor were occupied by doctors, nurses, secretaries, and the security people. The newspaper concluded: "Here we have the new Mystery of the Yellow Room. How could the Minister be abducted without the police guards at the door of his room seeing his abductors?"

[The presence of the Others constituted an obstacle to Amary's nocturnal repose. But, contrary to what he believed, it actually stimulated his work as investigator—especially the presence of Mickey and the Kid.

For years, whether in the large house in Geneva or in his room at the university, and before he took up politics, Amary had devoted himself to Science in the hope of discovering the secret of the universe, or at least the secret of energy, of that energy which contains a particle free of exterior forces as it travels through space.

He thought of himself as a free particle . . . with no ties, neither familial nor national. One day Doña Rosita, always garrulous and forked of tongue, told him: "You're no free particle. You're tied to us, to Teresa, to the Kid, to Mickey, and, most of all, to *Him*."

It was the typical ploy of an old reactionary female, and he could not allow himself to fall for it. She aimed to drive him into himself and force him to meditate on what she called "God." If he swallowed her line, the next hurdle would be Mickey and his ridiculous prayers.

"I am a man of Science," he would declare, trying to keep his composure, "and I speculate only on those things which can be known or measured."

Teresa laughed so heartily that her guffaws were heard through the door of the cupboard in which she was locked. The Kid simply smiled to himself.]

When Amary received his Marxist revelation, he understood what he had previously only intuited. He let his comrades, the four militants of his Comité, in on the secret: "In Einstein's theory of relativity, space, time, and matter are considered only as mathematical and physical objects in *our* system of energy. And so the unification of electromagnetic forces and interactions, weak as well as strong, is superficial, like the social democracy and radical socialism of our grandfathers. Physics makes sense if one thinks in terms of much greater energy. As in politics, it is worthy of consideration only if filtered through the infinitely superior energy represented by Marxism. In politics as in physics we are face to face with the Great Unification."

It was a simple enough exercise for the Master, one he called "familiar," to calculate in scales of "unsuspected" energy. (It was a feat of mental acrobatics that made Marc Amary's colleagues feel as if they had been called upon to walk a tightrope while juggling.) There was really no reason to be surprised at his dexterity in dealing with different scales of energy, considering his relations with what he called "the Great Unification."

[After all, did he not live with El Loco without Teresa being aware of his existence? Wasn't *He* situated in another world of values? Did he not perfectly understand the relationship between Doña Rosita the serpent and Mickey the tiny rubber doll? Not to mention the Three Condors, who spent the night outside, at the window, playing poker and carrying on with a pack of cardsharps until the Master himself was forced to remind them that they were only "guests" at the house.]

"Marxism has achieved what in physics we call the Great Unification; that is, unification associated with universal gravitation, as it brings Morality, Politics, Economy, History, and Science into proper relationship with each other."

De Kerguelen listened to him open-mouthed.

"Well," he finally said, "between the two scales of energies, the Social Democrats (as we know them today) and the Marxists, what is there?"

"A desert."

To speak of the desert was one of Amary's favorite locutions. Alluding to it, he could express himself clearly, and with a large degree of enthusiasm.

"We can assume that during the transition between actual energies and larger ones nothing of consequence will happen. That, at least, is the petit-bourgeois view of *avant-garde* physicists. The 'desert' will be terrorism's terrain. Marxist equilibrium, the Great Unification, cannot be achieved without it."

In order to achieve this highly desired Great Unification, Amary's Comité went on the attack. They proposed to frighten the bourgeois enemy and impress the working class "by exploding bombs in the proletarian consciousness." To serve this altruistic purpose, they made use of varied weapons, including howitzers, rockets, clock bombs, plastic explosives, antitank bazookas, and modest Molotov cocktails. Making use of this arsenal, they succeeded in blowing up the offices of Rolls-Royce in Paris, the United States consulate in Lyons, a building at the nuclear center in Creys-Malville, a police garage in Marseilles, the baggage checkroom at the Charles de Gaulle airport, a Renault parking lot at Flins . . . Amary could discern the "desert" beneath the craters.

The press coverage of what Amary's people called "actions of armed resistance" seemed only proper to the stupid incapacity of this transmission belt for Big Capital: "They speak of 'blind terrorism.' But we know why we kill. Nothing was ever better prepared than our attacks. We don't engage in blind terrorism: it is merely mute for the moment and invisible. Our silence matches that of our victims. But we will soon begin to speak, to issue communiqués, as soon as we enter on the final stage."

[The Three Condors sometimes arrived late. The Master was afraid of them; he knew that during the day they passed the time with *Him* at the apex of the universe. For his part,

Mickey often spent hours with his muzzle pressed to the glass of the window as he watched them playing poker. The doll's interest in the game only annoyed Amary.

"I'm really sick of seeing you watching them every night. What's so interesting?"

"The fact that they spend the day with *Him*."

"Don't be absurd!"

"When I find out how they play poker, I'll be able to understand how *He* thinks and reasons."

That a rubber mouse should give him lessons in anything was unacceptable to the Master.]

Amary summoned de Kerguelen. It was on a night which had a happy ending. A five-kilo bomb had gutted the Paris office of CII-Honeywell-Bull. Amary's planning had been perfect and so had its execution by de Kerguelen. The latter was expecting his mentor to congratulate him, but instead Amary announced: "I'm going to abandon the study of elemental particles. Beginning tomorrow I'll take up the genetic code."

Human beings are so peculiar! And unexpected. De Kerguelen, who was willing to risk his life carrying out the most suicidal acts conceived by Amary and who had "definitely" resigned from the CNRS for the sake of the Dimitrov Faction, received the news of Amary's latest project as if it were a personal affront. An unacceptable humiliation. After his return to scientific research, the genetic code had been *his* specialty. Amary could simply not stomp around in his garden like Attila's horse.

De Kerguelen strove to take hold of himself as he voiced an objection: "The Great Unification of the elemental particles is the number-one problem of physics today, and I thought you were on the point of resolving it."

"I found the answer. But the experimental confirmation can only be realized through the LEP, the project headed by Emilio Picasso, the long annular tunnel more than twenty miles in length which will be built someday . . . And it cannot reasonably be expected to be in functioning order before 1990."

De Kerguelen felt as if a dagger had been slipped into him somewhere. He was afraid of Amary's genius. Would not Amary be able, in a few weeks, to make hash of all the research he had carried out over a period of years? To make a discovery which would make him look ridiculous? He ventured an objection: "The genetic code surely cannot interest you . . . Tell me, what is your opinion of the model of unification postulated by Glashow and Salam?"

"In the first place, these two individuals, like most Nobel laureates in physics, work for the antisocialist army. And second, I would point out that the model uses both their names—because it was invented by Weinberg."

Amary was demonstrating his weak point: the irrational hatred he bore the Nobel laureates for the year 1971. De Kerguelen opened up the breach: "I'm sure you could *demolish* the theory. It would be a great step forward for science."

"The model was expounded precipitously, based on indirect and unconfirmed evidence, so-called. It has never enjoyed a shadow of support from experimental confirmation."

De Kerguelen grew bolder. He moved on in, attempting a feint: "Someone like you, investigating the Great Unification, could not get carried away by anything as microscopic as the genetic code."

Amary was on guard: "Despite the general opinion of our

185

'progressive' colleagues, the genetic code is the other pole to Marxism, thanks to which we'll find the origin of life, of man. Marxism will create the new man. And how can a man of Marxist science ignore molecular biophysics?"

Following this diagonal slash, de Kerguelen realized he had lost the initiative.

[When the Master arrived home, he found Teresa tied to the bed with a rope. The Kid and Mickey were in the act of securing the last knots. The three of them were laughing like crazy.

"I've forbidden you to engage in these beastly deeds! No more of these filthy doings! You, Teresa, back to your cupboard! I don't want to see hide nor hair of you around here again. You're allowed to go into my room only after I'm asleep, and then to lie down on the rug."

Teresa went off in tears. Or pretending she was in tears. And the Kid said: "It was just a game. We were putting her into 'infragreen bondage' in 'Technicolor.' But not to worry, we would have granted her 'asyntitic liberty.' "

"What kind of nonsense is that?"

Mickey attempted a clarification: "He gets everything mixed up. He's talking about 'infrared bonding' (not infragreen'), which occurs due to the fact that the quarks enclosed in the proton are confined in low frequencies, while 'asyntotic' (not 'asyntitic') liberty denotes the property they possess at high frequencies to act as free particles. 'Technicolor' is the color, that is, the electrical charge of the gluons in the technigluons and the techniquarks."

The Master was furious. "You've reeled all that off like a parrot, just to make fun of me and my research. Who taught you all you know?"

186

The Kid answered: "The Three Condors. They explained it all while playing poker on the sly. They know everything: *He* speaks to them more often than to us. They spend days together in the heights, at the top of the firmament."

The Master went off in despair to sleep with El Loco. Thanks to the Three Condors and Mickey, his authority, so necessary in maintaining the balance of the Others, was in shreds.]

The next day the two members of the Comité continued their mutual skirmish. For the first time in his life, de Kerguelen hated Amary. For his part, Amary, more easygoing than ever, said, or announced: "I visited the chief at your laboratory this morning . . ."

What nerve! What a provocation! De Kerguelen could have torn the other's buttons off with his fingernails. "Did you introduce yourself as a friend of mine?"

"No."

"What did you talk about?"

"We simply exchanged ideas."

"Doesn't he know that you're a friend of mine?"

"We didn't talk about you. He brought me up to date on the research into the structure, dynamics, and organization of DNA."

De Kerguelen was on the point of exploding. He dove deep: "You could have asked *me* about that."

"Your chief seems to have a knack for explaining things with great clarity."

So: they had hit it off. De Kerguelen lunged: "He's a reactionary Trotskyite of the worst kind. He never stops signing letters in favor of Soviet dissidents."

"That's perfect. His laboratory will be a splendid place to

escape being noticed. We've already come to an agreement. I'll go there from ten in the morning to one o'clock, just as I did at the High Energy Laboratory. Everything will continue as usual with the Comité. We can meet in the afternoon and continue our acts of armed resistance, naturally."

"What will be the subject of your work?"

"I want to find what your chief calls the 'magic word.' "

Such cheek! Such brazen impudence! De Kerguelen took off his protective mask and breastplate. "I've been working on that for years."

"I know that. You can be of help to me . . ."

Help him, no less! He proposed to turn him into his laboratory assistant or his groom. After years of "revolutionary fraternity," it was clear that the vices of a petit bourgeois remained *encrusted* in de Kerguelen's subconscious: envy, jealousy, *amour propre,* and, worst of all, individualism.

But Amary did not know the human heart, or the danger of humiliating a beaten man. Because of the actions of its chairman, the Comité was equipping a pressure cooker with rockets.

Tarsis is fishing by candlelight, Amary thinks, when the moment has arrived to use a trident or a harpoon. He sizes up the situation, moving his knight 19. Ktd2-e4. His rival will not dispose of the time necessary to convey his queen to safe haven before harpoons rain down on his king. It is the typical conceptual error of the temperamental player who confuses deep-sea fishing with fishing in shallow water. *He has bitten the hook and is ready to swallow the poisoned bait that I have left for him at a2.*

Tarsis considers the net spread by his adversary, sees trick-

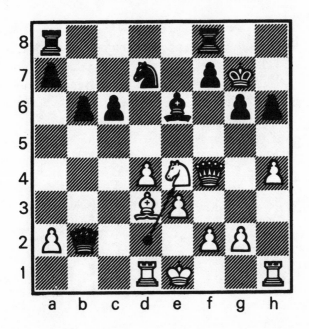

19. Ktd2-e4

ery revealing itself, and plays out line, taking the pawn
19. . . . Qb2xa2. *He's going to be left high and dry,* he thinks,
and so he does not bother at such a critical moment to ponder
his move.

Amary had published a problem in the review *Diagrammes*
which for Tarsis amounted to more than a declaration of
intentions. Amary's last move gives him pause and confirms
his initial surmise. Isvoschikov's abduction is clearly deline-
ated in it. The so-called originality of the terrorists' demands—as some newspapers have it—merely faithfully echoes
Amary's calculations.

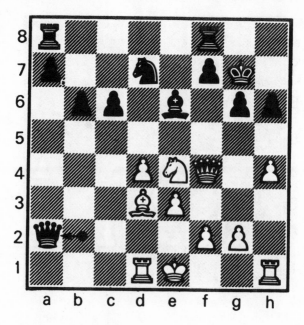

19. . . . Qb2xa2

During the first few weeks of the abduction, the kidnapper's blackmail appeared to be no more than utopian, a projection of the chimerically utopian spirit habitual in terrorists. They demanded, and continue to demand, as exclusive condition for the liberation of Isvoschikov, that the Soviet Union bomb the oil wells of Saudi Arabia, "whereupon the economic collapse of Western capitalism will be initiated, along with the fall of the most feudal regime in the universe." As the days grew into weeks, the authorities in Moscow became increasingly perturbed. As they considered the letters written by their comrade under torture, the members of the Politburo felt they were being personally attacked. And they were not disposed to let themselves be mocked. Many people believed that the "Machiavellian" demands of the terrorists were actually being taken seriously in the Kremlin. In addition, Moscow was convinced that the French authorities and the "bourgeois" police were deliberately protecting the kidnappers. For it was scarcely possible that, at the end of two months, not the slightest trace of the abductors had turned up. Meanwhile, the comrades were plugging their ears to drown out the cries of their tortured brother. How long would it last? Tomorrow it might happen to any one of them. And now, would they be forced to destroy one of the West's vital resources, thereby risking a world war, to save their comrade? Little by little, the terrorists' blackmail begins to seem like a serious matter demanding consideration: it ceases to seem like a piece of utopian craziness and more the terrifying project of a group of fanatics.

Tarsis is convinced that Amary wants a world war leading to a "desert," to a tabula rasa which would allow the construction of a new society. The truth is that Amary has always been intrigued by the well-known dialogue between Khrushchev and Mao, in which the Russian, after speaking of the cataclysm of an atomic war, concluded in an apocalyptic tone: "The living will envy the dead." Mao thereupon turned to his Ministers and commented: "What cowards these Russians are!"

In Amary's problem the one who plays loses:

The only possibility is to move the knight. The reply to that move would be 20. Ktd6 or KtxKt mate.

Chess players call this kind of position *zugzwang*, which denotes the obligation on the part of the player whose turn it is to move to make a bad move, since not to do so would obviate play.

The abduction of Isvoschikov was planned, Tarsis believes, to force the "liberating" disaster, the "desert."

Amary advances a pawn 20. h4-h5 to establish a bridgehead in his rival's stronghold. With this move he continues the siege of Tarsis's line of defense, thus freeing his rook, so that it will not become a castle in Spain but instead a field fortification: he's winding up the game. Tarsis is surprised that his opponent has not thought through such a complicated position. His own defenses are impregnable: the skirmish was the last gasp of a man in the death throes.

When they arrived in Nice, the three of them—Nuria, Soledad, and Tarsis—encamped on the top floor of a modest neighborhood house on Chemin de Pessicart. Their quarters were three ramshackle garrets with a rooftop on the verge of ruin. They soon transformed the place into three cozy rooms and a terrace covered with potted plants. Nuria and Soledad set about earning a living as cleaning women, and Tarsis went to work as a machine operator. Their net earnings allowed the trio to live comfortably enough. And to live like Spaniards. Their cuisine consisted of lentils, fried bread crumbs, chick-pea stews, paellas, meat and fish balls, and meat and vegetable turnovers. Their sweets were cream-filled pastries and rice pudding; they indulged in coffee breaks and drank thick chocolate as well; and they cured themselves of indis-

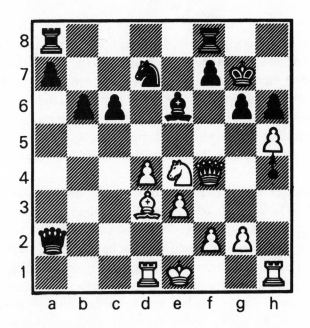

20. h4-h5

positions with linden and camomile tea. They not only ate in the way they had in Spain but they dressed and drank, spoke and acted as if they had never left their country. They established a Spanish Gibraltar, an enclave of their own in the very heart of the French Côte d'Azur without running into any diplomatic problems. And they weren't the only ones to do so. Spain-in-exile became an unsubmergible archipelago bathed by the waters of hope and melancholy, and it waged a solitary battle to avoid losing its identity. The rulers of the home country played no role in these dispersed microcosms of eternal Spain. The people were of a different sort, a race apart.

Tarsis made up his mind to conserve, to return to, some

of the rules of iron discipline which had marked his days as an *agapito*. He lived with Nuria and Soledad as if the three of them, and not just he alone, had taken the vows of chastity. The first days were truly difficult. He nearly gave in. When he came back from work, he could not avoid circling the two women as if he were held in a halter. He managed to subdue the burning desire which inflamed him, and like an ox, he found once again, as he had in the labor camp, that "man is a creature of habit." He became inured to the daily pyrotechnics. It was harder to go through the night and keep his hands to himself. He tried, but relief came to him in nocturnal pollutions; his fingers were wet when he awoke.

The three stayed married without having walked down the aisle. They were a rare married group, open and bigamous, or trigamous, by consent of the three parties. For them, matrimony was not a cross but an eternal honeymoon in which they went on eating at the marriage banquet. But without consummation by deed.

They practiced an eccentric religious life, in the course of which Soledad's viewpoint seemed to take precedence. In her imagination insects began to appear like a plague. According to her, the sacrifice of Jesus was equivalent to the death of the bumblebee at the moment of fecundation, and just as men for centuries received the communion of Christ's message, numberless insects carry the sperm of their dead male impregnators in order to procreate millions more. But then, carried away by Soledad's obsession, Nuria lived in a spiritual exaltation and rapture that might be characterized as *"mistico-insectil"*: not insectivorous, for, far from eating spiders or termites, whenever she captured a bug she would treat it lovingly and run her tongue over its shell.

Thanks to the scarcity of milling-machine operators in the region, Tarsis was able to find work at once in the shops of

APA (Atelier de Precision Achard), which constructed prototypes for such companies as Dassault, Thomson, Ferrodo, and the SNIAS. Schedules and salaries were far different from those that prevailed in Valencia, and so was the wage scale for advancement, and the ranking order. In Spain the ranking was as follows: apprentice mechanic, advanced mechanic, third-class operator, second-class operator, first-class operator. In France there were more categories, and advancement, in reverse order, was: *manoeuvre*, O.S. 1 (*ouvrier spécialisé* 1), O.S. 2, O.S. 3, P. 1 (*professionnel* 1), P. 2, P. 3, and to round out the honor role, a position which did not exist in Valencia, the "H.Q." (the worker who was *hautement qualifié*).

An older worker, in a nostalgic mood, told Tarsis one day: "Nowadays everything moves so fast. In my day there were only four categories: *apprenti, petite main, petit compagnon, compagnon*. I began as a woodworker, and I still miss the odor of wood. Whenever I go into a carpenter shop I am overcome with memories . . . I still preserve the tools I had to buy in those days."

Tarsis told him the latest: "They've made me sign an agreement that I could only read hurriedly. I know it mentions the death penalty for passing on our work plans to foreign powers."

"All of us have signed the same paper. As if we knew what we were doing! Before, when I was a model maker, I would help build a propeller and I'd see it later at the Auto Show. Now the most complicated pieces are required and they end up in the belly of an atomic submarine or in the fuselage of an airplane or in the middle of a missile's radar. And look, all that talk about military court-martials and you see how the plans lie around the shop without anyone's paying the least attention."

When he came home from work Tarsis would play chess by correspondence. The games he played against the former world champion, Estrine, and against the best player in France, Bergrasser, caused a sensation when they were published and analyzed in *Le Courrier des Échecs*. The rhythm of these games suited him fine. Sometimes, when the adversary was a foreigner, such play lasted for years.

Nuria and Soledad slept in one of the three rooms. Tarsis made use of the smallest. The third room served as kitchen, pantry, and dining room. The spacious roof terrace, a junk heap when they took it over, was transformed into a flower garden. In the summer they might spend a couple of hours simply watering the infinity of flowerpots which Nuria had placed about with the artistry of a watercolorist. Soledad called each of them by names which she herself had given them, for the most mysterious motives (Africana, Inés, Filigree, Docile, Rogue, Prankster), just as she had named the thousand-odd sheep in the flock she and her uncle had seasonally moved in nomadic fashion from Aragon in north Spain to the center of Jaén province in the south.

Nuria's breakdown, or perhaps it should be called an explosion, was foreshadowed by a series of wild eccentricities which Soledad and Tarsis found hard to deal with. Perhaps these extravagances were no more than subconscious cries for help. She not only licked the carapaces of bugs but let her tongue lick everything around her, as if she had a mystical obligation to perform a ritual at regular intervals, never more than fifteen minutes apart. Everything around her, plants or bugs, was subject to her ceremonial ministration. She licked them—but also she always rubbed her fingertips around them three times beforehand, as if blessing them, in a kind of benediction. When the object to be blessed lay on the floor, she would get down on all fours to carry out her ministrations.

And her "insectile mysticism" began to permeate every act. Soledad and Tarsis accepted everything she did: the three were spiritually united! Still, they were brought up short when they beheld her on the roof one day, kneeling before a dead pigeon and reaching out with her tongue to lick its beak.

Another night Soledad awoke Tarsis and asked him to go with her. "She doesn't sleep. She's been lying awake for hours."

Tarsis found Nuria sitting on the bed, her eyes wide.

"I dreamed of St. John the Evangelist. I told him: 'Johnny, you sure tell tall tales.'"

"Good enough, Nuria . . . Now go to sleep. Do you want us to make you some camomile tea?"

"My soul rebels against the Gospel!"

"You're overexcited."

"I was never so calm . . . I should drink more urine so as to purify myself."

"Calm down, Nuria."

"When Soledad first told me you were shut up in a labor camp, I realized you were paying for my sins."

"They put me there because I was a deserter."

"I was the whore . . . but you got punished."

"Go to sleep!"

From then on, Nuria spent her nights in vigil, praying, reading, or talking to herself. Soledad and Tarsis babied her.

"You treat me this way because you think I'm sick. But I'm in perfect health. Elias, I want you to know that I'm going to have a child as small as a scarab and as homely as a flea. He'll be like a sublimated Hannibal and a Saint John at one and the same time . . . I'll call him Francisco, María, and José. He'll be known as Ferdinand III of Liberty."

"You're suffering the torments of sleeplessness!"

"I need your intuition. *You* are *me*. My son will be born

on the fourth of September. He'll be an emperor, he'll be the most complete man of the century: a scholar, a musician, an architect, an ascetic. He'll be intuitive and logical. I'll conceive him without help from any male, like the mother of Buddha, who became pregnant when she watched an elephant going by, or like the Virgin Mary, who became pregnant when she was visited by an archangel."

Tarsis wanted to save her, but she wouldn't listen to him. She went right on talking, as if she were transmitting an urgent message.

"God and the Devil exist, you know that, and so do you, Soledad. But what you don't know is that Evil is about to invade the earth with unimaginable weapons. There will be a war of such butchery that at the end the living will envy the dead, as John says. I see it all clearly because I travel in a time elevator."

"I want you to sleep."

"Everything we do has some meaning. Even my having been a whore in Barcelona, even that my mouth kissed some of the clients' pricks."

"Shut up!"

"Beat me! I was a whore!"

"Stop yelling!"

"You don't know it, but you'll be the one to give birth to my son . . . through your forehead. At that moment, I'll go blind."

"Me? . . . a man?"

"Yes, you. That's why your head is so heavy. Ever since the night of time, you've been preparing to harbor my child."

Nuria continued her ritual of licking and blessing everything around her . . . but she also began to throw all "wicked" objects out the window, such as the money box they kept in the kitchen. One day, when Tarsis returned from work, Nuria, in a fit of trembling, announced: "The Martians are coming.

They're coming from far off. They've already colonized Venus. I've seen them as clearly as I see you. They have teeth like vampires and they live off our dreams. They've already told me that after the cataclysm we'll eat excrement. Urine will be the new sperm and we'll travel through space thanks to the energy provided by orgasms."

Without pausing for breath, she made assertions which Soledad and Tarsis found both novel and incongruent, and from her own affirmations she would deduce the most paradoxical conclusions: "The Devil manipulates us . . . that's why there are so many flies." "We must levitate . . . that way we'll get the better of pain." "I was an Indian slave in another life . . . that's why monsters are born in Japan." "The beautiful shall become ugly, and vice versa . . . and so termites build cannons." "In the end I'll have your intuition . . . and I'll speak from a wardrobe as if it were a television screen."

More and more perturbed, Nuria spent nights prey to a whirlwind of emotion. She assured them that her soul had taken up residence in the body of a cat; that there would be a giant atomic explosion; that the Martians wished to fornicate with humans; that she would stare at the sun—which is God—until she went blind; that the Devil is a part of God; that St. Francis of Assisi would be reincarnated as Frankenstein; that she and Soledad would turn homosexual, like Tarsis, for the anus is the center of life, while homosexuality would become the rule of the future; that worms would turn into lions; that we are about to live through a new Sodom and Gomorrah; that her heart would be stabbed seven times, like the heart of the Virgin; that the soul escapes through defecation; that the greatest sin is the sin of pride.

Tarsis felt he was witness to the dissolution of Nuria, who was obviously overwhelmed by some inner suffering, and he doubted he could help her.

"In Barcelona you used to beat me because I deserved it."

"No, no. I was simply out of my mind."

"And you'd cover my body with black-and-blue marks, and you'd say my skin was so fine! Bite me now! Make me bleed with your teeth!"

Nuria was so insistent, as if her life were at stake, that Tarsis felt forced to do as she demanded. He bit her arm so hard he feared he would tear off a mouthful.

"Look at my arm. Your teeth haven't left the slightest mark. I've already dreamed that it would happen this way."

Nuria went on talking and Tarsis examined her arm close up; there really was no sign of the violent bite he had given her. He was startled, even frightened.

"You think I'm sick, don't you?"

"No."

"I have no right to say anything against you, since it's you who takes care of me and makes me well. You could kill me if you want. I have only you . . . and Soledad."

Tarsis could not calm her down. She was like a defenseless child he could touch with his fingers but whose acoustic system he could not penetrate.

"Don't open the trunk in the kitchen. It's full of skeletons. They're the men I went to bed with when I was a whore in Barcelona."

"Forget all that."

She never let up talking about her child, her son who would save humanity, who would be lame, who would liberate womankind, who would suffer all the sorrows of mankind, who would pass through work camps like Elias, who would be locked up in a madhouse, who would proclaim that all of us are fragments of God, who would represent total confusion and absolute rationality, who would be nine times the size of a big toe, who would announce the truth hidden among a thousand errors, and who would fight against the Devil.

"Are you finally going to sleep?"

"I am falling in my soul like the cosmos fell in Genesis. I have only a thread of reason left with which to fight off sickness. You be careful: I'm going to kill myself and kill the two of you. I can't stop myself."

Soledad wept in despair. Nuria told her: "I can't feel pity."

And when Tarsis emerged later from the bedroom, Soledad sobbed to him: "We must save her!"

"She's so delicate," said Tarsis. "And her sorrow pains me deeply. Her anguish leaves me anguished."

Tarsis was truly overwhelmed by what was happening. He and Soledad followed the evolution of Nuria's sickness step by step. Tarsis was being consumed. Every night he was beset by her complex of confusions and her apparently unconquerable insomnia. They spent their nights listening to her describing her fantasies and visions, and all of them were aching in their bones. They tried a thousand ways of getting her to sleep, all without avail. Only sometimes, when they got her to take up to three sleeping pills at sundown, did she grow sleepy by dawn.

"You must sleep, Nuria, you're exhausted. You can't go on week after week without sleep."

"I have so much praying to do! Besides, when I sleep I can clearly see that life is cyclical, and recalling the past, I can foresee the future. I'd rather not sleep, and not see what is going to befall me. Tell me, Elias, do you want me to work for you? Do you want me to analyze your chess games?"

"I only want you to sleep."

"I could also be a whore again. I lack feelings. I don't feel anything; only others do and suffer for it. Do you know, Elias, when you give birth to my child from your forehead, that he'll stick his member in men's eyes and in women's ears? You'll carry him in your head for nine months, although, of course, nine months could go by in nine hours."

"And how do you know all these things, Nuria?"

"You've told them to me, Elias. Don't you remember?"

"When?"

"In dreams. In your dreams."

"In *my* dreams? You must mean in *your* dreams."

"No, Elias, you told me so in one of your dreams . . . in the form of a metaphor, of course, but I understood well enough."

What Tarsis understood was that Nuria's sickness was accelerating in the face of his incomprehension and inability to help her. He was overcome with sorrow and deeply wished

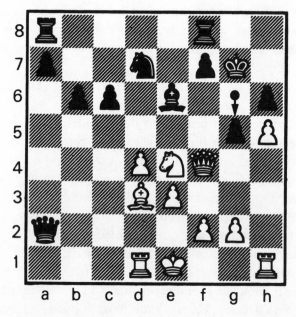

20. . . . g6-g5

that he had told her, before she began to come apart, how much he cared for her.

During a long eight minutes of serious reflection, Tarsis has been asking himself if Amary is all there, is he in his right mind. What is his attack if not a bout of delirium tremens? Tarsis slips on the straitjacket: 20. . . . g6-g5. And if the other man continues his lunacy, Tarsis will show him, in the twinkling of an eye, the place where the sun sets.

For the Politburo to issue a communiqué through the Tass agency without any express reference to the Soviet government or the Party is a highly unusual procedure. Apparently the members of the highest state organism in Russia, in response to the irregular situation, decided to address the French government and, even more directly, public opinion in France, in the same way as the abductors. It was a strongly worded text signed by each and every member of the governing body with their prenames and surnames. It thus demonstrated how far and how much they considered it a personal matter. They had come to the end of their patience. No more shuffling the deck. Their comrade's troubles have moved them profoundly. They announce that they are obliged to consider seriously the ultimatum issued by the kidnappers. And therefore, either the French police will effect the liberation of Isvoschikov or they will bomb the Saudi Arabian oil wells. Experts take the Soviet warning seriously, and announce that the situation has become a threat to world peace. Tarsis considers it a *zugzwang* position which only half hides his adversary's strategy.

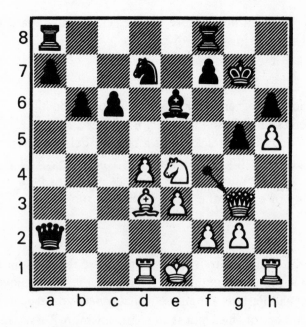

21. Qf4-g3

Amary corrects the course of his attack: 21. Qf4-g3. His rival's king-side is like a leaking boat almost on the point of sinking: the sacrifice of a knight at *g5,* which, at the time, jeopardized him, could not be made effective because of the possible intermediate check at *a5.* Tarsis's plan is like a ship without a rudder which will inexorably be cast adrift.

But as far as Tarsis is concerned, Amary's obstinacy is a reef which will sink him. He himself need only avoid the continuous threat of a check which would allow the other to reach port, and so he will navigate by the stars. And Amary will see stars.

The sight of a raincoat can cause vertigo or fury in a human being. Amary's raincoat provoked in de Kerguelen an overwhelming impulse to resign—or to accept an army research contract. He saw the coat on a hanger in the Molecular Biology Laboratory. *His* laboratory. Amary had installed himself and as a first move had taken over de Kerguelen's own coat hanger. For the first time, the latter was aware that the Comité-secretary's clothes gave off an assassin's odor. He also smelled the odor of a leech. And of an opportunist. Wounded to the quick, his heightened sensibilities led him to make new discoveries, aspects of the place he had not noticed in all his years there. The laboratory as a whole was made up of small sordid rooms boxed together on the third floor of a squat and sinister "turret," like some sixty others in the Faculty of Sciences, and each group of four surrounded little jail-like patios. He looked out the window and thought he could see that the top floors were protected by wire nets. It was not so; his dejection clouded his vision, though surely that was the intention of the architect, whose muse must have drawn inspiration from Alcatraz or Cuban political prisons.

The office where work meetings were held was known as the "house of assignation." Correctly so, he thought. They were all a fine lot of solemn whores. Beginning with his boss, who was now obligingly showing off his artillery pieces. He was like a cock of the walk with Amary, displaying his wares, his jewel of a laser, "which achieved impulses of 10 picoseconds." De Kerguelen felt as if someone were reaching into his underpants or reading his adolescent diaries. For his part, Amary contemplated the apparatus with some disdain. He did not deign even to look at the Spektralphontes Dmrio Zeiss. Why did his boss not realize that Amary simply looked down his nose at the joint efforts of his team to adapt these sophisticated machines to research into the genetic code? Amary would simply make use of the data which this horde—

the biophysical phenomenologists—would extract from the apparatus by dint of much brain power. The elitist revolutionary aristocrat would simply think it all through, lay his plans, make his decisions, and reach his conclusions. De Kerguelen hated Amary more and more at each stage of the present routine visit.

"With this centrifuge, which was built in accordance with *our* plans, we reach a speed of 60,000 revolutions per minute. In it we can treat the bacteria *E. coli*."

What airs he put on! He didn't fit in his own skin, and his apparatus didn't fit in this world. He went on and on. What a dreamer! As if Amary could be interested in any sermon delivered by someone else. Without ever taking off his white gloves, without risking the chance that a wandering *E. coli* would jump in his eye or a still unfrozen circuit burn his fingertips, Amary would be able eventually to make a synthesis of all the statistics and information that the worker bees had extracted in accordance with his directives. And then, in one sudden stroke, he would find the "magic word" which the entire hive had sought together for so many years.

[To the surprise of the Master, the Kid became a devotee of the genetic code. He would spend the night talking to the "Mosquito" through the chimney. The Mosquito was a rhinoceros who could not be lured out of the cellar for anything. According to him, he lived down there with a marquis. He was a well of wisdom, a fountain of science as concerned the genetic code. He had built up an impressive "library" behind the boiler.

What did he mean by a "library"?

Mickey didn't even know that a "library" was a collection of DNA sequences. Despite the fact that the Mosquito was only a rhinoceros, he had the memory of an elephant and could reel off the bases for all the sequences reported to date.

The Three Condors also disposed of a first-class "library": they would jot down the sequences any old way in the margins of their playing cards in the course of their cardsharping at poker. Or at least that was the Master's idea of it.

DNA, as the Kid explained it to Doña Rosita, "is formed like two spiral staircases joined by two strands which twist around and contain steps. Each stair is a base, and they can be only *A or T, G or C*."

Doña Rosita did not absorb the fact that these interminably repeated bases created a sequence. And that the repertory of sequences was called the "library." She was interested only in not missing any of the operas broadcast by France-Musique. And in smoking her horrible green Tuscan cigars.

"DNA's genetic code is all the information that the cell has. Thanks to it, it knows how to nourish itself, reproduce, and . . . kill."

"Kill its mother?" asked Teresa, merely to annoy the Master.

"Does the code contain any pornographic information?" asked Mickey, trying to be funny.

They liked to cut loose and have a good time. The genetic code amused them more than parlor games.

"Each of the two filaments of the DNA of the most diminutive cell measures more than three feet. That's how tightly wound it is!" The Kid was telling Teresa, who, putting on an imitation of Marilyn Monroe, only whispered: "Ask the rhinoceros to send us some shavings from his horn so we can make up aphrodisiac drinks."

A waste of time! Mosquito was ever so proud! He would never have allowed anyone to shave his horn; every night he wrapped it in a chamois cloth.

"That's enough vulgarity!" yelled the Master, beside himself. "If you don't shut up, Mosquito, I'll throw a harpoon down the chimney."

The rhinoceros's sardonic laughter was heard. He could imitate Louis Armstrong perfectly. In addition, he was a Maoist and knew about his own defensive properties, as exemplified in a statement made by his idol during the Long March: "History is like the hide of a rhinoceros. Disasters and massacres are no more than mosquito bites on its carapace." And so he called out: "Harpoons? Don't make me laugh."]

De Kerguelen knew that his boss was dreaming about the article that Amary would write, which, as the rules required, would be signed by the entire laboratory team. It would be a piece that would be outstanding because of its scientific exactitude and its inventiveness. And then goodbye to the lean years for the laboratory, the meager assignments from the CNRS, and the miserable grants. They would receive those ample contracts that are given to pals or for snobbish reasons. And then—why not?—a Nobel Prize! De Kerguelen was beside himself.

At one o'clock, when everyone went to lunch, Amary went to de Kerguelen's office. The latter was ready to tell him that he no longer wanted to be part of the Comité, and that terrorism—red, black, or chocolate-covered—was now out as far as he was concerned. The one thing he would not tolerate at this point was to be mocked by having his work as a researcher appropriated by someone else.

But Amary began the discussion: "For you and for me our work in the CNRS laboratory is of the utmost importance, vital for our safety. Thanks to them, we can count on the best possible cover as far as the police are concerned. More-over, as Marxists, we should begin to prepare the way for the men of the new society, thanks to the new genetic trans-formations, without letting ourselves be swayed by the ob-jections of our colleagues on the 'Left.' "

"Are you referring to genetic manipulation?"

"What reasonable person would refuse to make use of it if, as we can safely assume, it would lead to the creation of Marxist man?"

"Any research scientist with a minimum of morality . . ."

"You mean with a bourgeois morality in the service of the ruling class."

Amary spoke like a Fascist scientist. Had he taken leave of his senses? De Kerguelen was about to tell him to go away, to say that he no longer wanted to see him, when he guessed that Amary was reading his mind.

"Enver Hoxha said: 'Tito deserves spit in his face, a knife in his guts, and a bullet in his heart.' For years now, we've formed a clandestine group, and so we're bound together and risk our lives as one."

"We're not in Albania."

"It may be, de Kerguelen, that you're going through a moral crisis. We'll keep that in mind. And don't forget that *all* the information about us is in your hands."

"Do you think I'm about to inform on you?"

De Kerguelen had already learned, from reading the news-papers, that he was outside the Comité, though he hadn't been officially notified or "released." He had not been in-formed of or consulted in regard to the bomb they had placed at the Agence France-Presse, or the rocket they fired at the Palais de Justice in Paris, or the assassination of the direc-tor of the First National City Bank. He realized all of a sud-den that it would be best to say nothing to Amary about his feelings, nor did he feel safe enough to resign from the Comité.

[The Kid had everyone in an uproar with his gabble about the genetic code. They had more fun than if they were playing with puppets. They built a model on the carpet which they called DNA. The two arms were made of two ribbons, which formed a pair of spiral stairs wound around Doña Rosita. Then they began to stick signs representing A, T, G, and C in their respective sequences. They drove the Master mad with their nonsense and were delighted with themselves. For her part, Teresa went along with the game for reasons of her own, while Doña Rosita came and went with the greatest of ease from her place of confinement, and the Three Condors came in through the window as if they had every right to do so.

The Master was on the point of stomping on the ridiculous model, but Mickey, drawing himself up to his full minuscule height, as if he were a caliph in his court, warned him: "Don't even consider touching our DNA. I'll speak to *Him* . . ."

He said no more, and had no need to, for he well knew that this threat scared the Master witless.

They all gabbled at once in the general pandemonium. Only the deep voice of the Mosquito coming out of the fireplace was occasionally able to impose a few moments of quiet. The Master ostentatiously stuffed earplugs into his ears and took up reading the *Peking News*. But in reality he was dying of curiosity to find out where their game would lead them.

Mickey did not have any great understanding of the genetic code (though he was a whiz at elementary particles). He expressed his opinion. The Master thought it could not have been more reasonable.

"How do you hope to find the 'magic word' without a computer?"

The Kid replied: "You don't understand a thing. The 'magic word' is a researcher's mistaken notion. They're looking for a logical order in the strand's bases, while we have found the reason for this order, the rule."

The Master took out his earplugs and faced the Kid: "Are you referring to me? And are you making fun of me? Am I the researcher who is mistaken?"

He was being made to look ridiculous in front of everyone. The Kid explained the rule just as they had discovered it. Amary was stunned. Imagine this pipsqueak . . . And even that whore Teresa and the snake Doña Rosita knew all about what he had been up to for weeks, what he had been searching for with the help of the laboratory, and searching for unsuccessfully. He was beside himself.

"I'm leaving here for good."

Another dreamer's promise, thought the Others.

The Master went off to sleep with El Loco, and told him of his humiliation. But El Loco had to confess the truth, for he didn't know how to lie, and besides, he too had discovered the sequential rule.

"You!?"

"Yes, me!"

"How?"

"With a roll of toilet paper."

"Are you going to make fun of me, too?"

"I built a sequence with it, and on the margins I jotted down the series of bases A, T, G, C . . . until I came to realize how and why they followed the order they did."]

In the service of the revolution, de Kerguelen had planted a number of bombs in his time. But the bomb which shook him the most and changed his life carried neither an explosive charge nor a detonator: it was a twenty-page article, illustrated with sketches, titled: "Analysis of the Signs of Genetic Organization: Structure and Dynamics of the Problems of Stability in DNA."

He took barely five minutes to read it. And then he read it again. What a farce scientific investigation was! His own name, and those of his superior and of Ernest Byrrh, appeared along with Amary's as co-authors of the text. This was in accord with the hypocritical standards of scientific courtesy, which required that the names of members of the laboratory team should be given at the foot of each article. But if outsiders might be fooled, insiders knew well enough that Amary was the sole and exclusive author. As for everyone else: as usual, they would learn the contents of the piece when the second galley proofs were corrected.

The very worst of it was: Amary's thesis was irrefutable!

He began his demonstration with a proof: The pairs in the bases "A–T" and "T–A" are joined by two electrodes and those of "G–C" and "C–G" by three. From this fact he deduced that the former are less stable than the latter.

How is it, de Kerguelen asked himself, that none of the researchers had considered this property to be important? How was it that he himself overlooked such a significant certainty? Perhaps because it seemed so routinely self-evident.

And now, a barbarian, an assassin, a robot, had approached the problem in a different manner. He was not blinded by the apparent disorder in the sequences A,T,G,C, and he never went looking for the "magic word" which would lead to the secret, as the others had done . . . De Kerguelen hated him.

He had not uncovered the mystery through talent, but simply because of his lack of respect for the work done by all the others; and because of his egotism, which bordered on paranoia, and the total absence in his makeup of any shred of generosity.

"A sequence rich in A and T (that is, not stable) possesses biological significance . . ."

Son of a bitch! Cuckold! Faggot! He was damnably right! The series A,T,G,C of DNA should not be read as if it were an onomatopoetic phrase but as an open book of biological organization.

His entire life as a researcher gone to waste! The "magic word" buried forever . . . His years of work rendered ludicrous by a beginner without preconceptions, without scruples . . . a man of ice.

The text of the article finished with a revelation which would change the universe of molecular biology. Amary demonstrated that the *transcription,* that is, the transformation of the branchless information in the genetic code of DNA through branches which will produce proteins, for example, is always carried out in periods of low stability, that is, rich in the bases A and T.

De Kerguelen opened his window and hurled the article out onto the patio. Its twenty pages took flight, flapped like wings, separated in the air, paused there a moment, and began to fall slowly in a gliding motion; they seemed drawn to the squat dome of the giant computer center which filled most of the patio between the four low towers, and they ended up against one of its long gratings.

"Robot meat!" he cried. He was from Brittany and had never set foot in Spain, but he echoed a romantic Spanish phrase he had learned in school: "Better to die with honor than live reviled."

Amary would not have believed that after reading his article de Kerguelen was ready to sacrifice his life, if necessary, to destroy him and his Comité.

Tarsis advances his third protector: 21. . . . . f7-f5: his kingside, now disposed in order, will make his rival eat crow. And Amary is counting on nostrums and potions, when what he needs to fix him up is some strong doses of LSD.

The official in charge addresses himself to Amary and tells him: "I have received a note. One of your assistants gave it to me, and he said that it was of *vital* importance. Naturally, I can give it to you only if it is authorized by chessmaster

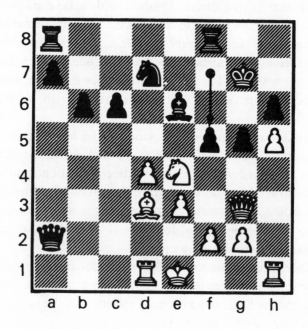

21. . . . . f7-f5

Tarsis. As chief official in this match, I may not transmit any outside message, which might contain information in code as regards the game, to either of you without permission from the other."

Tarsis thereupon is given the note and, after reading it, returns it with an affirmative nod. He does not wish to betray his own intense reaction. The official then passes it on to Amary.

The message reads: "De K. managed to get in. He discovered the refrigerator. He's given us the slip. We're searching. He can't get away."

Amary is so overcome that the paper drops from his hand. He stares at the board as vacantly as if he had received a blow on the back of his head, or as if he really had taken a large dose of LSD. He seems hypnotized when he moves: 22. Kte4xg5.

Unable to believe its eyes, the public is scandalized, and a murmur goes around the hall. They know that if such an absurd move were to be recorded in chess journals, it would necessarily be marked with the ignominious question marks, thus: 22. Kte4xg5??

Tarsis thinks he knows the cause of his opponent's dismay, and the meaning of the message: De Kerguelen has broken into the house at Meung-sur-Loire. He has stumbled on the hiding place where they have concealed Isvoschikov (the refrigerator is the secret passage). He has made an attempt to free the Minister . . . but the gang surprised him. He has succeeded in escaping by running down the passages, and he has taken refuge in one of the subsidiary galleries, perhaps in a camouflaged storeroom. They have him surrounded: they've manned the exit from the underground passageways . . . But they haven't found him yet.

All of Amary's plans, both for the chess match and for the

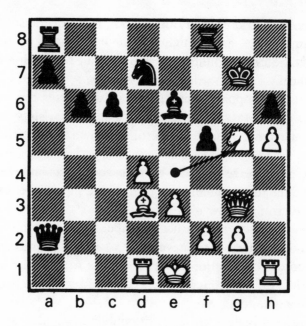

22. Kte4xg5

abduction, are coming unstuck. All that is left is to polish him off.

The Talmud almost led Tarsis to Salt Lake City, capital of Utah, but a few stalks of white hawthorn changed his destiny.

Tarsis and Soledad spent some sleepless weeks listening to Nuria's ravings without being able to help her much. And then, one morning, as Tarsis was going off to work, Nuria asked: "Buy me a bottle of champagne? I want to toast the birth of my child. And I'll wash out the toilet with what's left over."

Nuria's whim somehow pleased him. He had heard that the Talmud advised that there was no happiness without wine.

So this was a happy augury. And in Hebrew "Talmud" means "learning."

Still, he knew nothing about French wines. And after work he bought a dozen bottles of champagne for an absurdly low price. The only trouble was that it was not really champagne: despite the bottle, only someone as ignorant as himself could have been deceived. It was white bubbly, but certainly not from the Champagne region. He had bought a dozen bottles of Clairette de Die.

His generation of emigrants had fallen on France as if from the sky. Their fellow exiles from earlier years—those from the 1920s (the *"sudetos"*) and those from the thirties, beginning in 1939 (simply the "refugees")—called them, the newest wave, the "parachutists."

Soledad was waiting for Tarsis in a highly distraught state: "I've had a hideous day!"

"Did she sleep?"

"Three times she drowsed, but for no more than a quarter of an hour each time. She's more excited than ever. A few minutes ago she announced that a giant fart was the voice of God announcing the end of the world, for He makes use of her belly for pronouncements."

Sadly Tarsis went into Nuria's room. She became agitated immediately: "Don't leave me alone. And do let me live normally."

"Are we bothering you now?"

"The business about my sleeping . . . sleeping . . . I've slept so much I'll never sleep again. But don't go. Ever!"

"I've brought you the champagne."

The three of them sat on the bed. And they drank the first bottle almost in one nervous gulp. Drinking to her health, they got through the second as well. It was six o'clock in the afternoon, but they had barely started the day or begun to drown the worm of unease and alienation. The cork on the third bottle came out with such force that it shattered a light bulb, and they decided to trim the wick on the lamp. They'd begun to feel joyous and lit from within, and they swore to drown the thirst roused in them by the third bottle by opening a fourth. But their thirst was not slaked, and they began to wallow in their own liquidity. They lost count, sequence, and identification. When they awoke the next morning, they were naked and wound around one another.

Tarsis was never able to summon up the memory of what had happened that night. And much the same for the succeeding nights. And succeeding days. He had a diffuse remembrance of a wafting joy, but he would not have been able to name the details of that joy. He knew they had "known" each other, plumbed each other as if they had newly discovered one another. Nuria threw off all her torment. She slept easily and went from dreams to caresses, and from caresses to dreams and sleep. She was reborn, her hands took on a life of their own, her eyes shone with abandon, she shivered with delight. All their sorrows vanished, and they were engulfed in an abandon which bordered on exaltation.

Joined together, the three of them learned to gaze at each other, to touch each other, to love each other, and they went round and round like the small horses of a carousel circling their own intimate nudity, and yet maintaining their own orbit. They went from the unconditional chastity in which they had lived for so long to a stage of sensual frenzy. Their fingers and their desires, their eyes and their imaginations, their tongues and their fantasies collaborated in letting them act out the living dreams which kept them inebriated. In that spell, they often could not tell the difference between man and woman: they became both. Their naked bodies locked together might have seemed depraved, but they were learning to become part of one another and to love one another with a delicate generosity. They offered themselves to each other with both hands, offered up their very essence, their beings, their innermost texture.

They lived their triangular idyll without any thought of rivalry, as if it were the most natural thing in the world. The mysticism which had characterized the three of them was affirmed, and they felt themselves to be servants of God more than ever before. But they were practicing a highly personalized reformed religion with freedom of thought. At night they went through a delightful ritual which began with their kneeling before a statue of St. Francis of Assisi and ended with their lying together naked on the same bed. They went from contemplative devotion to active rapture as if none of the participants in the two phases of the ceremony had anything to do with this world.

They tried to get married in the cathedral at Nice. And they planned a white wedding, too. But the men of the Church, taken aback, showed them the door. Then one day they chanced to read an interview with the American actor Robert Redford in which he said: "My wife, who is a Mormon, wants me to marry another woman, but I refuse." The three of them were ready to convert to Mormonism. But there was no trace of that church on the Côte d'Azur. They ascertained merely that it was called the Church of Jesus Christ of Latter-day Saints and that it had been founded in 1830 by Joseph Smith. Nuria found further intriguing details in the municipal library:

"They were persecuted and jailed for the practice of polygamy. Joseph Smith was lynched. But they managed to take refuge in the state of Utah. Their Mecca is the capital, Salt Lake City."

They decided to make a pilgrimage to the city where their preferences were sacred. And they were delighted to learn that, for the Mormons, marriage did not end with the death of one of the parties but endured forever. The only points separating them from the disciples of Joseph Smith were the questions of original sin and the virginity of Mary. None of the three could find in himself or herself to deny these two articles of faith. Besides, for them, the Virgin Mary who had appeared to Tarsis was without any question the mediatrix of the human race . . . and theirs as well.

The terrorists, taking advantage of the stop made at Nice by the Paris–Ventimiglia train, placed a bomb in one of its mail sacks. The attack did not have the cataclysmic effect desired but led to only a minor accident, a strange event. The wounded suffered more from shock than from hurt.

Nuria and Soledad had looked forward to Tarsis's return from work by going to pick white hawthorn shoots. They wanted to lay out a terrace garden with a low stone wall covered with green hawthorn and wild roses. And they wanted to add white hawthorn, which they adored for its small flowers in combs and its serrated leaves, all so subtly fragrant.

The train went off the tracks. If it had done so a few hundred yards farther on, in the middle of the populated area, tragedy would have been a certainty. The bomb went off as the train emerged from the Carabarichel tunnel, before the engine had reached cruising speed.

Nuria and Soledad had chosen a stony area alongside the tracks: the hawthorn grew thickly there, forming clumps around an outcropping or even hanging from the high mouth of the tunnel. They uprooted a dozen plants with great care, not so much to avoid the thorns as not to do violence to the plant's arabesque harmonies.

The authorities breathed a sigh of relief: disaster had been somehow averted. They were able to point out that it was not even a true derailing, inasmuch as only two coaches "lay down" on the roadbed as the train emerged from the tunnel.

Though the terrorists issued no communiqué, they could not have been pleased. They had wasted a good deal of powder in salvos: seven kilograms of dry plastic explosive.

Nuria and Soledad had made up a lovely bouquet they knew would please Tarsis: it was composed of thyme, rosemary, and poppies. They would place it on his table next to the chessboard, while he analyzed his chess-games-by-mail. From time to time he would be sure to bend over and smell the thyme, and perhaps he would also break off an anther to perfume his fingers.

The accident constituted a media event. Television cameras appeared, as did press photographers. Minutes after the accident they were able to swing into action with legitimate pride of office. Despite everything, the photographs were not spectacular. But they were eye-catching: the locomotive and the two overturned coaches looked like pieces of a kid's toy train. The presence of firemen and two police helicopters added some spice to an otherwise pedestrian scene.

Nuria knew just where she wanted to plant the various hawthorn shoots. She would make a spectacular crown out of them. Soledad had already chosen a name for each of the shoots. They were both sure the plants would "take" on the roof-terrace wall. They would sing to the transplants if necessary, and later Tarsis would speak to them lovingly in his best bass voice.

The Minister of Transport openly vented his satisfaction, as was only natural, given the fact that the security services had functioned perfectly and the tracks were clear and circulation was reestablished within six hours of the mishap.

Nuria and Soledad were getting ready to leave, for in a few minutes they would be going to pick up Tarsis at the door of his shop, just like every afternoon. That particular afternoon the three of them would be taking a walk to Cap Ferrat to watch the sunset.

In reality the train derailment had claimed two victims. Fortuitously, the press and television had already left by the time they were discovered. When one of the coaches "lay down" on the tracks, this one actually a baggage car, it had crushed the two girls, utterly mangling them. They were holding on to each other at the moment the train hit them, and so when their brains burst they mingled, as did their rent bodies. In the end they were buried together in one piece, since it was impossible to determine which parts belonged to which woman.

The authorities interred the incident in silence. They considered it to be the only thorn, albeit benign, in a drama which had been so cleanly resolved. This silence, moreover, robbed the terrorists of any sign of success. The pair were buried quietly. Only Tarsis attended the burial of his two girlfriends.

His anguish was such that he could not relieve it with tears. Torn apart like two little birds, torn from him, Nuria and Soledad had left him utterly alone forever. A bubble of air traveled from his heart to his brain and back again: it was more like a bubble of molten steel which seared him as it traveled from his heart to his brain and from his brain to his heart.

Tarsis moves on to the denouement: 22. . . . h6xg5. *It's curtains,* he says to himself. *It's time for the stagehands to appear and carry Amary off.*

The iron sheeting yielded easily. It was poorly camouflaged by some cut branches. De Kerguelen raised it with little effort. He had decided against carrying any weapon whatsoever. He would not be able to openly confront Amary's partisans, his own "Comité comrades": Delpy or Delacour or

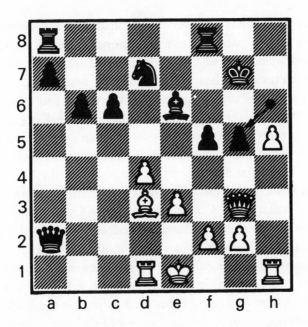

22. .... h6xg5

Hermes would kill him like a dog if they were to find him in the underground tunnel. More than a tunnel, the place became for him, for nearly a mile, a rabbits' burrow. At the entrance, the footprints and tire marks around it convinced him he was at the "secret" entrance to the manor house at Meung-sur-Loire, the one used by the Comité behind the backs of the gendarmes out front.

He proceeded along the tunnel with great caution, trembling the while. He carried a flashlight in his hand. And in his head a bright idea which seemed to him to be luminous: he would penetrate the house, through the tunnel into the cellar, and free Isvoschikov. In all truth, he was dreaming of stabbing Amary in the back and denouncing him to the whole world. He had finally convinced himself that with the article on the genetic code Amary had finished him off as a research investigator, thereby severing his tie to life. He would have to pay Amary back. An eye for an eye, a tooth for a tooth.

Amary had probably already guessed what was going on in de Kerguelen's head. The latter was assigned no further activity in the "urban guerrilla." But Amary had committed the error, the other realized, of allowing de Kerguelen to stay on the Comité—perhaps to keep an eye on him more closely while entrusting him with "secondary" missions. For example, he was asked to present a study on the Uruguayan Tupamaros, and then an analysis of the thesis promulgated by the Italian Lotta Continua and Potere Operaio. Naturally he was told nothing of the abduction of the Soviet Minister.

Meanwhile, with his heart in his mouth, de Kerguelen was making his way along the tunnel. He knew he had been right not to make a complete break with the group. His staying had led Amary to commit his fatal error, for the leader was such an opportunist that he had asked the near-renegade to draw up a report on Paris's underground tunnels and even on the secret entrances to the Marigny Palace, the residence assigned to guests of the President of the Republic.

When de Kerguelan handed over the documents he asked Amary: "Why do you want this information? Are you going to blow up Paris?"

"Those are questions that should not be asked a militant in a revolutionary group."

"Is it too important for me to know about?"

Amary would not be drawn in. He put the matter in another light: "An organization like ours should be able to count on a plan for escape, and the net of subterranean passages in Paris might serve us well someday."

Since he could not imagine that Amary was simply amusing himself, de Kerguelen decided then and there that he had definitively been excluded, as good as gagged.

Thanks to the second part of the study he had been asked

to do, de Kerguelen had little difficulty in imagining how Isvoschikov was abducted from the Marigny Palace. He had seen the building plans and had even copied them, and he knew that the Soviet Minister's bedroom contained, hidden somewhere in the room's majestic chimney, a concealed doorway which led, via a spiral staircase, to the cellar, which in turn gave access to a tunnel in subterranean Paris. The mystery surrounding the "yellow room," to which *France-Soir* referred in its reports, could be explained: the abductors entered the bedroom directly from the chimney, less than a dozen feet from Isvoschikov's bed; they drugged him with something like chloroform and then, with the help of a blanket or the like, they carried him to their makeshift prison at Meung. The Soviet guards saw nothing because they were posted at their chief's door . . . outside it, on the wrong side. (The police quickly discovered the secret door, but they preferred not to inform the press of this find. That was a decisionmade by the "crisis cell," also called the Council of War, attached to the Ministry of the Interior.)

After more than a quarter of an hour of reflection, Amary, unthinking, continues his attack as if he had not been disarmed, and moves: 23. Qg3xg5 + (Amary could not concentrate on the game following the previous play's mortal error).

[The Kid emerged from the bowels of the earth by raising the lid on the square *a1*. Confronting Amary by raising his head to the height of Tarsis's queen, he told him: "Teresa wants to go to bed with the black king. Will you allow her to come up before they pass judgment on you?"

Amary could see Teresa three steps down in the darkness, ready for anything, made up like a cheap whore and with an outrageous décolletage.

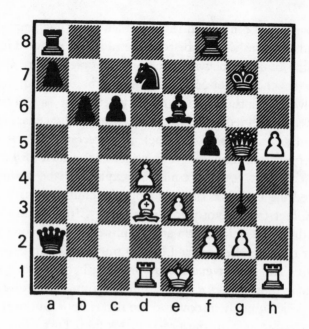

23. Qg3xg5 +

It was the final straw! Ever since the unfortunate experience in New York, he had forbidden them to leave the house . . . And now they had the brazen gall to appear in the middle of a world championship. They knew that they had no role to play, and yet they took advantage of the situation. Amary tried to stay cool, so that neither the official nor Tarsis, let alone the audience, would notice the untoward events at the chessboard.

Next, Doña Rosita put in her appearance: she had entered through the cellar of the black castle at a8 and was calmly smoking a green Tuscan cigar; she was wearing a sort of cassock. She told him: "We don't wish to disturb you. We know you mustn't talk, but you can answer the Kid by moving your head . . . and the king when he passes judgment on you."

Amary moved his head in a vigorous no.

Bold as ever, Mickey began dancing a Strauss waltz with the black queen. He was not beyond dragging her off her square at a2 and making her lose her balance and consequently the game. Around his neck he was wearing a hangman's rope. He told Amary: "You won't bother me as long as you don't eat Tarsis's queen."

Amary didn't feel like raising his head from his contemplation of the board. He heard the Three Condors debating the death penalty, and they were comparing the virtues of the gallows to those of the electric chair and the garrote.

Utterly brazen, Teresa walked up and installed herself in front of the black king, whom she tried to cajole; next she spread her legs and wet, the dirty thing! A big puddle stained the board. Amary's place was a mess.

He began to notice that the chessboard was swaying, and at the same time he heard the deep voice of the Mosquito. He understood at once that the rhinoceros had hoisted the board on his back and he need only shake himself a bit to scatter the chess pieces all over the board.]

De Kerguelen stumbled and was on the point of falling into a concealed well inside the underground tunnel. His heart pounded; he feared that Amary's gang might have heard him. He shone a light on the map he had carefully copied out: this gallery was not on it. Still, he felt he knew the underground tunnels better than Amary himself. He knew, for example, that there were two tunnels connected to the house: the principal passageway, which was the one he had taken, and a walled-up secondary one, dating from the time of the French Revolution, which led, at that time, from the mansion to the bridge over the Loire. This passage was a subsidiary of the principal tunnel some fifteen feet from the mansion's cellar and contained a small two-tiered cave used as a storeroom and wine cellar during the summer by the Marquis d'Arthuy, the mansion's proprietor in the eighteenth century.

If Hermes, Delpy, or Delacour were to find him, they would surely shoot him, and then, without the slightest remorse, they'd bury him forever in one of the passage's vaults. Who would ever reclaim his body? . . . Unless it was Tarsis! For de Kerguelen had alerted him. Now he could imagine the three partisans in the mansion's living room listening to the news broadcasts on the hour, impatient to learn the results of the chess championship, or waiting for a call from Mathieu Olive, who accompanied and protected the chief, along with Rode and Demy, the three of them sitting in the front row of the tournament hall.

When the impending championship match was first announced, de Kerguelen had sent Tarsis a letter offering his help: he proposed sending photocopies of Amary's chess analyses. Tarsis did not accept, however. But they entered into correspondence. And de Kerguelen began to develop such a feeling of affinity and affection for the man who was challenging his enemy that he revealed to him the existence of the Comité Communiste International and its varied terrorist actions, including the derailing of the bombed train at Nice. He suggested that Tarsis denounce Amary and the Comité to the police—in case he himself was killed for having "recanted" and become a "repentant terrorist."

Amary feared that no Soviet chess player would be able to stand up to the latest wave of young American and English prodigies. For him, as for Lenin, "chess should aid the triumph of Communism." He, Amary, had been much moved by the telegram that world champion Botvinnik sent to Stalin following his victory at Nottingham: "I have defended the honor of Soviet chess with a sense of great responsibility . . . My victory was made possible thanks solely to the Party and the government . . . Soviet chess collaborates in the construction of socialism . . . I am happy to have been able to carry out my struggle for socialism within the area and limits assigned me." Amary could not abide the notion that a new American prodigy, some Fischer or other, should put in question the intellectual supremacy of Communism—chess being the scientific game *par excellence.* His own intention was to win the World Championship and then reveal, in the course of the ceremony of investiture, that he was a Communist and that his victory represented the triumph of Marxism.

For his part, Tarsis had begun the first round of his attempt at the world crown, the zone championship, almost indolently, and by chance ("chance" was always linked in his mind with Andorra), but as Amary more and more seemed to be the likely opponent, and then when he heard from de Kerguelen, his passion to avenge Nuria and Soledad flared. The president of the Chess Federation of Andorra, who had read his brilliant games-by-mail, asked him to represent his country in the zone competition, the first step toward the top. The president considered that, thanks to Tarsis, his little country might finally stop being awarded the "zero points" which previous representatives of the principality of Andorra had scored.

After the death of Soledad and Nuria, Tarsis's world had sunk beneath his feet, and he barely managed to go on living—just barely. His heart had lost its wings, and it was almost by a miracle that he got through the obligations attendant on the first series of matches. He vegetated in his run-down rooms amid the rubble accumulating around him. Some days he measured time only by the passage of the bubble of air, or of mercury, or steel, or stone, which traveled from his heart to his brain and back again. De Kerguelen's letter, disclosing the part Amary had played in the train wreck at Nice, was the one thing that brought him back to life: the desire for vengeance began to animate him and to rekindle his reason for living.

Tarsis moves his king to his right: 23. . . . Kg7-f7. He uses up five minutes to make this obvious move because, instead of reflecting on it, he has been contemplating Amary. He watches him shake his head as if addressing his pawns or answering questions from his queen.

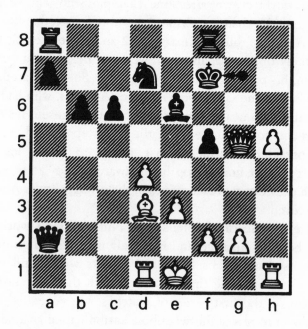

23. . . . Kg7-f7

He's in a state of shock, Tarsis tells himself. *If he were able to think clearly, he would make the only serious move possible now: abandon the game. There's nothing left for him to do. I've made him bite the dust on every side.* He could denounce him to the police if he wanted, revealing his plans and those of his followers (the letter from de Kerguelen would be sufficient proof), first to blow up the Paris–Ventimiglia train, and now the fact that they have Isvoschikov in their hands. He dreams of vengeance, but he is far from crowing victory. No one can give him back so much as one small afternoon on the terrace at Chemin de Pessicart, where he sat among the flowerpots between Nuria and Soledad. The withered blooms in the weathered pots will never again flower. For the first time he contemplates Amary without hatred. He has the impression that the odor of assassin that hung over the man has dissipated. *He's a monster right enough,* he tells himself. *But a poor monster, with infantile characteristics.* He examines the other's hands carefully, and once again notices that they are familiar, as are his eyes and his mouth. It occurs to him that years ago . . . somewhere . . . the two of them had stood face to face once before. But where or when? He has asked himself the same question since the beginning of the championship match.

Like an automaton, Amary, with a sudden lurch, takes Tarsis's pawn: 24. Bd3xf5. It's a beginner's blunder. The audience starts to buzz in the face of such irresponsibility. There are even outspoken complaints. One spectator asks in a loud voice: "How is it possible for a chess player to commit the errors of a novice?"

[The Kid places the wig of an English judge on the black king and smiles coyly at the Three Condors as he tells Amary:

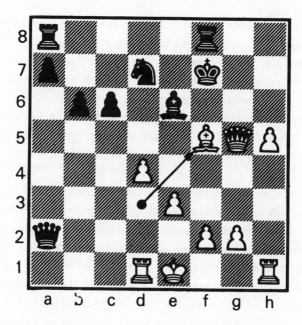

24. Bd3xf5

"The tribunal is going to call a meeting, presided over by Tarsis's king, in order to judge you."

They knew Amary couldn't talk, that the game official would penalize him if he uttered a single word . . . and yet they busied themselves organizing his trial! And, just at the moment that his situation in the game was desperate, Doña Rosita, solicitous, advised him: "We know you can't defend yourself in your present *situation,* and so we've hired the best possible lawyer. He's not an ambulance chaser but a regular lawyer with an office."

The Mosquito intervened with the natural grace of a rhinoceros: "Don't pay her any heed. Snakes have monopolized the legal profession. The lawyer they've hired is a shyster and she knows it."

Teresa was kicking El Loco and forcing him onto the board at *a6*. He was gagged and was wearing a toga covered with patches. Teresa sat him down forcibly at pawn's place *d4*. They were ready to humiliate him: they not only had discovered the Master's secret relationship with El Loco, but now, without the slightest hesitation, they were mocking him to his face. And, if El Loco was supposed to be the defense attorney, what kind of defense could he put up with a gag in his mouth?

El Loco gazed at Amary, terrified, his eyes big as saucers; he seemed to be saying: "What can I do? It's not my fault."

The Kid addressed Amary: "El Loco will represent you. And he will answer all questions from the judge in writing, so that they will form part of the record."

Amary wanted to protest but couldn't. It was obvious that they had all ganged up on him, and were ready to bring accusations against him at his "trial," and to take part in his execution without the slightest qualm. Mickey was already setting up the gallows on the black rook's roof. He was getting help from the Three Condors. The four of them were whistling a popular ditty.

In order to get a better view of the proceedings, the rhinoceros had opened a hole with his horn at h3, and from there he could command a good view of the tribunal and the accused. He advised the latter: "The charges include a long list of crimes—beginning with the murder of your mother. I'm telling you so that you can prepare a defense."

That was the limit!—to judge him for matricide, a murder carried out by the Kid, which he had tried to prevent. And then, to heighten the irony, the latter, in his role as jurist, announced: "I have been named prosecutor. But don't think that despite everything I'm going to take it out on you. I only want to help. By means of the law, of course, applying it

233

strictly." The Three Condors were applauding with their wings. Mickey, happy as a lark, was swinging the gallows rope.

Doña Rosita, between two puffs from her Tuscan cigar, shrieked: "Let them finish him off and make him dig his own grave."

The Kid pretended to admonish her: "Only Tarsis's black king has the power by rights to condemn him to the supreme penalty . . ."

They all set up a din: "Hang him before it's all over!"]

When de Kerguelen reached the end of the underground tunnel, he ran into a spacious vaulted wine cellar almost rectangular in shape, situated, without a doubt, in the basement of Amary's residence. With the utmost caution he made his way into it. He could imagine the Comité's fanatics overhead, a few yards away, armed and ready for anything. He also imagined running into Isvoschikov, chained to the bed and worn out with torture. The last photograph he had seen of the man was the one published that morning in the press: a photograph taken the previous day by the kidnappers, which showed him with wide eyes full of fear, an obvious victim of brutality.

For an hour, treading lightly, he explored the wine cellar. He examined rotting shelves piled with bottles, cupboards built into the walls now moldering around jugs of marmalade, a gigantic freezer, a dozen butane gas containers, screened food cabinets, and cheese boxes hanging from the ceiling. Meanwhile, he was not finding any trace of Isvoschikov. Whenever the sound of conversation came to him from Amary's gang in the living room above, his hair stood on end. Despite his fear, he was determined to continue his search, and so he consulted the chart he had made, spreading it out on the mildewed table and shining his flashlight on it. He could not find any indication of a secret chamber. He wondered if they might not have already murdered the Russian since the last photograph they had made of him and sent to the press. He began to feel along the walls again, trying to discover some exit. Finally he retraced his steps and entered the second passage. His teeth chattering, he proceeded until he reached the storage area for vats shown on his chart. As he investigated it carefully, he wondered if he wouldn't come across Isvoschikov's corpse. Just as his drawing indicated, a concealed opening led to a second story; he made his way to it through a narrow passage and found himself in an empty hollow barely large enough to hold a man in a crouching position.

Once more he went back impatiently to the cellar. And once again the rough laughter of Jacques Delpy made his skin creep. He would be a goner if they found him: death without mercy. And again he began his fruitless search of the place with mounting despair. He was about to retreat when suddenly the door to the freezer caught the beam from his flashlight and it occurred to him that some kind of passage might lie behind the big box. He opened the door to the freezer. Involuntarily a cry escaped from his throat. Isvoschikov lay there, his eyes open, his gaze fixed on infinity, immobile, frozen, dead.

De Kerguelen was paralyzed for a moment, unable to move his legs, as if hypnotized by the "lifelike" corpse of the Russian.

And now his cry must have alerted Amary's thugs in the living room overhead. For he heard their sudden running and knew that they could get down to the first floor in a couple of strides, then through the office and the kitchen, down the stairs to the garage, and then into the cellar, there to seize and kill him without further ado.

He didn't think twice but ran down the second passageway

toward the storage room. He was petrified, but he managed to squeeze himself into the tiny hollow he had come upon before. He hid his head in his lap, in the position of a fetus, as if unwilling to see the danger which had run him to ground. His heart beat so loudly that he had the demented thought that it could be heard outside by his pursuers.

He knew that the trio would take in the open freezer at a glance and even the chart he had left spread out on the table with notes in his own handwriting. They would have immediate proof that the prey they sought, the unwelcome visitor, was himself.

After what might have been a quarter of an hour of their running back and forth, he heard Delpy calling out to him: "De Kerguelen, we know you're hidden in the tunnel. You can't escape. Mario Circillo is posted at the entrance. We advise you to surrender. Immediately. If you don't, we'll kill you like a rat."

Footsteps approached the storage room.

From the very first de Kerguelen had deduced the reasons for the abduction of the Russian diplomat. Amary simply wanted to demonstrate that revolutionary terrorism was not necessarily financed by the U.S.S.R., and not organized under the command of Boris Ponomarev. He would thereby prove that convinced Communists, determined to destroy capitalist society, could act with total autonomy, with no help from Moscow and without training in the military complex of the Soviet bloc. Now that the Pope himself and so many other Western rulers had fallen under the spell of revolutionary Marxism, so too would a representative of the Kremlin be a victim to their power. He assumed the Russian government would react strongly against the abduction, but nevertheless the Soviets would be served by his devious maneuver. They might even be driven to actually bomb the Saudi Arabian oil wells. Still, he was not a man to drag utopia along by the hair, and so he assured his followers: " 'A world war would be more than welcome for the international workers' cause,' as Mao said . . . But we can't just dream. We haven't lost our perspective."

The kidnapping as such had lasted less than one day. When Isvoschikov woke from his drugged sleep in the cellar at Meung, three hours after his abduction, he found himself already gagged. He felt sharp pain from a rope tied around both the thumb of his left hand and his right big toe, and then around his back. He was feverish, and overcome by thirst. There was a taste of salt in his mouth, and he thought his abductors must have forced some saline solution down his throat while he was unconscious.

It seemed like an eternity before anyone appeared; it was Amary carrying a pewter water cup, a knife, and a pen. Without a word, Amary examined his prisoner's hands and feet; the bound portions had already turned as purple as two peaches ready to burst.

Coolly Amary told the prisoner: "You've been moaning for hours. We could all hear you in the living room. I imagine that your pain is unbearable. The bindings are pretty tight."

"Please loosen them."

"And you must have a pretty high fever. I suppose it makes you thirsty."

"A terrible thirst . . ."

"You're no doubt anxious to improve your situation . . ."

"Do something, I implore you."

"I'm in no hurry. I'm planning to go to see a film with one

of my comrades. It's being shown in a theater nearby. You don't mind if I leave you alone for three hours?"

"I can't stand it for another minute. Untie me! I'm about to faint."

"I don't think so. The kind of binding you have on your finger and toe only exacerbates the pain. It seems worse every moment, as you can no doubt confirm. Naturally, it will get worse. So does cancer. But you'll be able to bear the pain."

"I can't stand it. I'll do whatever it is you want."

"Well then, I'll give you proof of my good will. I've brought a glass of water and a knife to cut your bonds. But before I put an end to your discomfort, I want you to write nine letters, exactly nine."

Isvoschikov, using his right hand (his left remained tied to his back), wrote the nine letters, exactly as Amary dictated. Each letter was dated on a Wednesday, a week apart, to cover the following nine Wednesdays. When he was almost finished writing, Isvoschikov muttered: "Are you going to kill me? Is that why you have me writing letters with dates in the future?"

"Don't get distracted. Just write. You have only one letter left to do and then I'll cut you loose."

Once Isvoschikov had finished the ninth letter, Amary kept his word and gave his prisoner water to drink.

It contained some grams of arsenic.

Only then did he cut the cords. The sudden release of the bonds which had cut off circulation caused such an overwhelming rush of pain that the Russian fainted. He suffered no more. Never again.

Tarsis puts a finishing touch on the game by moving to check: 24. . . . Qa2-a5 +. *After losing his knight, he'll lose his bishop. Why doesn't he resign? Tarsis says to himself. Why is he gesticulating in silence? Is he going crazy? . . . Could he be going through the torments I suffered after the train was wrecked?* Tarsis would like to savor his vengeance but is not able to. He even finds himself looking at Amary with a certain tenderness at one point. *Where have I seen him before?* Tarsis is thinking that at some point in the past—in his childhood?—they have crossed paths. When was it?

Trembling in his hiding place, de Kerguelen listened to the approaching steps of his pursuers as they closed in on him. Suddenly there was a yell directed at him: "Surrender, you son of a bitch! If you don't we'll finish you off."

He had a vision of how these fanatics would "finish him off" with savage refinement. They had been capable of murdering the Russian Minister and of keeping him frozen for

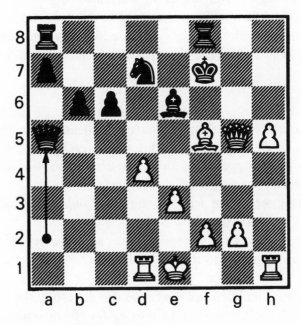

24. . . . Qa2-a5 +

weeks so they could take photographs of him, as if he were still living, propping the latest issue of a daily newspaper under his chin. They had turned the dead man into a frozen mannequin whom they took out of the freezer once a week, powdered and spruced up for the farcical presentation. As for de Kerguelen himself, how would they get his eyes to shine?

When de Kerguelen saw the glint of his pursuers' flashlights through a slit, his blood froze. They were breathing like wild beasts and seemed only inches away. They went over the storage room with a fine-tooth comb; meanwhile, the hideaway's heart was pounding or, rather, seemed to him to be exploding in noisy detonations. He was sure that they would simply look up, discover his hiding place, and, like a pack of wild animals, tear him limb from limb. Panic made him tremble all over, including his imagination . . .

In actual fact, it never occurred to the pursuers to think that the storeroom might contain a hidden niche and they didn't even look. They simply went away.

Amary has less than a minute left to carry out his final moves. If the large hand on his watch reaches twelve, indicating that his two hours and a half are up, he will have lost the match.

[The Others have occupied the board and are yelling: "Kill him! There's no time left! Skin him!"

Teresa makes an obscene gesture, as if she were choking Amary's white king with her bare thighs, and gives vent to a randy laugh.

Mickey climbs the gallows rope dangling from the roof of the black rook, and when he reaches the top he dons a hangman's hood and cries out: "How long do we have to wait